FISH ANTH

2023

www.fishpublishing.com

Nothing matters but the writing.
There has been nothing else worthwhile
… a stain upon the silence.

— Samuel Beckett

Published in Ireland by
Fish Publishing, 2023
Durrus, Bantry, Co. Cork

The *Fish Anthology 2023* receives financial assistance from the Arts Council of Ireland.

the arts council an chomhairle ealaíon funding literature

ISBN 978-0-9956200-6-3
A catalogue record of this book is available from the British Library.

Cover Image – *Gate* by Mary Martin (www.marymartin.info)

For details on Fish Publishing's annual competitions write to:
Fish Publishing, Durrus, Bantry, Co. Cork, Ireland
info@fishpublishing.com
www.fishpublishing.com

FISH ANTHOLOGY
2023

Winners of the 2022/23

Fish Publishing

Short Story Prize

Flash Fiction Prize

Short Memoir Prize

Poetry Prize

Edited by Clem Cairns

Fish Publishing
Durrus, Bantry, Co. Cork, Ireland
www.fishpublishing.com

Contents

SHORT MEMOIRS

POETRY

BIOGRAPHIES

Acknowledgements

COMPETITION JUDGES

Sarah Hall ~ *Short Story*

Kit de Waal ~ *Flash Fiction*

Sean Lusk ~ *Short Memoir*

Billy Collins ~ *Poetry*

SPONSORS

Arts Council, Ireland

Anam Cara Writer's & Artist's Retreat
Ireland (www.anamcararetreat.com)

COPY EDITOR & DESIGN

Jula Walton

E-CONSULTANT

Phoebe Bright
(Vivid Logic)

ADMINISTRATION

Fizz Collingwood

COVER IMAGE

Mary Martin
(www.marymartin.info)

WEB DESIGN

Ergo – Tom Walton & Justin Bowley
(www.ergo.agency)

EDITORS/READERS

Mary-Jane Holmes

Simon Humphreys

Tina Pisco

Nancy Laforest

Judith Hinman

Tessa Gibson

Adam Wyeth

Paul McMahon

Guy Simpson

Pierre Antoine Zahnd

Cressida Peever

Nicholas McLachlan

READERS

Ray Travis

Epi Lagrilliere

Jo Hopkins

Introductory Note

What a joy! What a joy to experience in these stories the many versions of us, told in so many different ways, small episodes pushing up against big themes, propositions and provocations that expand any restrictions we might make for ourselves, socially, politically, or textually. What a joy to be transported to so many different places around the globe, and into speculative futures, and back into the disputable past.

In this anthology there are ten short stories, ten flash stories, ten short memoirs and ten poems – winners of their respective competitions, with the writers coming from many places around the world. From 5,746 entries, these 40 pieces came through a grueling process and forced their way to the top. The writers here deserve huge credit, each piece is unique and brilliant, and our wish at Fish is that their writing careers continue to flourish.

Sarah Hall judged the short stories, Kit de Waal the flash, Sean Lusk the memoirs and Billy Collins the poems. An enormous thanks to them for their time, attention and wisdom.

This Anthology is a *showcase of disquiet, tension, subversion and surprise*. So buckle up and enjoy the ride!

Clem Cairns: June 2023
Quotes from Sarah Hall

Short Stories

Vietnam

Letty Butler

The day we met two things happened: I started going grey and my period came back after six years. It was as if my body woke up and said *a-ha, here he is* but at the same time *oh shit*.

The body always knows.

It was a Christmas party I'd forced myself to go to. I wore a red dress and felt too tall. You stood in front of the microphone and apologised for dressing like Alan Partridge. That was probably the moment.

We went for coffee a week later. I knocked mine over. You ate a chocolate slice with a knife and fork and when I asked you why you said you didn't know. We talked for two hours. I tried to work out if I liked the strange timbre of your voice, the high pitch of your explosive laugh. I felt you looking through me, beyond the jumper, beyond the skin.

As the cafe closed, you made a casual reference to your partner. I felt ridiculous. We parted in the snow and I shut the box of you in my mind.

You unlocked it five days later with a text. All it said was *Happy Christmas*. I had a visceral reaction, a tiny explosion somewhere in my gut. I waited and sent one back: *Happy Boxing Day*. Twenty-four hours later you replied. *Happy Post Boxing Day* it said, and I thought *I see*.

We kept finding reasons to communicate. A book recommendation, a creative opportunity. The smattering of texts became flurries followed by days of silence, most of which I spent berating myself for being so affected by it. I'd just about manage to shut the box again, when you'd send a new offering – a link, a question, a video of snow falling. I would vow not to respond, then draft replies in my mind as I paced the slushy streets of Sheffield. You were a scab I couldn't stop picking.

We met again, this time for three hours, during which a silent negotiation took place: we would not mention Her.

I became a cliche overnight. I couldn't eat or sleep. You frogmarched me out of my fussy little life into a kind of glorious hell. The texts came daily. Each one a shot of espresso. You sent songs. I listened to them repeatedly, googled the lyrics and tried to understand you. I had too much energy. I started dancing in the flat. I lost weight. People fretted. It was like a disease.

One Sunday morning, you sent a message asking if I would help with your stand-up routine. You knew my background, had seen the films. I felt important. You arrived, drenched from football, and wrestled your enormous bike into my tiny flat. I sat with my back against the oven and watched your set. I wasn't sure if it worked but I couldn't believe your bravery. I would never have taken such a risk in front of a potential lover and took it as confirmation that my feelings were not reciprocated.

But we are not all the same.

And there is no one quite like you.

We got into your Fiat 500 and drove to Clowne in the pouring rain, which you said was funny in itself. You were brilliant that night and I knew I was powerless. In the bar afterwards, all I wanted to do was touch the soft skin behind your ear.

You are so beautiful.

I became your director of sorts. It was strange being back on the circuit, rediscovering the world that almost buried me. I saw it anew, and it was not so terrifying with you in it. Something inside me stirred and whispered *the lights, look at the lights*.

On the way to gigs, we played *Snap!* with our life stories. Did we match? Could our lives tesselate? There was a certain freedom about being in the car – two people side by side heading in the same direction. I felt I could ask you anything, so that's what I did. Excluding the obvious, obviously.

The goodbyes were abrupt and clean. You never touched me. Every time I closed the door, I felt absurd. I was terrified you could sense the depth of my desperation, smell it on me like cigarettes. But I am nothing if not proud. I didn't linger in the doorway. I took my cues.

* * *

It was February when you invited me to a DJ night in Crookes. I turned up in a jumpsuit and you said I looked like a communist factory worker. We danced for hours. It was my first sober night out having ditched the drink two years before. I think you were simultaneously impressed and annoyed by my abstinence. I left at 2am and you sent a message asking why, then another, then another. They said everything and nothing. We'd crossed some sort of invisible line. We both knew it, but not what to do about it.

You ignored me for a week and I thought I might die.

When you finally got in touch, you asked if I would co-produce and perform in your comedy cabaret, which was going on a short tour. All my friends told me not to do it. But I didn't have a choice, not really.

We met in the Dorothy Pax and made each other laugh for five hours, ad-libbing full blown skits and finishing each other's sentences. The place filled up, day turned into night and you got drunk with a focus I hadn't seen before. It was exciting. You poured it in, until it all came pouring out: the spats, the suspicion, the slamming of doors, the fact you could not sleep for I was in your head.

We kissed. And it was everything.

But you did not want to feel this way. The guilt, the mess, the timing. We left and walked back to my flat, ice-air knocking the breath and bravery out of our lungs. Silently stumbling along the pavements, your drunken arm draped over my shoulder, the weight almost too much to bear.

There was no discussion on arrival. You climbed the stairs with a kind of tired resignation. Inside – hands, lips, tongues and teeth, soft bodies smashing against hard surfaces, kisses interspersed with half-hearted attempts to stop and dramatic declarations. You wished I was ugly. You were useless at relationships. You would destroy it without knowing how or why. On and on it went, one hour, two. But then you unpeeled my dress, looked at my body and sighed. It was a disaster you said, a disaster. You kissed me again, the full inebriated weight of your 6'4 frame leaning down, down. My face reaching up, up. I thought my neck might snap but I held my ground. I took your weight and it was not so heavy.

But you were drunk. It was late. I sent you home.

Two days later, the same soft bodies against the same hard surfaces, only both of them sober, standing, not stumbling. I touched you and you came on my stomach. Suddenly silent, seething with something ugly, you washed your hands. Of me? I did not know and I could not ask. It was all so fragile.

I have never felt so emotionally silenced by another person.

The next morning, a text came asking if we could delete the last week. I fell through the floor of the cafe I was sitting in. You may as well have asked me to forget my own name. You didn't want me to get dragged into your breakup, did not want to hurt me. If we were to pursue things romantically, you wanted to feel excited and joyful about it, not guilty and sad.

If? I thought. What is this *if?*

When the aftershock subsided I realised it was a noble thing to want. I replied and told you no, I could not delete it, but I could give you time and space. I would go on my adventure, and we would wait and see.

The next day she contacted me on Facebook and I felt sick. She said I was welcome to you, as if she and I were bidders at a meat auction. I'd finally been cast as The Other Woman, a role I have been studiously avoiding for my entire life, having watched my mother destroy herself playing it for the best part of fifteen years.

It's in the blood. Everything's in the blood.

Ironically, the message became the scrap that would sustain me over the coming weeks: you must have told her, which meant I was important.

Now that was an assumption, and they are always dangerous.

I didn't tell you about the message because it was an off-limits topic. I knew this by osmosis. We were keeping things professional, huddled back under our trusty old umbrella of co-creativity.

But the universe had other ideas.

It was Friday, close to midnight. I was coming back from a party when I saw you walking towards me. We stopped and stared, both asking the same question at the same time. *What are you doing here?*

She'd thrown you out. You couldn't or wouldn't elaborate. I later discovered it was because she'd found the texts, not because you'd told her. Writing this, I imagine how she must have felt in those dread-filled days leading up to it, when she knew something was wrong, but you couldn't or wouldn't elaborate.

I wonder if you'll ever be able to communicate.

You'd parked outside my flat but realised it would blur the lines so you were *just walking and thinking*. I was glad I was your first port of call, even if I was just a parking space. Perhaps you would sleep in your car you said.

We both knew you wouldn't.

I made you a sandwich and you sang a song about swans. It should have been funny but the atmosphere was peculiar, uncomfortable. I suddenly felt I didn't know you at all. I asked where you wanted to sleep. You said the bed would be fine. You cleaned your teeth while I put on the biggest pyjamas I could find. I did not want any of that desperation seeping out.

In the dark, I closed my eyes and tried not to think about the soft skin behind your ear. Forty torturous minutes later, you pulled my arm around your ribcage. It escalated. Quickly, quietly. Too far, too soon. It felt wrong, robotic and cold. Halfway through you froze. I didn't know what to do. It had been a very long time since I'd been intimate with anyone. Perhaps I had forgotten how? Perhaps my body repulsed you? I lay down and recognised that slick, wet heat between my legs. I asked if you had come inside me, and you said yes. You asked if I was *covered* as if I was a car with an insurance policy. You didn't hold me or talk to me or touch me. When I asked you to say something, you told me an anecdote about Beatrix Potter.

There is no one quite like you.

I lay there, listening to your laboured breath as you thrashed your way through the dregs of the night. I could feel the beginning of the end, like a butcher's hook to the gut. The body always knows. You left at 5am. I cried in the tangled mess of sheets. Later I went to Boots alone and got the morning after pill. You never asked me about it. For all you knew, I could have been pregnant. I actually think I was, such was the aftermath of that small white swallow.

Another thing we'll never talk about.

* * *

Gone were the texts, the songs, the invitations. You treated me like a PA, ending emails with things like *cheers*. It was insulting and cruel. I suppose you thought I either did not notice or did not mind because I didn't cause a scene. Well I did notice and I did mind.

At night I paced in the dark, wondering if I had imagined it all.

But the show must go on.

I channelled all my energy into making it a success by being an exceptional PA. I wrote press releases and got interviews. I spoke when spoken to and didn't ask any questions. It was the most unfulfilling role I have ever played. I rebelled and booked a one-way ticket to Vietnam. I didn't tell you, because you didn't ask. You never ask me anything.

One evening, I had to rehearse a burlesque number in front of you and you alone. It was the most exposed I have ever felt, with or without my clothes on. To put myself through it after you had rejected me so profoundly, was humiliating. But I did it. Because I knew how much the show meant to you. It was the only light in your newly, dark world. I understood that my creative currency was the only part of me you wanted or would allow yourself to have, so I gave it to you. Because that's what love is – self-sacrifice and insanity.

But it wasn't pure altruism: I'd missed the camaraderie of a rehearsal room, the thrill of being on stage. And besides, if I left, you'd know how hurt I was. And I am nothing if not proud.

* * *

The show came together and brutal though it was, we made an excellent creative team. I was good at feeding the cast and maintaining morale, while you dealt with technical issues and venues. Together we battled our way through the inevitable production challenges and found something stronger in our shared goal – respect, friendship, integrity. We grew comfortable with each other again.

A week before the show, you went to Lanzarote and found it lonely, while I tried to get my head around Vietnam. I had five jabs in one day and vomited in a car park. I bought a head torch and a water purifier, with no idea why.

The day you got back we rehearsed. You looked brown and better. You asked if I had plans that night. I did. I'd made very sure of that. I didn't want to risk being that lame little dog again, silently begging for scraps of your time. You gave me a lift to the bar where I was meeting friends. On the way you said *So Vietnam?* I said *Yes*. You said *When?* and I said *The day after the last show*. You nodded and changed gear. *For how long?* I glanced sideways at your profile and said *I didn't know*.

It felt like a small victory.

We staggered through opening night. It was stressful and shambolic, but it gave us a baseline to work from. It was my first time on stage in five years. I was home again and it was all because of you. I will always be grateful for that.

The tour was a success, despite some major hurdles. The worst was Lincoln – your hometown. You rang and told me we'd only sold eleven tickets. I could hear the embarrassed disappointment in your voice. We went down a day early so we could flyer outside the venue. It meant we had to stay with your parents. And then just like that, we were back in the car again – me asking my questions, you ranting in all your sardonic glory.

Side by side, heading in the same direction.

When I met your parents, you finally came into focus. We stood in their modest kitchen while they gave you both barrels about your life choices, your chaos. I just stood there, holding a Tupperware box of flapjacks like the middle-class idiot I am. It made me realise how hard it must have been growing up with parents who did not understand this thing, this essence of you. I felt lucky in comparison and wondered if you wanted to punish me for it.

Where's she going to sleep? came the question suddenly. *In my bed. I'll go on the airbed.* You replied. Your Mum looked at me then, with something like a question.

We all ate together at 6 o'clock. Chilli and jacket potatoes, with fruit salad and cream for pudding. It was delicious. I asked your father whether he'd ever seen you perform. *About fifteen years ago* he said. *And what did you think?* I asked. *Bit long*. He said and you laughed. But I knew the impact of that butcher's hook.

The airbed squeaked like cheap shoes every time you moved and it gradually deflated through the night. *This is silly* I said at 4am, *get in here.* And you did. We did not touch each other – we did not have to this time. And we slept like kings. In the morning, we got the laptops out and did admin in bed.

Side by side, heading in the same direction.

We flyered all day and managed to flog forty odd tickets for the show, but the band got stuck on the motorway and missed the first half. It was a quiet audience but you gave it everything you had. I could see your father's poker face in the half light.

You cried in the interval and I have never loved you more.

We flew towards the finish line from that point. On days off, we performed at spoken word nights together and watched Kenneth Williams documentaries afterwards. We didn't touch or kiss or say the unsayable. You started asking questions about the trip. Was I all packed, did I have everything I needed. *Almost*, I said*, almost.*

The final show came. We spent the day setting up in the usual way. It was unexpectedly sunny so we had a picnic, the air hot and heavy with the unsaid. You were tactile with me and I knew you were thinking about Vietnam. As we packed down for the last time, the anti-climactic sadness loomed, threatening as the sea.

That night, we went to Hagglers Corner. I broke my abstinence because I knew it would make you happy and it did. As the alcohol flooded my veins, my body sounded alarm bells. The body always knows. But that's what love is. Self-sacrifice and insanity. The night wore on, taxis were called and we got in one together.

Back at the flat, I could almost feel the minutes ticking away until I would be on a train to Heathrow, a plane to Hanoi. Eventually we ran out of jokes and just stood there staring, willing someone to say something. But you are a coward. And you never ask me anything.

What I need to know I said, *is whether I am going away to get over you or get ready for you*. You couldn't answer and I was too tired to cry.

We went to bed, fully clothed. I turned on my side and blinked into the abyss.

But you found me in the night and undressed me, and it was good and pure and right. We were slow and careful with each other. I kissed the soft skin behind your ear and you told me I was rare. My heart was so full, I thought it might explode and fill the flat with butterflies. When I allow myself to think of it, it makes me cry. You left in the morning but came back with croissants and a half-wrapped present – a cash belt and microfibre towel – the two things I'd forgotten. How did you know? You'd written funny, beautiful words on a card. I am looking at it now from my balcony in Con Dao.

It's been a month since your last message, which was clipped and cold. I've been here for six weeks now. I've thrown myself down waterfalls, trekked the mountains of Sa Pa and got a tattoo. I've driven a motorbike, been sick on a boat and slept under stars. I've kayaked through Halong Bay and karaoked in Saigon. I've eaten crickets, drunk weasel-shit coffee and started smoking again, nursed jellyfish stings and nosebleeds and sunburn. It doesn't matter how many drinks I drink, you are still there, refracted in the wet glass at the bottom.

I am not proud anymore.

They say the right partner finds you in pieces and leads you to peace. The wrong one finds you in peace and leaves you in pieces.

I know which one you are.

And now my phone is ringing. I know I shouldn't answer.

But there is no one quite like you.

The Longhouse

Nicholas Petty

Harald sits in the longhouse, watching the logs take flame. He twists his hand through his beard and breathes. Oak and smoke and tar; the air warms his lungs. Pale morning light flickers through the beams. He closes his eyes and listens. The slosh of water in a bucket, the clatter of counted spears and shields, clucking hens – and there, faint but undeniable, the bleep, bleep, bleep of a reversing forklift, the hum of refrigeration units.

The schoolchildren will be here soon. Harald seals the safety gate surrounding the fire pit and scatters the fake furs he slept on last night. He straps on his sword, hitches his heavy coat onto his shoulders, and pushes out through the double oak doors into the Danelaw Recreational Village. Five thatched buildings, painstakingly recreated. A mill, a smoking house, a guard house, an actual house, and the longhouse, all within a palisade, surrounded, until recently, by woodland and fields, the A1 audible only on still, winter days. Harald averts his gaze from the village's southern flank, but his eyes flicker that way to trace the unnaturally straight lines of the Catero warehouse rising above the palisade. The warehouse created 300 jobs. Surely they didn't have to paint it yellow.

Harald reaches the *Althing*, a tree stump situated in the middle of the village where they gather for the morning briefing. Agata sits on the stump, chewing at her thumbnail.

'Still no sign of Eric?' Harald asks.

'More money at Catero,' Agata says. 'With forklift license, more money. I tell you this.'

Harald gives a small laugh. 'I was hoping he could see past all that.'

Agata pokes at the ground with a stick.

'No bother,' Harald says, already performing the calculations. They will have to consolidate the children into larger groups and move them through the stations more quickly. Not all the kids will get a turn on the millstone, and they will have to fit eight to a bench in the smoking house. With the pony long since dead, larger groups might even make dragging the plough more manageable since the fields turned to sludge. The warehouse messed up the waterboard.

'How many spears and shields do we have?' Harald asks.

'Seven shields, eight spears,' Agata says.

'It's not enough.'

'Can't you do some more whittling?' A strange word in Agata's accent. She must have picked it up from him.

'It takes a while to get them right.'

Agata shrugs.

'The kids on guard duty are going to have to share,' Harald says.

'Like Stalingrad.'

Harald only vaguely registers the comment, his thoughts moved on to Aethelred the Unready, the Saxon raider. Eric always played Aethelred, and he did it well, threatening enough to make it seem real, but with a comical slant that made it interactive and memorable. 'I'll figure something out.'

The rumble of tyres and the hiss of hydraulics from the car park. Harald issues some final instructions but Agata knows what to do. She strides off through the gates towards the reception centre. It used to be Harald who met the children by the bus, to joke about the steel dragon in their midst, but he realised it was impossible to conjure the genuine fear a Viking would exhibit when confronted by such a monstrosity, while also briefing on fire safety. The anachronism tainted him for the entire day. And he's never liked talking to the teachers about payment and logistics. That was Liv's job.

Now, Agata meets and greets and gets the kids into tunics, her exotic, albeit Slavic intonation containing enough mystery to bridge the gap between the modern world and the village. Then, she leads them past the field and the hens, until, as Harald envisions it, the children see the smoke rising from the chimney of the longhouse, where Harald awaits them in the elders' chair, his head bowed as if in some long, historic sleep. And when they have all filed in and sat down, he slowly lifts his eyes, causing an anticipatory hush, which he breaks with a strong, low whisper: 'Welcome to Danelaw.'

A large crash from the Catero warehouse and the sound of glass smashing. Harald sighs and thinks of Liv. Did she leave him before or after the pony died? He shakes his head and trudges back to the longhouse.

The village was her idea, Harald had always thought. Liv was the one with the degree in it, or something like it, and she was the one who loved kids. But when they were in the midst of a legal battle with the Catero lawyers – when Harald had received that cease and desist – she had claimed the village was his idea all along.

'Then I did it for both of us,' he'd conceded as they sat by the fire in the longhouse. 'To get you away from that awful school. And I needed a change. That place, it just wasn't *me*.'

Even five years later, thinking of his work made his stomach churn. The slow yet persistent increase in responsibility. Meaningless, bureaucratic responsibilities, but responsibilities nonetheless. He would not call it a burnout. It was not a burnout.

Liv took a slow sip of beer and stared at the smouldering logs.

'You were stressed,' Harald continued. 'They worked you too hard.'

'Everyone gets stressed sometimes,' she said.

'Well, they shouldn't.'

A hiss of air through her lips, like a punctured tyre.

Harald looked down at the lawyer's letter in his hands. 'I only said "pillage". And it was a joke, mainly.'

'We'll have to shut the village down when that place goes up. If they don't shut us down first.'

Harald screwed up the letter and threw it onto the fire, then quickly fished it out and set it to one side. 'We're not shutting down.'

'Maybe it's for the best,' she said.

'How can it be for the best?'

She hadn't answered that. Then the pony died, then she left. Yes, that was the right way around. Sleipnir died first.

Harald is thinking of all this as he roams the longhouse, one hand resting on the hilt of his sword, the other clutching a horn of mead. It's lunchtime and, despite the staff shortage, the morning has gone well enough. One of the benches in the smoking house collapsed but Agata managed to prop it up on a couple of rock-hard hams, and there were only a few tears over the weaponry shortage.

The children are eating bowls of vegetable broth served with bread and apples. It's about all the village can afford, and the children don't care. They are having too much fun banging on the table and belching, a Viking custom Harald has permitted for their time in the longhouse. Occasionally, he stops to ask them about their day so far, framing the question in the stern manner of a chieftain demanding productivity from his people. A boy claims to have made bread purely by turning the millstone quickly enough. A couple of girls giggle and talk about the smoking house, mainly about the smell, like soggy bacon. The children who performed guard duty are the most enthusiastic – especially the ones who got a spear.

'Keep your eyes peeled for those treacherous Saxons,' Harald warns in a grisly voice. 'Aethelred the Unready has been spotted in these parts.'

A burst of some kind of siren floats in from the warehouse. The children turn towards it. Harald forces a smile. Agata leans over with a fresh jug of berry squash.

With lunch nearly over, Harald walks back towards his seat to give a final toast, a final belch, and send them out for the afternoon rotations. Halfway there, he stops. A pale light glows beneath the table, a boy with his head tilted towards it at a severe angle. A phone. Harald catches glimpses of the game the boy is playing, hears the rattle of gunfire. Some kind of army simulation, trench warfare. The child sends droves of soldiers over the top or machine-guns them down from the other side, it's difficult to tell. Harald considers moving on, telling a teacher, but he suspects the other children have spotted him looking at the phone, and to not react would bring his whole character into question. He clears his throat, squats down to the boy's level and in a friendly, fascinated manner says, 'What is this magic you hold?'

The boy looks up. Broad-faced and missing four of his foremost teeth, top and bottom. He waggles the phone at Harald. 'It's a Samsung.'

Harald clears his throat. 'Do you talk of the famous Sami reindeer herder, Sam Sung?'

The boy responds and the children around him laugh, but Harald isn't listening, already turning over the potential anachronism of his ad-libbed retort. Would Danelaw Vikings know of the Sami? An arm swoops in to pluck the phone from the boy, who grasps after it with babyish, straining sounds.

'Dad,' he complains, to little effect.

The man turns to Harald. Early forties, also with a broad, flat face. Wearing an expensive-looking coat fit for arctic expeditions. Not one of the teachers, a parent running support. A dad, moreover. The mums are easy enough to entertain, encouraging, even, if Harald can ignore the slight weariness behind their eyes. But a dad, that's something new.

'Sorry about that,' the man says, 'he must have taken it from my bag.'

Harald flounders, stuck between eras, social norms. 'Thank you, strange wizard,' he says.

The man gives a plastic smile. Even through the thickness of his coat, Harald can smell his aftershave. Like herbal tea and honey-roast ham. Harald has started making his own soap.

'I'll let you get back to it,' the man says, and shoots a warning look at the boy, now sulking.

Harald watches him go, then drains a mouthful from his horn, looks down at the children nearby, and attempts a Viking belch. Nothing comes out. From the warehouse, the sounds of a barrel being poured down a drain.

The next time Harald sees the man, he is leaning on the palisade, talking on his phone. Harald is organising the latest recruits for guard duty. The man's boy is in this group. He has managed to obtain a spear and shield all to himself, while a dreamy, unarmed boy walks around karate-chopping. Harald considers pulling them up on it, both the hoarding and the kung-fu – and that man on his phone – but he is tired. This is the last rotation of the day and he has until now split his time between the village defences and the plough. His feet are soaked and his hands are red-raw. Also, Agata blew up at him for reasons unknown – in front of the children but in Polish. He looks forward to the end of the day, when he can sit by the fire in the longhouse, and, if he feels like it, fall asleep on a pile of furs. He feels like it.

The children quickly pick up the basics of the shield wall. The wall is not only historically accurate but serves a practical purpose: the discipline keeps the more excitable children from engaging any Saxon raiders in one-on-one combat. Afterwards, Harald sends them out on patrol around the perimeter of the ploughing field, with a warning echoing in their ears: that Aethelred the Unready has been spotted nearby. A commitment on Harald's part, and one that causes him some stress. Aethelred is the highlight of the day, as the village comes together against a common foe, but he still hasn't figured out how to organise it. He had hoped Agata would step in to play the Saxon but he is hesitant to ask. She might run him through with the longsword, and besides, the children would recognise her accent. So Agata will have to run the defences while Harald himself dons the Saxon garb and storms the palisade.

He is still lost in the details when the man appears at his side, his hood up and his hands tucked into his pockets with performative coldness. His face half obscured by the hood, the man turns bodily to talk to Harald. 'They're having a great day out,' he says.

Harald clears his throat. 'They have worked well.' And then, with the man looking at him expectantly, adds, 'Though the day is not yet through. I sense trouble is afoot.' He will keep his stint as Aethelred short. Flee almost immediately.

The man gives him a sideways glance and smiles. 'Afoot.' Then he takes out his phone and films his boy on guard duty, who has paired up with Karate Chop, walking behind the defenceless boy and poking him with his spear. The man shakes his head and presses stop. He catches Harald looking at his phone and says, 'I'll quit with the wizardry.' Harald bows his head with what could be quiet authority.

'So when did you start this place?' the man asks.

Harald clears his throat. 'Around 870AD.'

The man gives a hollow laugh, and they stand there for a while longer, looking at the plough, which is totally stuck.

'It's nice to get the day off,' the man says.

Harald snorts. He's not sure what he means by it.

'I'm Tom Parker by the way.'

Something in the way he gives his name. Both barrels of it. Professional. As though Harald should already know him. He's a banker, Harald decides. Or no, a project manager, which leads Harald to once again think of his days in the office, a hollow sense of something not good in his stomach. A different him surrounded by what he now considers a bunch of total strangers. Everyone pretending. In the wrong way.

Tom Parker has his hand outstretched. Harald hesitates, then takes it.

'Harald,' he says.

'Spelt with an *a,* I take it?'

'Two *a's*, that's right.'

'Actually? I guess you had to go into something like this with a name like that.'

Harald changed it a couple of months after Liv left.

Tom Parker's boy, who has now launched the spear into a bush and commanded Karate Chop to retrieve it, looks over at his father and waves. Tom Parker waves back, then says with a smile. 'He's a terror. Got any of your own?'

Harald pauses, finds something in his pocket. A fake coin. He turns it through his knuckles. 'No.'

Tom Parker looks across the fields then says, almost absently, 'You're good with them. The kids, I mean.'

The coin falls from his fingers and down through a seam into the lining. He forces a sigh through a thin gap between his lips. 'This place, it's demanding,' he says.

Tom Parker turns to Harald once more. His eyes flicker around Harald's face, but Harald can tell that Tom Parker's mind is elsewhere, that he never properly entered this conversation or meant what he said. Tom Parker is no doubt back on that call, thinking of his schedule, packed with more calls, the school run, the children's dentist. Harald has a sudden urge to push the man over, flick him hard in the face.

In the field, the plough tips over on its side and the children fall into the sludge. Harald should go over to help but he doesn't. The day is getting darker. He cannot delay any longer. Aethelred must rise.

'If you'll excuse me,' Harald says to Tom Parker, but he isn't looking, his head bowed at a severe angle towards his glowing pocket.

The path leads from the back of the village through the trees to the reception centre, where they keep the Saxon gear. Harald walks along it, past the ventilation units of the Catero warehouse, visible through the bushes and a new wire fence. He stood here with Liv once, staring at the machines when they had first whirred to life. She was wearing a cagoule with a luminous orange hood; he remembers that.

'I suppose we could move the village,' she said.

'We're not moving the village.' And then, failing to catch the words before they left his mouth, 'This is our home.'

Liv had kept staring at the machines, her face stretched with a new and deeper tiredness. 'Our home is 14 Bartholomew Avenue,' she said slowly.

'I wasn't being serious,' he said.

'Weren't you? Because you've been sleeping in the longhouse for how many nights now?'

'You know we're busy.'

'With grinding flour and whittling spears.'

'If we're going to do it, we're going to do it properly.'

'There's a middle ground, you know?' she said. 'Those guys we spoke to at the motte and bailey – they were doing okay.'

'They were total fakes.'

Liv kicked at a pile of leaves. 'I don't know,' she said. 'Sometimes I feel you're lost in this place.'

'I'm not lost.'

'Hiding, then.'

Harald sniffed a laugh. 'Hiding? From what?'

For a little while longer, they'd both watched the ventilation units, the steam dispersing in the cold air. Harald idly looped his fingers through the wire fencing and shook it a little. Liv picked up the wheelbarrow, laden with Sleipnir's saddle, feed bucket, and the last of his shoes, and walked off towards the reception centre.

Harald hates the office. A sunless little room with a lethargic PC that even under modest stress clicks like a swarm of insects. Piles of half-made historic objects. The half-burnt letter from the lawyers. Sleipnir's saddle. This was Liv's domain, Agata's more recently. Harald comes in here only when absolutely necessary, which is basically never.

Aethelred's outfit is in the corner, the helmet askew on top of the stiff leather jerkin, as though Aethelred himself sits propped against the wall, mortally wounded. Harald removes his chieftain gear and puts on the outfit. The chainmail is too big and rubs at his neck. The helmet pinches at his forehead. He wriggles it around a little violently, cross about something he can't quite put his finger on. It doesn't feel right, dressing as a Saxon. He moves to the door, longsword in hand, and glances once more at the neglected office. He wonders what Tom Parker would make of this space, of the clash of his world and Harald's. Mud trodden across unopened letters, a keyboard lost beneath piles of moth-eaten tunics. Tom Parker's office is probably large, organised, cleaned by others. Glass-walled meeting rooms where they draw charts and plan warehouses, a hundred at a time.

'Tom Parker, Tom Parker,' he mutters, and he is vaguely aware of how mad it sounds. The name is definitely familiar, or at least of a familiar ilk. His eyes rove the room until they land almost purposefully on the half-burnt lawyer's letter. The top and bottom were charred by the fire in the longhouse, leaving only the body of the letter, the accusation, Harald's apparently terrible words, which he can't remember now. What he can remember, what he is sure of – or at the very least can picture – is some bland name like Tom Parker signed across the bottom. Harald kicks at the printer and the empty paper tray falls open like a mouth.

Harald doesn't often approach the village from the front, preferring the back gate, or, better, not to leave the village at all. But he always liked the view from here, rounding the wild hedgerow to reach the head of the track leading up to the gates, smoke rising from the longhouse chimney. But today, striding out from the office in the garb of an intruder, the village looks different. Tom Parker is still leaning on the fence, his phone fully out in the open now. He seems large in comparison to the thatched buildings, as though he could topple the palisade with a push. The warehouse rises over the village like a polluted wave. This is what Liv must have seen when he'd handed her the last of her things and told her he wasn't coming to the car. Harald, standing before his failing village, in fake furs, a drinking horn tucked into his belt.

'You've met someone, then?' Harald had said.

'No.'

'But you will?'

Liv shrugged. 'You're sure this is what you want?'

For a moment, Harald feels like waltzing through the village's pitiful defences and burning it all to the ground, the warehouse with it. Then he sees Tom Parker again, his phone held forward, filming. Harald makes a sound close to a growl, some kind of certainty brewing inside him. Before he can stop himself, Harald is marching towards Tom Parker. He hoists his shield and draws his sword, picking up the pace to a jog. A charge? Perhaps. Tom Parker doesn't move at first, watching the spectacle through the screen with a small smile. As his jog turns into a sprint, or as close as he can manage to a sprint, Harald starts shouting, something even he can hardly make out. 'Magic! Fuck off!' Tom Parker's smile falls away, and, still filming, he draws himself up to his full height. He is taller than Harald, but that doesn't matter: Harald has gone berserk.

A crash against his helmet brings Harald to a stop. The shock and the pain cools him, the red mist parting; he should be unstoppable, practically invincible. He is not. He looks down to see Tom Parker's boy retrieving his spear from the ground. He has thrown it at Harald and managed to hit him square on the head. Where did the boy even come from? He should be in the shield wall. Looking around him now, Harald cannot see anything resembling organised defences, cannot hear the bell that should have warned of Aethelred's approach. The children are scattered through the fields, all of them looking at him. Agata stands by the gate, watching him too. Harald can't remember if he actually told her of his plan to have her marshall the defences, whether the conversation he remembers now was totally imagined. He tries to signal, but she doesn't move.

Tom Parker's boy is advancing, his gums bared. 'Get back,' Harald says. Somewhere distant-sounding, Tom Parker gives encouragement and quiet video commentary. The boy jabs with the spear. Harald feebly wafts his sword. He is too slow to block. The jerkin is thick and the child is weak, but the blow is not painless.

'Get back now,' Harald says. The boy advances. Harald steps away, off the road and into the muddy field. 'I said stop it.'

Another prod, this time in the back of his calf. It's Karate Chop, suddenly armed. How? Harald cannot think. Tom Parker's boy has been joined by the one who milled a whole loaf of bread, and behind him come the two girls who giggled at the smell of the smoking house. The rest of them are approaching now, encouraged by Harald's slowness, his lack of fight, his total stagnation. Harald tries to move, but his boot is stuck in deep mud. More jabs, whacks, high-pitched laughter and cheering. He tries to lever himself upwards with his sword, but it sinks partway up the blade and is lost. He is on the ground. Hiding behind his shield. Which he loses too. On his back. The jabs hurt. Harald whittled those spears too sharp.

It is dark outside the longhouse. The children have left. Tom Parker was almost apologetic and promised to delete the film footage, or at least not to share it, not widely. Harald throws the last of the logs onto the fire, and then a handful of firelighters. The flames are bright but not all that warm. He pulls his furs tighter. Hazy light blinks through the beams. The security bulb over the staff door of the warehouse. People coming and going. Harald closes his eyes. The refrigeration units hum; the low thud of dropped crates. To Harald, it sounds like chanting. It sounds like beating on the longhouse door.

Autophile

Dylan Garity

I.

The notification chimes a few minutes after midnight.

Marcus had turned the lights out at 11:55, like Mom always would after it was just the two of them. Keep each day from bleeding over into the next. A steady schedule makes a steady mind. Now, the soft blue-green of the Connection screen illuminates his narrow room. It's a peaceful color, like being submerged in shallow water with blurred trees above, so peaceful that for a moment, it makes him want to close his eyes again and sink.

But he promised he would try, so he picks up the phone and opens the App.

The Connection is with Amy, age twenty-nine, astrological sign left blank, a graphic design manager who loves hiking, strong coffee, and mystery novels. In her first photo, she's sitting on the floor in the middle of a party. She's laughing at someone's joke, her legs tucked under her chin in a pair of side-zipping block heel boots. Her curly brown hair is cropped short, just above her shoulders, and a small nose ring glitters in the lamplight.

Marcus doesn't remember coming across her profile, but he feels a rush of warmth looking at the picture – like he's the one sitting across from her making her laugh, like he could be. Awake now, he taps the messaging window.

Hey Amy, he types, *I …*

He stops, and a moment later the gray text pops up, filling in the rest.

… really love those boots. Did you get them at that little shop down on Harvey?

That's good. Specific, attentive, complimenting but not aggressive. Exactly what he was looking to say. Marcus knows the shop, a vintage clothing store kitty-corner from the park near his office. He taps the words and they turn black, then he clicks to send.

Amy writes back a couple of minutes later.

Hey! Haha, you nailed it. Have you been there?

He pauses again, thinking. After three seconds, the autofill icon appears – a little animated hand scrawling a letter. Marcus ignores it, starting on his own.

No, he types finally, *not …*

The predictive text fills in, *really my vibe*. That seems risky – what if it comes across as him saying he doesn't like her style? But it continues*, It always looked super cute, though. I walk by there on the way to work, and I think I saw those in the window a while back.*

Did he actually see them? Marcus tries to remember. The boots do look familiar, but maybe they're just in style lately. That's not the point, though. What's important is that it sounds like him. It is him, really. That's the promise of the App, to help you be yourself. It knows how he writes, how he sounds, so it helps him come across better, authentically and efficiently.

From gray to black, making the words his own. He sends.

She writes back quicker this time. *Yeah, it is. One of my favorite spots. So what's your style then? Photos all look a little normcore – not bad on you though.* Three images follow: man in a turtleneck, eye roll, winky face.

Marcus smiles and sits up, pulling a second pillow over and propping it behind him. Amy's right – all of his pictures show off the same dark jeans, gray hoodie combo. She's making fun of him a little, but in a way that feels welcoming, how she might if they already knew each other. It puts him at ease.

What can I say? he types, and the App fills in, *I'm a simple guy. Who knows though, maybe surprises hiding underneath – rainbow socks? sparkly boxers? It's a mystery.* Then a little animated graphic of a book opening.

It's goofier and a bit more flirtatious than he was thinking, but now that he sees the words, they feel right. And the App knows her too, of course, so what's the risk? It wouldn't suggest something that would turn her off. He sends it, and Amy replies with immediate laughter before she starts typing something else. Reaching over, Marcus turns his lamp on, takes a sip of water, and sinks in.

They write back and forth for a while. He lets the App take over entirely at points. It turns out they know a couple of the same people, old college friends of his that she recently met in a rock-climbing group. She talks about an author she loves, and he sends her a song from a new band that was picked for him this week. When she mentions her recently adopted kitten, he shares a video of a monkey grooming a cat at a South African sanctuary, and the heart-eyes she sends back in response almost fill the screen.

They say goodnight, with a plan to meet up over the weekend, and Marcus glances at the clock – one thirty. So much for Mom's advice. Miss you, always. Yet he feels energized in a way he hasn't in months. He's looking forward to the morning instead of dreading it, eager to figure out the details and see Amy in a few days.

As he scrolls back through the messages, their CouldBe photos pulse gently at the top of the screen, and he taps on one to enlarge it. There they are, hiking together, Marcus helping Amy over a fallen log blocking the trail. He swipes to the next. A bar patio, where Amy sips a dark cocktail, Marcus a glass of wine, a few unknown friends out of focus down the table. Then curled up on his couch, a little older, Amy in his lap, reading while Marcus rubs her shoulders.

He smiles and turns out the light again, his mind filled with the images, their faces and their bodies pieced together so seamlessly he can almost remember the scenes.

II.

The morning of her date with Marcus, the complimentary ListenIn arrives in Amy's mail in a blue-green tie-dyed box. The device itself is a semi-opaque, colorless plastic, shaped like a scythe. It feels comfortable as she slides it over and around her ear. After a few seconds, Amy reaches up in surprise. Did it fall off? No, it's still there. She just can't feel where her skin ends and it begins.

An old-fashioned greeting card pops open at the bottom of the box, revealing a handwritten message.

Hi Amy,

Congratulations on your First Date. With ListenIn's natural language AI, you never have to worry about the right thing to say. Just think of it as an extension of you, subtle and discreet.

To turn the earpiece on, simply swipe from the top of your ear to the bottom. To turn it off, run your finger along the back of your ear, like you're scratching an itch.

Your Casual subscription comes with two free weeks of ListenIn. If you like what you find, consider upgrading to our Dating or Committed tiers for continued access. Who knows? If things go well, maybe you'll even stick with us for a Lifetime!

Amy closes the card and sets it on her pillow, then stands in front of the full-length mirror on her bedroom door. Behind her, the mini bamboo and kangaroo fern hanging in the window sway with the spring breeze, haloing her reflection in green. She bought them from a local garden store just over a year ago now and has kept them thriving the whole time. They remind Amy of her grandmother's yard, that tangle of branches and leaves that once felt infinite enough to get lost in. Usually the sight of them overhead comforts her, but right now they feel like another life intruding, like something that doesn't belong to her anymore.

Brushing a dark coil of hair back, Amy tilts her head. The earpiece is nearly invisible, just a slight glint when it catches the light. She reaches up and slides her finger down from her hairline as if smearing a streak of paint, tracing the straight edge of the device.

A brief crackling sound, like someone rustling a candy wrapper inside her skull. Amy shivers and takes a deep breath, letting it out slowly. Then silence again, but a new frequency of silence, the silence of waiting.

* * *

They're meeting at an upscale bar called Raymond's Tavern, about halfway between their apartments. The tables are lit by small candles, and a muted piano filters through speakers in the corners. Amy's been there a few times before, but it was Marcus who suggested it.

A couple of minutes early, she grabs a high-top in the corner, where she can see the door as each new person enters. Her heart scurries around inside her chest. What will she say? What will he feel like, sitting across from her? When did she get so nervous about meeting someone new?

There are the horror stories, of course – that musician Natasha slept with, the one who used a banned CouldBe plug-in. Arm around her, nuzzling her forehead after sex, he'd told her how he watched them fuck a dozen times before they met up that night. "I wanted to see what it would be like with you," he whispered. "You weren't as perfect as how it showed you – you were better."

Amy feels violated just thinking about it. But still, safer to meet someone screened. The App doesn't allow harassment – it permanently locks out anyone who shows even a hint. In his messages, Marcus has been kind and thoughtful and witty, and there's something in his eyes, something that makes her want them to be staring right into her.

That's not what it's about. She just never used to be like this. In college and over the few years after, Amy was confident, the one who approached strangers when out with her girlfriends at the bar, merging groups and sending the night off on unexpected rails. A self-assuredness that felt as much a part of her as bones and skin. She could say anything and it came out right – and if it didn't, it was forgotten a moment later.

When did she lose that? It slipped away somewhere, without her noticing. Had she changed, or had the world? If she had, it was without her permission. Please revert. Roll back to previous version.

Marcus walks in five minutes after eight, and she recognizes him immediately. She's wearing a black silk top tucked into a red polka-dot pencil skirt, while he's ditched the hoodie for a slim button-down with rolled-up sleeves, though still the same black-gray palette from head to foot. Normcore plus, Amy thinks with a smile as he makes eye contact and heads over.

They greet each other by name and Marcus apologizes for being late, something about a bus crashing into the bike lane a few blocks ahead of where he was riding. As she starts to ask if people were okay, the waiter comes over. They pull out their phones to look at the menu. Marcus gets a "Risky Ginger" and Amy goes with a new red ale from a brewery down by the river.

Once the waiter's taken the order and left, they teeter into an awkward silence. That dread fills Amy again, somehow racing and heavy at the same time.

After a moment, she swipes her finger down in front of her right ear and sees Marcus do the same, mirroring her. "Anyway," she says, and then the earpiece crackles and speaks to her in her own voice. *"You mentioned you were going to see your dad in Oregon next week …"*

She hesitates for a second, then says the words aloud.

And as she does, the voice continues, *"Is that where you grew up?"*

Amy says it quicker, too quick almost, the words stumbling out in a rush. This will take a little getting used to.

Marcus waits for a few seconds, tilting his head to listen to his own earpiece. Then he speaks. "Sort of. My parents split up when I was twelve, and my dad moved down to Portland." He hesitates again. "So I ended up trading time between there and Seattle, where I lived with my mom."

"Oh, that must've been a lot," she says, and it's already easier. She's listening and speaking nearly together now, forming a harmony in her head. "Mine got divorced when I was around the same age, but they ended up living down the block from each other. So they kind of just became neighbors."

They settle into a flow after that, Marcus talking about a punk show he's thinking of going to the next night, some local band playing, and soon Amy's dread has slipped away without her noticing. They talk lightly and intimately, they joke and they commiserate. She speaks in short, confident sentences. She does not say "I" too much. They ask each other questions and she never has to worry about coming up with another. Each time ListenIn speaks, it feels just like that internal monologue in her own head, like thinking what she's going to say before saying it, but now she doesn't have to.

They have such a good time that when the voice suggests they head back to her place, with her roommate off camping for the week, she almost says the words before she hears them.

At the apartment, she turns and kisses Marcus while he's still closing the door behind them. In her bedroom, the earpiece switches off by accident as she pulls her shirt over her head. She leaves it that way; something would feel wrong about it. The sex they have is comfortable – it does not shatter her, it does not make her see new constellations in the stars exploding behind her eyes, it simply feels warm and good.

When they're done, she brushes her hair down, turning it on again.

"Hey, I know this might be ..." she says, and her own voice comes to her, soft and familiar, leading her into this dazzling new world. All she has to do is listen. "... a little forward, but do you wanna meet up again tomorrow? Go see that concert maybe?"

Marcus smiles, pausing for only a second. "I'd love to."

III.

Before Marcus knows it, they've been going out for three months. The second date was the best time he'd had in years, even though the band was terrible. He and Amy ended up drinking in an alley behind the venue for the back half of the show, where they could hear themselves speak and watch the hardcore kids shove each other until a bouncer came out and halfheartedly broke them up.

Since then, they've seen each other a few times a week, and ListenIn has been magical. Their conversations feel endlessly spontaneous and original, unfolding like the pages of a book. They reveal themselves, and welcome each other's revelation. He feels closer to Amy than he's felt to anyone he's dated before. Even when they fight, the resolutions only leave them more connected. He wonders what their future will be like together, and has the App generate CouldBe after CouldBe. The pictures fill his mind, let him envision all the moments they will strive for.

Marcus finds himself wanting to tell Mom about her, once even reaching for the phone to make the call. Where before this would flood him with sorrow, now he's just glad that he's found someone who makes him happy. She would've liked Amy, and she would be proud of him, so proud.

Sometimes he comes across posts criticizing the App and the device – how using it is dangerous, debasing, giving up your humanity. But for him, the whole thing is freeing. So much of dating is performance anyway, he thinks. Why not embrace it? If he were acting in a play, he wouldn't write it himself. And it would be a far better story than any he could come up with. All the great love stories are stories, after all, scripted for us. He and Amy are living a perfect relationship, and one that no one has ever lived before – novel, singular, crafted anew from their very essence.

One week it has them go to the local zoo, something Marcus hasn't done since he was a kid. They marvel at the butterfly garden, the impossible array of colors flapping from bush to tree, a few even landing on their arms. They wave at the gorillas and talk about how human the mother seems, nursing and carrying her infant. When another one charges at the edge of the enclosure, Marcus shouts and jumps back out of instinct, and Amy laughs but then wraps her arms around him and leads him on toward the lions.

Another week they write beautiful poems to each other. The words make Marcus cry. The words that come from Amy's mouth and hands and the words that come from his own. He isn't always sure they line up with what he's feeling, but they seem like such wonderful things to feel. At times, it's so profound he just doesn't know what to make of it all. He doesn't know what to think.

In early summer, he wakes in Amy's apartment and finds her already up beside him, sipping coffee, messing with some generative artwork on her tablet, switching and prompting and combining. Her legs are tucked under her chin like in her first photo, and for a second Marcus can only stare, remembering that time just before midnight that feels so distant now it was like a different person lived it.

His earpiece crackles as he rises. *"Hey, let's take a long weekend and go on a trip next week."*

Amy smiles when he groggily says the words out loud a second later. He's always a little slow in the morning. "That sounds wonderful. Where are you thinking?"

"Have you ever been to Glacier? I've driven through Montana but never gone all the way up there. Only a couple-hour flight. I hear the hiking is absolutely incredible – and of course the views."

Amy's eyes brighten. "That sounds amazing. Let's do it."

They haven't been anywhere outside the Cities yet, and a rush passes through Marcus at the thought. "I'll book it all right now," he tells her.

"There's this great combination discount site that takes care of all the details," and the earpiece gives him the name of the site, and he says it aloud and pulls it up, and after they have it all planned out, the rush of adventure doesn't fade for the rest of the day. It fills him and keeps him full.

When they get back, sunburned from the thin atmosphere, muscles aching but satisfied, they agree to move in together, fully Committed.

IV.

Sometimes, as they settle in for the night in the new apartment, Amy finds herself telling Marcus a story and questioning whether it's real or not. Did Natasha really say that funny thing at brunch the other day? Did ListenIn record it and remember it, while for Amy in the moment it slipped right by?

Other times, she's sure it isn't real, but she says the words anyway. Memories of growing up, formative moments. One night she tells him about when she was a kid and broke her ankle flying off a swing set into a tree in the park down the street from her house, a park that didn't exist, how years later a group of boys tied her to the same tree and joked about what they'd do to her. How they ended up letting her go when one of them got freaked out.

Nothing like that ever happened. Worse things did, but she doesn't talk about those.

This is the longest she's been with anyone since college. Marcus is great, he really is, perfect for her – she can't risk turning the device off now. What if she no longer knows how to talk to him? What if he's not interested in whatever she wants to say?

The apartment they found is just right, on the third floor of a five-by-five that finished construction a month before they moved in. A huge bedroom and an office for her and Marcus to share, the sleekest kitchen she's ever seen, light pirouetting in through the windows in the corner living room as they look out toward the skyline at sunset.

But as the months go on, something's missing. They still go out on dates, they still have sex, more than her other long-term couple friends from what she hears, but sometimes in the morning she doesn't remember a single word they said the night before. Doesn't remember what they did beyond the loosest sketch. Some days she doesn't feel like she's thinking at all, really – like her mind isn't inside her anymore but somewhere else entirely, somewhere she can't reach.

More and more often when they're out together, Amy sees couples with visible earpieces, some almost wearing them like jewelry, colorful and gaudy. The ostentation feels wrong to her, as if they're afraid of being criticized or made fun of, and responding preemptively – like dropping your pants because you're worried they might fall down during an important speech. But it's what all the ads for the App say now – *be more. More than who you think you can be, more than just human.*

One Saturday, they drive out to a wine tasting on a farm in the suburbs and take cute couples photos by an abandoned barn in the falling leaves, something she never would've dreamed of doing. Neither of them even likes wine all that much, but at least the suggestion got them out of their normal routine. Amy's cold and tired the whole time, and Marcus seems miserable too by the end. They both tell each other how much they're loving it and what a perfect day it was, and when they get home she avoids him until bed, staying in the office so they don't have to speak.

* * *

A week later, they fight all night.

Their fights have been growing frequent, and recursive. Maybe the model needs them to have more fights for it to continue to learn from, and then they can finally be productive again. But to Amy it feels more and more like sliding onto the same tracks, locking in, rushing toward a broken bridge.

This one is the worst yet. Marcus has an opportunity in Colorado, a promotion, managing the six-month installation of a new wind farm. He's been out to Boulder a couple times already and he loves it, thinks he might stay when he's done, and he wants her to move with him. Amy's not ready for that yet. Not ready to leave the Cities, not ready to start all over, not ready for what might be a Lifetime. It's that dread again, heavier and faster than ever.

The fight takes them from the couch, where they were just sitting down to eat sushi, to shouting across the marble counter in the kitchen, to the balcony outside after Amy retreats there, where they keep every word at a spitting whisper so their neighbors won't be alarmed.

"Maybe we need to take some kind of break," she tells him, and it feels like what she's been wanting to say the whole time.

"A break? What's that supposed to mean?"

Marcus looks less angry now, more disbelieving. His eyes glaze over, like he can't see her anymore.

"Not forever," she says. "Just see how it feels."

"You can't do this. You can't just decide you love me, but not quite enough. Either you love me or you don't."

"Of course I love you. That's not what I'm saying."

"Then don't break up with me." He storms inside again, and she follows. "If you mean that, don't leave me."

"Marcus, I—"

Back in the kitchen, he reaches up above the stove and pulls down a liter of bourbon, unscrewing the cap. They don't drink much at home, so the bottle is almost full, sloshing around near the top. Amy doesn't understand what he's doing.

"If you break up with me," he says slowly, the words jerking out through sobs, "I will drink this entire bottle. I swear I'll do it. I'll drink this whole bottle tonight. I will fucking lie down in the street in traffic because that will hurt less."

Amy freezes. A buzzing fills her head until she can't hear the words from the device. She's not in the apartment anymore, she's back in high school, shaking her friend Carmen on the cold tile floor of an upstairs bathroom. There's vomit across her face and down her shirt, and Amy tries to lift her, calls out for help, but Carmen is already heavy and cold.

He won't actually do it, will he? How is it telling him to say this? But even as she thinks this, Marcus lifts the whiskey to his lips and begins to drink, his face contorting as he swallows, once, twice, again.

The earpiece repeats itself, over and over until she hears it and chokes out, "Marcus, stop. Stop, we'll figure things out."

She's sitting on the hallway carpet, rocking with her arms wrapped around her knees. Marcus stares at her from the kitchen, leaning against the wall, the bottle limp in his fingers, still more than half full.

After a minute, he lets it drop to the counter, his face calm now. Then he walks past her toward the bathroom, tilting his head the way he sometimes does still when he's listening.

"Come on, honey. Let's just brush our teeth and go to bed. I'll give you a massage." Marcus turns back to her. "Maybe we'll feel better if we physically connect instead of talking around in circles. A reset."

Amy stares up at him.

"Okay. You're right. That sounds nice," her voice says in her ear.

"Okay. You're—"

But it doesn't sound nice to Amy. It sounds insane. She doesn't want to be anywhere near him right now. She doesn't want to be anywhere near herself, not this version of her. Amy wants to be whoever she was before, long before all of this. Eager and unafraid.

Reaching behind her ear, Amy turns the device off. In the dark, she's not sure if Marcus can see her do it.

"No," she says, and the word sounds so strange and thin on its own. "No, I can't – do that."

He turns around in the bathroom doorway.

"This is me," she says. "This is me, Marcus. I'm saying … every word. They're my own."

His eyes widen, and he shakes his head, then opens his mouth to speak.

"No," she says again. "I don't think it will fix … but talk to me. Just you. Please."

Amy walks up to him and slowly, like reaching to pet a frightened animal, stretches her hand out toward his ear. He shakes his head. She can see him listening again. Like on that first date, when he was just learning. But now it's not the lag of keeping up with the device – he's trying to decide whether to say the words or not.

Marcus takes her hand.

"Come on," he says, "we can just take a shower and then get in bed. I'll read something to you. Maybe it'll feel a little better if we just do something else for a while before we sleep. Start fresh tomorrow."

Amy squeezes his fingers. I'm sorry, she thinks, and then she says it aloud. He's still standing there when she walks out and down the stairs and into the cool night air.

V.

Late the next spring, in one of those weeks when half the trees are in full bloom and half are hard and bare, when crossing to the next block can feel like stepping into a different season, Marcus sees Amy on Fourth Street, waiting for the bus. She's wearing the same red skirt from that first night at the bar.

He walks past her. He's unsubscribed. The earpiece is buried somewhere in the closet in his new apartment, and there's nothing for him to say.

Endangered

Roger Vickery

Finbar scorns the hippie music of his generation. He loves music that bites or flies. When Kinky Friedman, 'the last of the Texas Jewish cowboys', is belting out *The Wild Man from Borne-o-o*[*], Finbar shakes his big hands and gyrates around a Bang and Olufsen quadraphonic turntable like Joe Cocker on back street speed.

Sal and Finbar rent an arthritic, semi-detached brick cottage in a dog-leg street that juts into Edgecliff Road, four kilometres from Sydney's centre. The semi is scheduled to be demolished if the Eastern Suburbs railway line goes ahead at the end of 1978.

'Never happen,' Finbar says. Sal is not so sure.

Their backyard runs onto a half-acre block of lantana-choked land strewn with logs, wooden crates, planks, pipes, bricks, screws, nails and sheets of asbestos fibro and corrugated iron. Under cover of darkness, wealthy neighbours stroll there, furtively discarding consumer goods like prisoners of war spilling escape tunnel dirt from their trouser legs.

Finbar calls the block *The Twilight Zone.* 'I can forage there for firewood and treasures without meeting anyone except an occasional Rottweiler with a child in its jaws. Position, position, position.'

Their low-beamed front room houses hundreds of blues, jazz and country LPs that stand erect and ready on plumb-level, hand-planed shelves. All else is chaos.

Finbar gave up working on building sites in 1976 after right wing thugs took over the Builders Labourers' Federation and began dismantling the union's green bans on heritage sites. These days Finbar is employed as a part-time audio-visual officer in the Building School at Sydney Technical College. On the weekends he works as a kitchen hand at *La Dolce Vita* restaurant in Leichardt. That was where he won Sal's heart.

---

[*] Richard 'Kinky' Friedman, 1974.

'How could she refuse me?' he boasts. 'I am the life of the sink.'

Sal adores Marilyn Monroe, feels guilty about leaving school at 15 and is wading through the 50 most influential books in world literature as part of a Workers Education Authority course that has been outsourced to the Leavis wing of the Sydney University's English Department.

* * *

I met Finbar when Sydney Tech hired me as an assistant film and TV producer.

The panel was impressed by my CV: BA Hons, 1-year political liaison in Canberra, 3 years' cutting copy for the Grey Advertising agency, 2 years' peddling freelance stories from Africa and South America ... and only 27.

They didn't know my gut was inflamed courtesy of Ghanaian guinea worm, my self-esteem was shredded thanks to Wilhelmina from Amsterdam deserting me for a Masai prince, and my literary aspirations had been punctured by Peter Carey–my boss at Grey–who said my writing was ... 'florid, over-detailed and besotted with the rule of three'.

A red-faced manager with Marty Feldman thyroid eyes briefed me on my first job. 'We need you to ride shotgun on a 16mm training film called *Re-studding a Californian Bungalow.* Finbar is turning the thing into *Gone with the Wind.* He's a big, bolshie bugger but he won't monster you, just as well, you being a short arse. Blarney is his go, watch out for his blarney.'

Marty pointed at a door plastered with a poster declaring *Monsters Live Here* and blown up photos of Angela Davis, Einstein, Gandhi and Howard Hughes. Country music was blaring out from behind it. I knocked, got no answer, walked in and found Finbar hunched over a neatly dismantled Steenbeck editing deck. All else was chaos. Strips of film were dangling across walls and chairs and spilling out from plastic bins and open filing cabinets.

Finbar grinned, showing an impressive set of ivories. 'That's Kinky Friedman on the eight-track, crooning out his sentimental ballad: *They ain't makin' Jews like Jesus anymore*[†]. So, pilgrim, are you ready to

[†] Richard 'Kinky' Friedman, 1974.

create a technical masterpiece?'

I needed a place to live. Finbar offered to rent me his spare room but there was a caveat. 'Sal's been turning down potential sub-tenants. They weren't arty enough. Don't be afraid to *allude*.'

Sal greeted us on the stairs holding a book in one hand and supporting a precariously tied towel across her breasts with the other. 'I'm not an aficionado of clothes in summer,' she announced, descending with the grace of a catwalk model.

'Nor winter,' Finbar muttered. 'What're you reading, foxy?'

Sal held up a green Everyman paperback. '*Gerard Manley Hopkins: The major poems,'* she said, gliding in my direction.

As she drew level, my Ghanaian wormhole stirred and my gut erupted, releasing a burst of quiet, nasty gas. I began back-peddling, trying to minimise the damage. But Sal kept gliding into my gap. I didn't know her sense of smell had been ruined since her second stepfather broke her nose when she was 12.

Sal hemmed me in against a bookcase. 'I hear you're an intellectual. Finbar, why're you fanning your nose? Quit it, you clown.' She turned back to me. 'Do you know Hopkins' poems? Do you like Hopkins' poems?' Her voice had a husky 'happy birthday Mister President' cadence.

I nodded.

'Maybe you could quote a few lines?'

I swallowed, coughed and mentally bellowed out for Sister Josephine.

'Or … are you another one of Finbar's bull-shitter mates?'

Sister Josephine believed the best prompt for a tongue-tied boy shivering in the wings of an Eisteddfod performance was a nonchalant clip across the ears. I felt a mild sting and the opening lines of my performance piece in a 15-years-and-under Verse and Drama section came welling up.

'His rash-fresh re-winded new-skeinèd score …' I declaimed. *'In crisps of curl off wild winch whirl … and pour and pelt music … till none's to spill … nor spend!'*

That was it. My memory tank was sucking air until Sister Josephine sank her knuckle in my back. Sister believed a fancy genuflection could sway an undecided adjudicator.

'The Sea and the Skylark, middle stanza,' I declared, bowing low from the hip.

Sal located the poem and read it, moving her lips with each word.

I felt another sting. 'Sprung rhythm, inverted syntax and coined words ... the triple threat,' I added.

'Smart arse,' Sal said, grinning. She looked towards Finbar and gave him a thumbs-up. Then she fell over and began fitting.

Finbar rolled her into the foetal position, covered her with his jacket, wiped dribble from her face and cooed like a mother pigeon until the thrashing eased.

'No spoons or keys, never prise the jaw open,' he said. 'It happens every month or so. No obvious trigger. Stay with her until she surfaces and help her overcome her embarrassment. Hey! There we go! Hello foxy.'

* * *

Sal keeps pushing Finbar to do something with his life.

'No need,' he grins. 'I'm one of Sydney's golden bums.'

The high ground above us is occupied by a row of dilapidated 1890's mansions. They loom over *The Twilight Zone* like a crumbling pueblo village. Their Peter Pan tenants come and go to our semi bringing books, wine, joints, hangovers, gossip, invitations and get-rich-quick schemes, and none are more extravagant than those that fall from the mouth of Tennyson Ho, a Bruce Lee look-alike, who vaults our back fence with the grace of a Kung Fu master evading a phalanx of spears and enters our kitchen, as if he is Joseph Smith bearing Moroni's golden plates.

'Tennyson is the human equivalent of a cassata ice-cream on a hot day at Bondi Beach. I could lick him to death,' Sal says, leaning on my shoulder, as she watches Tennyson murmuring to Finbar about a container of instamatic cameras at Port Botany docks that two Ninja-types with night vision goggles could scoop up and unload for a tasty profit.

Bradley, a squatter in the largest pueblo, warns Finbar against going along with Tennyson's plan. 'It's illegal, physical, and risky. I know how we can make real money, legitimate money.'

Bradley wins bets at White City tennis courts with a switchblade backhand, moonlights as a sultry psychic at Paddington markets, complete with a Sabu the Jungle Boy turban and a fake gold tooth, and he keeps two sets of books for Cadrys, a carpet dealer on Edgecliff Road. Finbar is sure the guy won't die poor.

He invites Bradley into our kitchen and listens intently as his new consigliore waves a cigarette in the direction of some sleepy cockroaches moving across the floor.

'They're Germans, ugly brutes, but slow and easy to spray. The American hash browns are real buggers. They're costly to eradicate. Find a nest of hash browns and you've got opal miner's rights.'

Finbar and Bradley enrol in a pest exterminator course at Sydney Tech.

Sal isn't impressed. 'You're nearly 30,' she tells Finbar. "Where do you want to be in five years? Stuck here … scrubbing pots, nuking cockroaches and hatching loser schemes?'

Finbar lifts her in the air. She wriggles and gives him a half-hearted slap. Eventually, she locks her legs around his hips.

'You think once women get stuck on you, they can't get away. But you're no tar baby and I ain't no Brer Rabbit.'

Finbar grins. 'I hear you, foxy.'

I look away.

The duo's first major assignment is carrying out a practice fumigation. They set about de-lousing our kitchen wearing respirators supplied by someone−who knows someone−who knows Tennyson. Sal finds them choking and retching in the backyard and drives them to the emergency ward at St Vincent's Hospital. They know us in emergency.

* * *

Sal's tutor slithers into our garden. Derrick is a 40-something hobbit on a short-term secondment from Oxford University. He laces his classes with anecdotes about drinking sprees with Sylvia (fortified sherry) and Ted (real ale) and other literary luminaries in a late-night Richard Burton drawl. He invites gifted students to his flat for martinis, fondues and 'quality music'. Sal loves walking bare footed across Derrick's tribal rugs. Opera is beginning to make sense, she says.

The serpent flies home and posts Sal a signed copy of Plath's poems.

Three weeks later it's a poster of Marilyn kissing Olivier in *The Prince and the Showgirl*. A business class ticket for one with British European Airways follows.

* * *

Finbar finds Sal's goodbye note.

Tennyson rushes us, in someone's Alfa Romeo to the international terminal and uses his contacts to get us past security and into the BEA lounge.

Sal groans as Finbar strides toward her.

'Foxy,' he pleads.

Sal shakes her head. 'You're an endangered species. One day you're going to vanish into your own Twilight Zone.' She dries her eyes, retrieves a flute of champagne, and waves us away.

* * *

Sal torments us with postcards from the city of dreaming spires.

In a newly acquired rococo script, she lets us know she loves playing Marilyn to Derrick's Miller.

* * *

A burly bloke in a houndstooth suit pounds on the semi's door and hands Finbar a notice to quit. The Eastern Suburbs railway is going ahead.

Finbar reaches for his firewood axe. Swinging it, nunchaku style, one-handed, he crams the notice into his mouth with the other, advances on Houndstooth and deposits a wad of soggy paper on the server's ox-blood brogues.

* * *

We hear rumours that evictions are being outsourced to bouncers from *The Pink Pussycat* night club.

The pueblos fall outside the demolition zone; for now, at least. Bradley and Tennyson urge us to recognize the inevitable and move in with them. I re-locate to Tennyson's floor. But Finbar refuses to shift.

A week after we finish *Re-studding,* Sydney Tech promotes me and sacks Finbar.

He blows his payout on the latest Canon Super 8 and begins following us through his eyepiece.

He labels the first cassette: ENDANGERED.

Fur

Allegra A Mullan

Lila killed a dog this morning. She hit it with the car. Now she watches Anna as she tosses bright green leaves in a wooden bowl.

Anna looks at her friend and says, 'That dog was already sick.'

'What?'

'That's why you could hit it.' When she doesn't turn around Anna says, 'Dogs aren't stupid, especially the ones here. They survive. If you could hit it there was already something wrong.'

'Maybe.'

'We can stop talking about it if you want.'

'We can keep talking about it.'

The ice in Lila's drink makes a sound against the glass. She is looking out towards the sea. The sea is a flat grey line between the Christmas palms. The glass is tinted, it takes the light away from the outside, the same way a storm does.

'I'm sorry you feel bad,' Anna says. 'You will feel better about it by tomorrow.'

'I know. It's happened to me before.' She says this to surprise Anna, and because it's true.

Anna asks, 'What do you mean?'

'With a dog.' It goes quiet. The birds switch in the air above the powerline.

After dinner they talk about it again, Lila and Anna, and Anna's husband Rudy. Lila and Rudy are sitting in the main room of the apartment, on two white sofas that sit facing each other, with a coffee table between them. On the table a candle burns calmly in a glass container. Next to it is a vase of long-stemmed pink dahlias that Anna bought in town. They look strange in the candlelight. They have so many shadows inside them.

Rudy says, 'How's the car?' His wife looks irritated.

'... Rudy.'

'It's my car.' Rudy raises his eyebrows at Anna and smiles.

Anna says, 'Leave her alone,' and moves towards the kitchen. Lila puts down her glass,

'The car is fine.'

'Good.'

'But I wonder ...' She catches herself.

'Yes?'

'I wonder if I should go and talk to them, the family.'

'Who owned the dog?'

'Yes.'

'How do you know who they are?'

'It's Maria's dog, you know?' Anna calls from the kitchen. Rudy shakes his head. 'She works at the chemist, I had lunch with her once – she lives at the end of Moruga. It was an Alsatian, I think.' Lila watches Anna through the door to the kitchen. She pours water from the Brita filter into the kettle and sets it to boil.

Lila explains to Rudy, 'I just think they would probably like to know. They might not even know what's happened to him, I mean, imagine if it was Mouse.' At the mention of his name Mouse slinks in from the kitchen. He is a Spanish greyhound, huge, and silent, swinging his head to look at them both. He lumbers over to Rudy and settles there, with one last empty gaze around the room.

Rudy doesn't look at the dog, instead he says, 'They'll only want money out of you.'

'I could give them money.'

'You don't have any.'

'I do.'

'You mean our money?'

'I have money.'

'Not much.'

'Some.'

'And you would give that to them and that would be a mistake.'

'Why?'

'Once you did, they would ask for more.'

Anna returns. She has brought fresh drinks for Lila and Rudy. White wine with ice. 'Lila can do whatever she wants with her money,' she tells him.

'You're the one who says she's so fragile, Anna. I'm only trying to help. She'll end up giving all her money to these people and then we will have to keep looking after her forever.'

'I love having Lila here.' There is a pause.

Rudy says with a gentler tone, 'You're welcome to stay as long as you want Lila, of course.'

'Thank you.' Lila takes the drink. She thinks about the bag of ice in the top drawer of the freezer, ice and plastic in the freezing dark.

'But no more animal sacrifices.'

'Stop.'

'Relax.'

'Don't make fun of me.'

He hooks his ankle under Lila's, and gently jogs it up and down to a certain interior rhythm. She moves her foot away. She says, 'Anna you decide.'

'Do what you like.'

'But what would *you* do?'

'I don't know.' Anna looks down. Lila turns to Rudy again.

'You see, here's the thing … I can't stop …'

He interrupts. 'Thinking about it?'

'Talking about it.' Rudy leans back in his chair. He breathes out, hard, through his nose. He has one hand making small circles on Mouse's head. She looks at the dog. It has a long silver muzzle and thin translucent ears. Light comes through the cartilage. She says, 'I can't stop talking about it.'

'It's done.'

'Maybe – maybe not yet.' Behind Rudy she can see her own reflection in the glass. It is dark outside.

The next evening Lila goes to Maria's house. Rudy brings the car round for her, the same car, the Audi. She waits in the courtyard of the apartment complex. On the outside the building is tall and white, with rows of lit windows on each floor. It has a circular drive and in the centre is a koi pond. Lila stands by the edge and watches the heavy, blunt-nosed fish nuzzling the concrete.

Her mum had had a dog. Once, she had rang Lila, crying. This was when Lila was still living in the old apartment, and she had sat on the leather sofa in the lamplight with a blanket around her knees. This was when her mum had just got the dog, and she had explained shakily over the phone that she just couldn't keep him.

'I can't live like this.'

'Like what?'

'I love him so much. I'm just so terrified, I know he is going to die.'

'Why would he die?'

'He will die, one day, and I just don't know what to do. It's all I can think about when I look at him. He is going to die and it will break my heart. I won't be able to cope.'

'He's so young.'

'I can't leave him in the house, Lila. I can't go anywhere. I worry about him so much. But I can't look at him, I can't. I can't stop crying.'

This was the first dog Lila hit with a car.

In the Audi she turns the air conditioning all the way up. It is getting dark. Here the darkness starts between the leaves, and on the ground. Everything else darkens slowly. Last to go is the sea. The flowers for a while stay luminous. Lila knows their names and she lists them if she sees them: hydrangea, oleander, hibiscus. When it is really dark the only light comes from windows, and neon signs in the town.

The house swings up under her headlights. It is one storey, a few yards back from the road, painted white, with a shallow roof. It has a wooden porch covered in thick, pink bougainvillea. Underneath it there are two white plastic chairs. She parks the car by the road. They have heard her arrive. The screen door opens. She calls, 'Hello,' and then, 'Maria?'

She locks the car.

'Hello.'

'I'm Lila.' She walks up to the porch. 'I'm sorry if I'm disturbing you, I know it's a little late.' Behind Maria she catches sight of a child, his face against the screen door, watching her.

'Is everything alright?' Maria asks.

'Yes, I'm a friend of Anna's. I wanted to talk to you, she said this was your house.'

'It is.' Maria smiles, 'Would you like to come in?'

'Yes, that would be good.' She climbs the porch steps. The little boy shuffles away from the door, and his mother opens it.

Inside the room it is hot and dim. Cupboards run along one side, panelled with blonde wood. There is an oven, a sink, a humming white refrigerator. In its centre there is a pale blue formica table. Around it there are four chairs.

'So you are a friend of Anna's?' Maria asks. 'How is she?'

'She's well. Thank you.'

'And you wanted to talk to me.'

'Yes, I did. I did.' Lila's voice trails off a little and she looks at the boy. He is holding a toy, a digger.

'Hello,' she says to him. He narrows his eyes.

'Teo?' Says his mother. 'Why don't you go and play outside?' He pulls at his t-shirt. 'Teo?' She repeats. He gives her an offended look but does what he is told. Lila feels nervous.

'Shall we sit down?' Maria offers. They sit opposite one another. 'What do you need to talk to me about?'

She is waiting.

Lila says, 'I'm sorry.'

'For what?'

'I'm so sorry, I – I was out driving last night, and I hit a dog, a dog that came out in front of the car. I think it was your dog. I thought I should come and see you. It looked like your dog.'

Maria presses her lips together.

'I would have done something but,' she turns her palms upwards, 'he was dead.'

'She.'

'What?'

'She was a girl.'

'I'm so sorry.'

Maria is looking at some space behind her, just over her shoulder.

'I feel terrible.'

'It's a bad thing to happen, we are all very sad.'

'You found her?'

'My son did. She was a very lovely dog. Very clever.' Maria exhales and gives Lila a small smile. Lila likes her, likes her gentleness.

'Would it be okay – could I have a drink? If you have one.' Maria nods and rises and disappears.

She is gone for a long time and when she comes back, she is carrying a bottle of white rum. Maria opens it without speaking. When this is done she sets it in front of Lila, along with a thin stemmed green glass. She fills it half-way.

Lila says, 'I'm sorry, thank you.' Then adds, 'I'm nervous.' There is a little dust around the neck of the bottle. She drinks.

'She was our first dog,' Maria tells her. 'I was very scared of them when I was young.'

'Were you bitten?'

'No, or I was, but I don't remember.' Maria seems very calm. Lila turns her glass in semi-circles on the table. 'Maybe I was when I was very young. But I used to cross the street when I saw them, and my uncle had a dog and I was so terrified of it that when he brought him round I used to cry and cry.' She laughs. 'And it was a tiny dog.' She shows Lila how small it was with her hands. 'It was stupid. My mother would be so angry at me, but I was too scared of the dog to be scared of her, so I would just stay incredibly still, crying the whole time.'

'What changed?'

'What do you mean?'

'You got a dog.'

'I got used to her. She was a puppy, and she slept under the fire escape where I work. And I saw her every day, so helpless, and I got used to her. I liked her differently.'

There is a click and Maria tilts her head up towards the door. Lila turns.

He stands with one hand on the door. He looks at them both with a blank expression. He is tall, and young. She doesn't know how young. It's hard to tell with teenagers. He has the slight, sinister body of a man who has grown very quickly, very recently. He has short dark hair. He is very thin, elongated, his body all limbs, all knuckles and ankles and pale skin. She looks at him. She dragged his dog into the sagebrush and left it to die. Maria speaks to him,

'Luca, would you like to come and sit with us? We are talking about Mika.' He stiffens. He sits down next to his mother, taking an unnatural languid pose, leaning back in his chair.

Next to each other Lila notices that they have the same pretty, aquiline features, similar soft mouths. She remembers his dog. Its heavy head and the spit and blood on her hands – even on the back of her hands. Part of its jaw had been hanging off and its eyes had gone fluorescent in the headlights. She remembers the thrills that went off in her body again and again that probably meant nothing.

'I have come to say how sorry I am,' she tells him.

'About what?' He wants her to say it, so she explains again what happened. As she does she studies his long eyelashes, the white rims under his eyes. The bones of his shoulders show through his thin t-shirt. Sweat has made bright places on his body, his collarbones, his temples.

She looks at his mother. He just sits there, breathing hard.

Then he just says, 'So why are you here?'

'I wanted to explain.' He stares at the formica. Lila refills her glass. 'I also wanted-' she directs this to Maria, 'I wanted to see if there was anything I could do for both of you. Maybe I could help you out with getting a new dog, or something to remember her by.'

The boy says, 'No.'

Maria adds, 'It's a very kind offer but I don't think it's appropriate.'

'Okay. I'm so sorry, I had a dog once too, I know what this can feel like.' Lila senses a strange pressure above them, like they are deep underground, or in the belly of a ship. That perhaps they are in some low hot cave, and a river is flowing above them. She can feel the rush of it, the weight.

The boy says, 'You can go.' She doesn't move.

She says, 'If you change your mind about the money, or if there's anything else I can do…' He sits up, angles himself towards her.

'Do you know what you can do?'

'What?'

'Why don't you give us your dog?'

'I'm sorry?'

'Your dog, I've seen you with it.' He has a peculiar lightness to his tone. She looks at Maria to test if he is serious. Maria presses her lips together, she might be laughing.

'It's not my dog.'

'The greyhound?'

'It's not my dog – I'm a guest.'

'That's what I want.'

'I can't do that.'

'You took my dog?'

'It's not my dog.'

She gives a little static breath of disbelief. He is leaning half-way across the table now, and she is aware of his height and the lean force of his body. He says, 'Why are you laughing?'

'I wasn't laughing.' She turns to Maria. 'I want to talk to you, maybe we should talk without your son here?' Maria raises both hands up by her face and her fingers are spread and she has an expression that should be kept inside. She looks like she is having bad thoughts. Lila feels a pang of betrayal. She wishes she had stayed at Anna's. Right now she could be vaping in her room, hearing the sound of dinner being made, playing on the drum machine. The room is contracting, pressing, contracting around her like the walls want to touch her. She feels annoyed.

She says, 'Look, I have said I'm sorry.'

The boy is shaking. He says, 'I don't like you.'

'Okay.'

Maria says, 'I think you should go now.' Lila stands and moves towards the door. Then her lip curls up over her teeth.

'I was doing a good thing,' she tells him. 'I was doing a good thing by coming here. I really didn't have to tell you about this.' She pauses, 'I am a good person for doing this.' She takes another step and without looking says, ‘and your dog should have been on a fucking lead.’

She hears the chair hit the ground and turns before the boy has reached her. He stands over her and she has a sharp kick of adrenaline – she had thought he was going to hit her.

He just stands there trembling. She feels another sharp rush, a drop somewhere in her body, the dull hard vibration she felt when she killed his dog. They stare at one another. His eyes look hot. He is going to cry. She says, ‘Baby.’ She almost spits it at him.

A short burst of pain and then just heat. She puts her hand to it. He looks so frightened. She tells him, ‘You just hit me.’

She leaves and the screen door clicks shut behind her. Outside it is as hot as in the house. There is no breeze. The light comes through the windows and onto the porch, the frame leaves solid slants of shadow over the street.

She leans against the painted breezeblocks, feels the coolness through her shirt. She stands there and puts her hand again to her cheek. Some things are wrong. It is wrong to hit someone. This is because you could hurt them. You must not hurt people, except in an emergency. She stays very still. What could they do to her now? She feels very young. For a moment, in the night, she feels the warm weight of her mother’s dog pressing against her thigh. A petal drops from the bougainvillea onto the asphalt. She realises she is smiling.

Teo is looking up at her. He has been playing by the door, probably listening. He has the digger in his hand. She breathes.

She says to him, ‘I was just talking to your mummy.’ He chews his thumb and looks at her wide eyed. ‘About your dog.’ He nods. ‘I was saying that I’m sorry that she’s not here anymore.’ He says, ‘Luca is feeling sad.’

‘Yes, he is. Are you?’

‘Yes.’

‘I’m sorry that you’re feeling sad. But you know what might help?’ She crouches down next to him.

‘What?’ He says carefully.

‘If you said goodbye to her.’ Lila waves up into the black night. ‘Goodbye.’ Teo scrunches up his face.

'That's stupid.'

'Why?'

'She won't know what I'm saying.'

'Why not?'

'She doesn't speak like people.' He lowers his voice confidentially. 'She can only speak dog.'

'How do dogs speak?'

He gives one single, high pitched bark. She asks him, 'Were you saying goodbye?' And he starts barking again, a proper goodbye. She barks with him. His sounds are sharp, clipped, hers are lower than she expects. They come jumping straight from the throat. They are loud. It feels good. It feels so good that she closes her eyes. She has to put her hands on the ground to steady herself. They are wonderful, raw, rhythmic, short bursts of sounds that keep coming out of her. They bark together, clear, triumphant, like laughter. Behind them, on the porch, Maria and Luca stand in a square of light, watching.

Hitch

Emma Neale

We were driving along State Highway 1 at night, after visiting family who lived out of town. Even as we travelled nearer the city again, the highway was spookily deserted. It was a week or so after our national lockdown lifted, and I wondered if people across the region were still hunkering down, experiencing the foreboding I'd felt the very first day we were allowed beyond our neighbourhoods. That day, among dozens of other people out walking along St Clair beach, beside the rolling immensity of the South Pacific, I'd felt exposed: nerves as raw to the elements as grazed skin. Days later, the sensation of freedom trickling back after weeks of isolation remained unexpectedly disorienting, even discomforting, like frost-nipped fingers tingling with red thorns of heat as they slowly begin to thaw.

Perhaps this undercurrent of unease sharpened the jolt when, like a flare, a figure split the darkness ahead. Our headlights had caught the yellow reflective jacket of a solitary figure hovering at the roadside, next to a broken-down car.

After larkspur-blue skies all day, the temperature had plummeted the instant the rugged crags of the Silverpeaks hid the sun. As we got closer to the driver, we saw his hands were tucked into his armpits, his shoulders hunched to his ears.

'We should stop and see if he needs help,' I said to my husband.

'He'll be fine,' Rick answered. 'He's prepared. He's in safety gear.'

'But it's freezing out there!' My voice pitched unnaturally high. 'And someone stopped for us.'

* * *

I meant the time, over a year ago, when I'd been the only adult in the car, ferrying three children down the same route. After a long, relaxed Saturday beachside picnic with friends up the coast at Karitane, we'd set out homewards just before dusk. On our trip back towards the city, nightfall arrived so swiftly that it reminded me of that Katherine Mansfield line: the one that starts, 'There was no twilight in our New Zealand days …' As I tried to recall the rest of the passage – something about the 'half-hour when everything appears grotesque' – we saw someone heading in the opposite direction. I dipped the headlights. There was a sudden bang, as if our undercarriage had hit something. Black, toxic-smelling smoke billowed from the car's hood.

Jake, our teenager, swore. I let that go, even though it was in front of his little brother, pulled the car over and said, 'We need to bail. Get out, quick! On the passenger side. Away from traffic.' All of us scrambled, running from the car in case it burst into flames, movie-style.

This far south in Te Wai Pounamu, even in late summer, the air was chilly after sundown. Despite our jackets, we ended up shivering on the roadside, the two teenagers – Jake, and his friend Lani, with us for a sleepover – sidestepping and jiggling to try to stay warm; Lani tucking her long, loose hair around her neck and under her collar like a scarf for extra warmth. Our eight-year-old, Ewan, pressed in close to me. His teeth chittered as he talked; I realised he might actually be shaking from delayed fright. I took off my coat, gave it to him, hugging him till the chattering stopped; then as I hunted around for my phone, guessed it must have fallen out of my handbag somewhere in the car.

We were on a rural stretch of the motorway: nothing but farm paddocks and scrubby remnants of fragile alpine forest on either side of us; yet there was fairly frequent traffic. As driver after driver careened past, I thought things through aloud: 'When the smoke dies down, I'll head back to hunt for my mobile.' It was like whistling in the dark, trying to reassure both myself and the children. An old station wagon travelling south slowed down and drew up alongside us. Packed to the gills with bags and bedding, with a fabric lei, a blue god's eye bead necklace, worry beads, feathers, and a lanyard of some sort dangling from the rear-view mirror, it also held two sunny, tangle-haired young women. The passenger cranked open her window, and in a cheerful singsong she asked if we were all okay. We told them what had happened, and they offered us blankets, and even some baking. 'Mum made us muffins for uni,' the driver said, with fond amusement. The passenger, who might have been her sister, loaned me a cellphone to make an AA call. I got through to the helpline relatively quickly but the woman who answered said the tow truck would be at least an hour. They only had one guy on night shift; he was way out at Green Island at the moment, on the other side of the city. Oh, and his truck only had room for two extras in the cab.

The students, no hesitation, offered some of us a ride home. I had to make one of those rapid internal parental judgements about who was safer where. *Should I keep Lani out here on the motorway in the glacial dark, or do I send her away with strangers? What would her parents think? Little Ewan's freaking out, but if I sent him home with her, and kept Jake here, she'd need to babysit. And if I …*

I turned to Jake and Lani. 'Do you two feel okay about catching a lift?'

'Totally!'

'*Ioe*, awesome!' They loved the 'cool old retro' music the students were playing on their stereo; the car would be warm; the muffins looked delicious. I made a dash back to our now smoke-free Toyota to scrabble around for my phone. The students and I exchanged numbers so that eventually I could return a blanket we borrowed, which my eight-year-old was now wearing like a cape. I waved the teenagers and their rescuers away.

Beyond the road edge, flax, manuka, gorse and broom made dim shapes: unsheathed swords, crouched haunches, bowed heads, curved spines. Each time the occasional ute, van or car roared by, we'd be spot-lit, the glare of headlights seeming to intensify our isolation and the penetrating cold. Ewan started to talk about how we might get murdered out there in the dark.

Memories flickered in my head like broken lights. When I was just a little older than him – only by a year or so – there was a news story in the early evening slot my parents often watched when we lived in America. As the bulletin unrolled, the terrified knowledge it gave me felt like a kind of losing grip. Poster-thin blue and white pieces of reality threatened to peel off and blow away, to leave a swirling chasm beneath.

The report was about a young girl in an unhappy home situation who had been trying to get a ride somewhere on her own. She accepted a lift from a stranger because she thought a man old enough to be her grandfather would be safe.

The visceral horror of what she went through that night seemed so extreme, even when I recalled it all these decades later, that I wondered: had I misremembered this? Was it a sinister urban legend, a macabre, contemporary *Little Red Riding Hood*, evolved to discourage girls from wandering and travelling on their own? In my hazy memory, the news story dated from around the same time that girls at school began to hold seances and tell ghost stories at slumber parties. Two recurring tales even centred on hitchhiking: in one, a driver picks up a man who is really a murderous ghoul; in the other, the young girl thumbing a ride turns out to be a phantom, haunting the crossroads where a car accident killed her.

Yet I could still see the young Californian hitchhiker in my mind's eye, with her long, wavy, dark hair, her serene and gentle face, and the reminders of the savage violence from that night: her pale prosthetic arms, their metal hooks. I've looked up her story since: it was not a legend. The young girl, Mary Vincent, is still alive. Her torturer, thank God, is not. It feels like an indictment of him, even from my subconscious, that I had recalled absolutely nothing about him: not his name, nor his face.

This chilling story; others in the news over the years; memories of one man's hands at my throat; of an angered boyfriend jabbing between my legs with a broken branch; a stranger breaking into the room where I slept; another forcing me down onto a bed, too strong for me to roll him off – all filled me with charged dread, out there in the bitter, motorway dark.

Yet I couldn't cave in to fear. My job as a mother was to lead Ewan out of his breathless, tightening spiral. 'You know what, sweetheart? The only people who have stopped, out of dozens driving by, just gave you a chocolate muffin. That's exactly the opposite of what you're scared about.'

He buried his head in my chest, and I rumpled his hair. 'It's okay, little man. Hey, have you noticed the stars? You can see so many out here, away from the city lights. They're amazing.'

He peeped at the sky. 'They look like icy dust.' He shuddered. 'We could die out here. We'd be frosted bones by the morning.'

'We're going to be okay, Ewan. The tow truck will be here soon.' I encouraged him to tread with me a little way up the berm that was wild with grasses, nettle and other weeds, so we were even further out of the path of any traffic. While we were shuffling towards the farm paddock's wire fence, a 4WD Hi Lux with a cage trailer barrelled past. In the distance, it started to do a U-turn right in the middle of the highway. My spine braced. What if someone else, inattentive or overtired, hurtled up out of the dark, unable to stop in time? The Hi Lux doubled back and drove past us again, stopping up some way ahead of our abandoned car. A strong, solid-looking man in reflective coveralls got out and strode towards us.

'Someone coming for you?'

My mind jammed on his phrasing.

'My wife said we had to stop,' he said. In the pitch dark and at that distance I couldn't see any passengers in his vehicle, but something warm, pliant, in the way he said *wife* felt like the lowering of a gun.

'Oh, thank you,' I said. 'Yes, I've called the AA. They said they'll be here as soon as they can.'

'Right-oh. Not sure what else I can do for you, but here,' he held up a lime-coloured fluorescent vest. 'You could do with this. I'll need it back for work so I'll give you my number. Assume you live in town?'

I said yes, took his number, thanked him again, profusely. He said a no-bother 'Che-roo,' in a laconic, South Otago way. After re-wrapping the blanket like a toga around Ewan, I slipped the luminous nylon vest over his head and settled it across his shoulders. It came almost to his knees, but he did a quick little sideways dance at being the one who got to wear it.

After the Hi Lux and trailer sped off, I said, 'People have been really kind. Aren't we lucky?'

'Mum,' Ewan said, in that seamless, senior tone kids can deliver with such devastating disapproval. 'Why do you do that thing where bad stuff happens and you say we're lucky? Our car just caught up on smoke, and we're standing in the freezingest middle of the night.'

Tomorrow promised a storm of mood swings if I couldn't get this boy to bed. I checked my watch. It was nearly ten o'clock. All I could do was try to distract by prattling happily. My imagination was fried, though: fried and pinned to our immediate situation. I scraped around in my head and all I could come up with were anecdotes of the other two occasions I'd caught rides in big trucks. Ewan was in a dragons phase, though; my big-rig accounts held no dragons; he was flatly unimpressed.

When the AA tow truck finally appeared, *I woo-hoooed!* and squeezed Ewan tight. He jumped up and down, with zero relief or gratitude, just reiterating, 'It's so cold!'

A stocky, bespectacled man swung down from the towie's high cab with a genial weariness. He told us we were right to be waiting on the roadside, not in the car, despite the temperature. Too many people, he said, had been killed by other drivers slamming into stranded vehicles they hadn't seen until it was too late.

I still had to ignore a prod of apprehension over getting into the truck. What other options did I have?

As it happens, our conversation was low-key, a bit dutiful: but the driver genuinely seemed to like helping people. My first impression – that he moved with the achy erosion from working long, physically-draining shifts – lightened when he talked about his young daughter, whose photo was on the dashboard. He sat up taller, glanced over at me now and then, gave a bouncing laugh about how much kids cost. His daughter loved kapa haka, netball, ice-skating, Taylor Swift, and ever since she turned thirteen, 'That Teeks,' he said. He fell into a slightly wistful reverie then, but he got us safely home, offering good advice about auto-repair shops, and leaving our wiped-out car in the driveway for us to deal with later.

The kindness of strangers, I thought, as I collapsed into bed later that night. *It's a thing. What was I so worried about?*

* * *

As my husband drove past the shivering man marooned on the highway, every detail about that other breakdown pushed into my chest.

'Rick!'

'Okay.' He slowed and pulled over. 'I'll have a word.'

In the dim light, and watching Rick's profile, I couldn't quite read his expression. Was he pissed-off, wary, preparing himself for messy social complication, or a little sheepish that he hadn't felt that Samaritan impulse himself? Whichever it was, I cupped his knee to thank him for stopping. He covered my hand and squeezed before he stepped out of the car.

While he walked back to talk to the guy on the roadside, the children and I went over the story of that time we were rescued, trying to confirm particulars: the smoke was black, right? There really was a bang? And the long-haired, bubbly students, with Pulp and Oasis playing on their stereo, and the muffins with chocolate and toffee chunks, remember them?

Soon Rick and the stranded man were at our car, climbing in. The stranger was slight, his face stubbled. He was shorter than both Rick and our eldest son, and younger than me and my husband: his hair brown. Ripe brown, it seems to me, now that silver spiders at my temples. Do young people know how colourful they are, how vivid, even when they're a little scruffy, a little worn around the edges after heavy days and screwed-up nights?

'Real good of you, thanks,' the guy said, atonal. It made me think of thin metal foil rolled out, an unmarked sheet.

'All right,' my husband said, as if he understood a plan of action – not as if he was saying, *happy to help*. Both kids were sleepy after the day's out-of-town trip, had to have it explained that they should move over, to make room for our passenger. Even then it took them a few beats to actually do it. It looked like reluctance, not drowsiness, and I felt a pinch of frustration. *Manners,* I thought, and *we'll discuss it later*. They also had to be told to gather up their detritus to make space: hoodies, single shoes, an open bag of corn chips, Ewan's craft book, *100 Paper Dragons* – which was a bit of a rip off. It was basically a book of origami paper, printed with different skin, feather and scale patterns: the 'dragons' were just paper airplanes. We'd made Ewan bring the book along to try to keep him off screens. Jake scooped up half a dozen planes Ewan had made earlier; Ewan, overtired, started to fuss about him bending the noses. Jake pulled his woollen beanie down over his ears: makeshift soundproofing. 'Dude,' he said irritably. 'Not cool.'

'Ran out of petrol,' the guy said, as he put on his seat belt. 'Forgot to fill up after my shift. If you run me into town and drop me at the north-end BP, I'll be set.'

'Yup,' my husband said.

The following silence quickly felt too stiff, too tight.

'Whereabouts do you work?' I asked, twisting around a little in my seat.

'Macraes. Fix up the trucks and mine machinery and all.' His voice was flecked both with splintery pride and a glint of hostility.

I felt myself turning this over in my mind, the way I might probe a broken-edged toffee in my mouth, testing its roughness. I tried to find the link between running out of fuel and being a mechanic. As I hunted around quietly for some other small talk, the smell of alcohol, like a rotting tropical flower, pushed into the front of the car. It hit me with something I'd completely overlooked in my urgency to get Rick to stop and help. I wound down my window a little, belatedly thinking of the virus, transmission, ventilation. 'I'd forgotten,' I said. 'We're still meant to be social distancing, right?'

'Ah-ha,' the man said. It was less a laugh than as if I'd unwittingly revealed something oppositional, an idiocy. And then, in a tone that was languorous yet stern, 'I can assure you. I have a completely clean bell of health.'

I was listening to several things. There was the way his answer fell into separate parts around the pause, like kindling cleaved by a hatchet. There was the way he got the saying a little crooked. Sometimes, when that happens, it has an accidental poetry. Tonight, I wondered what he saw when he said the phrase; what he felt it referred to. The bell you hit with a 'test-your-strength' hammer at a carnival? The one that chimes at the top of the pharmacy door as you leave, on a day you've been buying lip balm, or nail-clippers, no need for prescription medicines? But I also wondered about his tone. There was something in it of surly scepticism: of *don't come at me with your bullshit.*

The reek of drink was still there, even with my window cracked open. Usually on the motorway, my husband asks me to wind the window up after a few minutes, despite the fact the car's air conditioning is broken. He routinely reminds me about drag and lower fuel efficiency. But a second or two later, Rick lowered his own window too. It was one of those rare situations where it seemed our thoughts exchanged as clearly as folded notes passed from seat to seat.

We'd probably just saved the guy's skin. If a cop had found him out there, he'd have been breathalysed, and done for drink driving. The fact he had run out of fuel might have actually prevented carnage on the road. Yet his slightly abrasive, fume-soaked air of devil-may-care heightened the fact we could now be endangering ourselves, cooped up with his breathing: virus particles released with each exhale. (Those particles which, under the electron microscope, look like sinister, spiked medieval flails.)

We travelled on in an unaccustomed, electric silence. Our boys usually talk constantly to each other, a mixture of jokes, hoots, brays, fights, admonishments and stories about the 'sussy' things other kids have said or done, at school or online, but they leaned against each other, not scrapping about it, just whispering, with their jackets rustling as they adjusted posture in the squash now and then. I glanced around at them once, but they were both gazing abstractedly out the window. I turned back, ignoring the occasional shifting and muffled crackling, trying to let the cat's-eye road markers become as hypnotic as they were in my own childhood; each one gleaming orange, then whipping past like campfire sparks caught by the wind.

Rick slid a Marlon Williams CD into the car's ancient stereo. The swift canter and cry of 'Miss Lonesome', the sound of the engine, and our wheels on the road became a distraction. We were getting somewhere, they said: the weird tension in the atmosphere would soon be gone. When we finally pulled up into the gas station the guy said, 'Cheers, mate. I'd offer you cash but I've got none spare on me.'

'No worries,' Rick said. He looked up into the rear-view mirror to see whether anyone was arriving behind us, wanting the pump we blocked.

'It's a pay-it-forward kind of thing,' I said, turning around again to watch as the guy undid his seat belt.

'Youse are good people,' he said, but again his tone was ironed of feeling, dull and automatic, as he clambered out of the back. Once he was standing on the station forecourt, he ducked down a little to look into the car. I started on my *good luck* smile, about to say goodbye, when we met eyes. His gaze was filled with a direct, undisguised dislike. Something cold slid past my ribs and finned into my stomach. One of my hands clenched my seat belt, the involuntary animal part of me readying for something: *fight goes to your arms, flight goes to your legs*, where did I read that, about the direction of adrenaline surge in the body?

The man drew out a yellow, plastic-handled box-cutter knife from his jeans pocket. The forecourt lights slid and trembled on the angled metal tip. With an oil-stained thumb he moved the blade silently into the safety position, then pushed it into view again: a talon sheathed, unsheathed; a snake's tongue flickering in and out of its mouth.

When I looked up from his fist, his stare locked again with mine. He returned the knife to his pocket, then took out his mobile, dialling beside the petrol station's *no cellphones sign*. 'Yo,' he said, into the speaker, then slammed the door.

'Jesus. *That's* shut,' said Rick, eyes at the wing mirror, as he released the handbrake and gunned the car.

'Freaky vibe,' said Jake, unfolding his long limbs into the freed-up space.

'Did you see …' I faltered. I wasn't sure what to say about the Stanley knife. It was a nothing moment, from one perspective. Would he have even been capable of serious harm, in a car with four people trying to stop him? Why would he think of doing anything violent, when we'd plucked him out of a shitty situation?

I wanted to believe the best of people. But the thing is, I hadn't needed to see the knife to know what was in his eyes. When I thought of the loathing there, and how to convey the chill and the certainty of it, I had to haul myself back from that unpeeling disintegration, the dark-grained abyss that I first felt opening when I was nine or ten, and I learned what some men could do to women.

'I could smell a *lot* of beers,' Ewan said, then added lightly, 'but he gave me this that he made.' He leaned forward into the gap between our front seats, his small, pale hand shaking something back and forth.

I had to ask him to stop and hold it steady for me to see what it was. It had the silhouette of a dragon. Details like the fiery breath, the claws, the spines on its back and tail, and wings a little like the long, graceful fins on a koi, were all sliced away, sculpted like a stencil, into one of Ewan's sheets of origami paper.

'Oh,' I said. I swivelled around quickly, craning to look back over my shoulder, but the petrol station was already well behind us. I felt an unlatching, as if I'd let something small yet vital slip from a hasp. 'Did you say thank you?'

Ewan slumped back down into his seat, and draped the stencil over his face, treating it like an eye-mask for sleeping. A few moments later, he was peering out at street lamps and traffic lights through the lacey paper incisions, with the curious, stilled wonderment of someone using an old-fashioned View-Master for the first time.

When we arrived home, and piled out of the car, there was a snowfall of tiny red and white scraps littered all over the rear seat. For a moment, it looked as if something had disintegrated back there. But as I brushed them into one hand, those papery shards make me think more of a kaleidoscope. Or really, of how a mind could be like one. A person turns this way, or that, and in an instant comes the rapid tumble of memories, feelings, assumptions, unwitting prejudices: radiant or lacerating. All the vivid, angular pieces seem to seize, then just as suddenly keel and jostle: dread, fear, misreading, trust, delight, hope, shame.

Readmission

Josephine Rowe

The girls' dresses are rancid with coconut oil. Ordinary cooking kind, scooped out of a jar and palmed over their already summertoned limbs. A cloying, unpleasant smell trapped in the polymer for weeks, maybe months, turning foul. But there's themselves in it, too; parallel cosmologies she huffs in deep before bundling the dresses into the hamper.

Irresponsible. Him letting them go out like that. With *accelerant*. In late summer, no less. New colours in the heat chart – as if the UV index weren't enough.

I tried, he says, pocketing his hands. They told me not to tell them what to do with their own bodies. Started up about the patriarchy. Who'd they get that from then, hey?

She is momentarily proud of them, while allowing room for the possibility that he is bullshitting about this last part.

They know that I'll be here when they get home?

It's all they can talk about, he says. Practically had to kick them out of the car at the school gate this morning.

It would've been alright, she says, for them to be here. When I got here. Wouldn't it?

Just thought you might want a little time, settling.

She nods, and wonders where the cat is. Do we still have the cat?

Ferdie's around, he says. In the garden, probably, waiting for the birds to fall out of the grevillea with heatstroke.

He goes out to get the rest of her things from the car. A new car, paid for by insurance. The old one sold off cheap to students who didn't mind the blistered duco, the heat-warped tint. Poor old car, she thinks, even if it was complicit.

What she wants now, more than anything – more than the gin that is perilously low in its bottle, more than decent coffee, or to bury herself in the clean white drift of her own bed – is real food.

Opening the fridge she recognises his sister's work; a heavy glass bowl of Dana's cold stewed plums, purple-black from her own tree, that will be both too sweet and too tart. A thick quiche cross-hatched with meticulous ribbons of red and orange capsicum, cherry tomatoes studded around the edges of the high crimped crust. *Women's Weekly* colours, from 50 years ago, a minor time warp. The food is never exceptionally good to eat, but typically comforting to look at and uncannily of a time. An era which – they are around the same age – neither of them actually lived through. The orange-brown-red era of ratatouille and white sugar, pineapple upside-down cakes.

The meaning of the food is not lost on her: a party, a 'welcome home' of some description which she will have to find a way to hold off. Her husband no longer knows how to touch her, even how to speak. A new quiet caution in his voice that makes her want to put her teeth through something, to lacerate, to rend. A frustration that is almost carnal, bordering sexual.

The girls will be home in three hours and she might know, then, whether she will be able to stand it, any of it. She suspects she will not be able to stand it.

A pile of unopened letters on the table. And cards, postmarked and not, her name – familiar and formal – written over and over. Too soon.

She hefts the quiche out from its place on the refrigerator shelf, revealing a cake – a fucking cake – armoured in peach buttercream. Her name (again) looped in silver icing. Just her name, because what other words could they have possibly found? *(Sorry, just so sorry…)*

She hacks a wedge from the quiche and carries it cold from the kitchen, plateless. The obsessive busywork of the overlapping strips is faintly unsettling. She eats one-handed – real butter, but also some kind of chalky insoluble fat that coats her teeth and tongue – while drifting from room to room, noting what has changed and what has not, letting crumbs fall on the hardwood floor. Had there been a rug, before?

They've kept her houseplants alive, between the three of them. Or simply replaced the dead predecessors, once they knew she was coming home: she can't recognise for certain. Even the maidenhairs and the orchids, assembled in the bathroom for the steam, are going strong, their soil fed with some kind of slow-release nourishment.

In their bedroom the porcelainflower is thriving. The sun comes through its umbels and leaves and projects their shadow across the room like a photograph she's always loved. A sense of accomplishment in this, in establishing, re-inhabiting a life that so fluidly mirrors art. In the wardrobe, there are her dresses, her coats, her shirts. They will mostly no longer be suitable. She remembers as a younger woman – in her 20s, chronically dysmorphic and unaware of her hectically fluctuating shape – believing that a person (or persons), known or unknown to her, had broken in and stealthily replaced all of her clothes with slightly bigger versions of the same. Remembers hunting out the small details that a stranger would surely have missed, and could not possibly have known to replicate: allegorical stains, ripped pockets, the mismatched button on a shirt cuff, the cigarette burn in the lining of a second-hand jacket. But they were all there, these private insignia. And so she had to conclude that the person, or persons, whoever they were, had been exceptionally thorough, acting with forensic, Orwellian precision.

Her hands are empty, but she still feels a hollow hunger, runs her tongue around her gums and sucks her teeth. She takes something long sleeved and floaty from a hanger and lays it flat on the bed.

On the dresser, a miniature cityscape of perfume bottles. She uncaps one and sniffs the nozzle, returns it to its place. No dust, on the bottles. Or on the carved Icelandic seal, or the crumpled origami jewellery box one of the girls made. Nothing of hers has been allowed to gather any dust. Someone has wiped each object down and put it back in its place. Not something she can imagine him doing. Perhaps her sister-in-law, again. Or he'd started hiring a cleaner. But of course there were facets of a person that you just could not know, could not know, however long you'd loved them.

She sprays her wrist with the smallest bottle. A perfume composed of a single note, that supposedly interacts with the wearer's natural scent and registers differently on everyone. Not always favourably. She'd always found the scent calming, clarifying. On her it started quietly then opened out into a large cool room, with white clay walls, a polished stone floor. Little or no furniture. Just somewhere to sit, maybe, austere but not unwelcoming. A large window onto deep cedary shade, some captive silverly thread of water, and the sound of it trickling in. The image is so vivid she must've stood in such a room, at least once, felt its dimensions or at least seen it pictured, somewhere? Or else the scent somehow conjured it from scratch.

Anyway, it doesn't now. Conjure that place. She rubs her wrist to get rid of the scent, the unfamiliar space it now evokes.

She smells different now, she knows. The medications she ingests as well as the topical salves and ointments. Some of her skin isn't even her skin; lattices that have taken and healed whose origin she strives not to wonder too hard at, beyond a murky gratitude.

She slips the shirt off its hanger, turns the sleeves inside out and shakes, before turning them rightside in again and slipping them over her bare arms, buttoning over her crinkled décolletage all the way to her throat, despite the heat. 19 years in this city, and still she turns her clothes inside out, shakes the bed clothes, expecting small yellow scorpions or other desert biters to tumble out and scurry for shelter. Habit.

It's her, she knows: she will no longer know how to accept their care, their kind acts.

Outside, the tall rampart of poplars that screen them from the road are sashaying, waving their many limbs in conference. *As if* in conference, she corrects herself. They wink, glint with something. Glass. Strings of party lights. A table has been set up out there, wood silvering in the weather, mapped with tributaries of candle wax – white, red, purple – the stubs fused to saucers that had belonged to her grandmother.

Folding canvas chairs, their seats stained from the mulberry tree. A bright towel abandoned on the grass, spread out and weighted at three corners: a small blue radio, a gold-foiled sandal, its mate.

A garden is the total … the totality of the world, she remembers from somewhere. The smallest parcel and the totality.

They will be careful with her, her family, will not tell her anything too harmful, or even too joyous, about their own lives.

He comes back into the house. The sound of him setting her case in the hall.

Then he's beside her, his eyes red. He'd stayed out there, in the new car, probably, to cry.

He puts his hand to her shoulder and she flinches. He apologises and touches her face, where everything is more or less the same.

He swallows, then finally says out loud the lines he must have been rehearsing for weeks:

In the moment I thought, it's what you would have wanted. It's what you would have done.

She nods. She has no answer for that, no definite answer to that.

Because if I thought there was any chance. Even a snowflake's chance…

She watches his eyes, where they land. Nowhere.

You know, Miro. You know.

She nods, again. Thinks about fucking him. If, ever again. Thinks about who she will think about.

Their youngest daughter comes through the door, far too early, hair blown into snarls by the northerly, bands of her socks grubby with sweat and sun lotion. Her school shoes swapped for glittery Keds.

What's happened? her father asks. It's barely past one.

There's a look passed between the two of them; a breach, a threat Miro observes but can't read. Private language, developed in her absence.

What happened to school? He asks again.

Sophie drops her bag on the slate. I left at lunch. I walked.

What about your sister?

I didn't ask Nik, she says, trying to manoeuvre past her father. Couldn't find her, she adds, her eyes bright with the lie. *You're like the doorbitch from hell,* one of them said to him, once.

Mama, Sophie says, and ducking past his arm and coming for her.

Gentle, he warns. Gentle, gentle.

No proper hugs yet, Miro says, and kisses her daughter close to her chapped lips. Hot orange, in the grain.

What colour's that?

Nuclear Tangello.

She is tall enough now to reach her ear, to whisper into it: Mum, I have to show you something. Outside. Pulling her by the fingertips toward the back garden.

Whatever it is can wait, Sophie, her father calls after them. Your mother has to be careful, with this sun.

We'll stay in the shade, Sophie says without turning. It'll only take a minute.

Outside, the air crackles with heat, its own subaudible language, too hot even for the insects. Sweat beads her lip, instantly, and her new skin tingles, tightens.

You shouldn't have walked all that way, Soph.

I had water.

But I do like your shoes.

Mum, that's code.

What?

Saying that about shoes.

Right. She knows that, or used to.

They stand in the shade of the mulberry, in the baking rot. Each breath a rasp in the lungs, northerly-borne dust and atomised oils from distant eucalypts.

Ferdie shouldn't be out in this either, she says. She calls out for the cat.

Her daughter looks embarrassed for her. He won't come, Mum. He ran away.

Oh.

Dad said we should wait to tell you. That you were already dealing with enough shocks to your system.

Well, she says. That's very sad.

We can get another one, her daughter says. When you're ready.

Maybe he'll still turn up.

Yeah. I don't reckon, though. It's been a while.

Okay. She can feel her smile, her skin tightening. What are we looking at out here?

Sophie waves back at the window, where her father is standing, and turns her back to him. She holds her phone out for her mother to look at. But it's only for show, a prop.

The counsellor says we're not supposed to blame anybody. Dad and Nik would be upset if I said anything. I'm not blaming anybody, I'm not. But we called and called and you didn't answer.

The phone in her hands, with its charms and paste diamonds. Its lock screen shows a picture of a chinchilla. The mulberries are dried brown rattles on their stems, haven't fallen. Her daughter keeps speaking.

I told them to turn back. But they wouldn't. Dad wouldn't turn the car around. Everybody was scared, nobody was thinking right. Nobody was brave. Dad, he said – they both said, too late. Dad said you'd know what to do. Cos of how you grew up. He said you'd know how to –

The girl is sobbing now, heaving with tears. She cries with the same breathless violence as when she was small and in trouble, lacking the stagecraft to convince them of her innocence.

A lie or not, it is enough for now. She makes it enough; holds her shaking daughter closer, who in her distress forgets, and clings too tightly.

I know, she tells her, stroking her ravelled hair. I know.

Her older daughter, when she comes home, will say much the same, with fewer tears. She knows each of them believes just as fiercely as the other. And she will believe each of them, fiercely. In the same way she convinces herself that she loves them, equally. Because the alternatives are not survivable.

They will each come to ask, in private moments, what she remembers.

She remembers everything. Or would, if she allowed herself, had not worked to keep it all on the other side of a wall of flame.

She tells them: a wall of flame.

The truth is she felt like a god coming down off that mountain. Manifesting in the middle of the highway like the smouldering urban legend she would soon become. Her clothes singed, soaked with sweat and creek water, her hair raked down with clay.

She'd left them at breakfast, hiking alone the three-hour mid-grade loop from the cabins, bouldering and scree. Nearing halfway when the wind swung, and brought smoke – too early in the season – and she pelted the way back in less than a quarter hour. Towards the fire, toward her family.

When she saw the car was gone, she ought not to have gone inside. Ought not to have seen: the bowls and plates and cups abandoned, the stray clothes hung from chair backs and doorhandles, their laptops and phones and carry bags gone. The television still blaring; a cable channel that said nothing of fire. She turned the shower on and stood for three or four seconds under the stream, fully clothed. Then she ran.

Too early in the season, she fought, reasoned, pleaded with something.

She found the creek, the broken thread of tannic water. She bent her face low to the water, and she went. Scrub and trees close to the creek edges, catching alight, raking her back. Ember rain. Her shirt dried and tore and singed in no time and she flattened out again and again to drench her clothes in what was only sometimes water, sometimes mud and damp stones. She pawed up handfuls of thin silty clay and dragged it through her hair, over her face. She bent lower still and prayed (to what, to whom?) that this gravelly seam would deliver her to something: a river, a catchment, a road.

A road. *Angel of the Argales*, one of the tabloids called her. It didn't take. Small mercy that it didn't take.

It was to her mother (of course her mother) that she prayed. To whom she reasoned: *too early… too early in the season.*

She smells her wrist again. Wonders how to get back to that cool quiet space. How long it will take.

Her daughters outside in the cicada-mobbed evening, speaking low in their new code, sharing one of the covert cigarettes Niki has lately taken up, or simply stopped bothering to hide. One of them has kept a scrapbook of the news clippings that call their mother *miraculous.* The other cannot stand to look at them.

She has imagined it, was given all the time in the world to imagine it, lying half-drugged in the overburdened burns ward. If it had been him, as good as gone on the mountain. If it had been herself at the wheel. Heart pounding in the driver's side with the air sizzling around them, the wind already carrying smoke, bits of burnt leaf. Their two girls in back – begging her to stay, to wait, or urging her to go, go, just drive – would it have mattered? Would it have made a lick of difference?

Not a second. Her foot would not have left the gas. Not for a second.

She could admit this to him, make a gift of it.

Penelope work, she once heard it called, the diligent art of forgetting. Of deciding what shall be warp, and what shall be weft.

The party will go ahead. She will not flinch when they come for her, hold their arms out to her.

It is only the cost of readmission, of knowing them. Pouring champagne over the antibiotics and laughing under the clemency of prescription dope. Standing in the dusk calling for the cat, shaking his box of biscuits to coax him out of hiding. Refreshing his water dish every few days, just in case. Lying facedown in the garden in summers to come, amidst all the sweet rot, coconut oil rubbed into the tender new skin on her back and her arms and listening from under the shade tree as they talk carefully, and then recklessly, about their lives.

The Parts He Missed

Josh Wagner

Garrett responds to the medical student's ad with an offer to injure his own body. So you can repair it, he types. The medical student assures him no damages will be necessary. She follows this up with a smiley face. I'm just in it for the free healthcare, he replies. He asks if mole removal falls within her wheelhouse. She appreciates his choice of words. I could do it with my eyes closed, she says.

They meet for coffee and get on well. Myra is twenty-two. Blonde hair, bluntly fringed. He finds her energy both arresting and liberating, but feels too awkward to say it out loud. This isn't a date. What she needs is 240 volunteer hours with live subjects – one last hurdle before graduation. He allows her to perform a cursory examination right there at the table. She fingers his pulse. He piles on the melodrama, acts like he's dying. She snorts when she laughs. He teases her without meaning to; a coyness in her manner seems to invite this. They schedule a time the following week for her to swing by his apartment.

Garrett trims his fingernails and toenails and stores the clippings in a green glass bottle from the 19th century. He shaves his head, chest and legs. He presses a Sharpie against his right calf, drawing a small circle around the mole which has developed asymmetrically over the past year, and he waits for the medical student to arrive.

Myra brings a salad. They sit on the sofa and share conversational sketches of their lives. Her passion for medicine; his love of dance. When she insists on seeing a few moves, a profound shyness comes over him, but he dims the lights and tells her to pick out some music. Her eyes gleam with exacting scrutiny. Just a few ideas I'm playing around with for my dissertation, he says. She tells him it's like watching cold oil drizzle over an expensive rug. He appreciates her choice of words. I could do it with my eyes closed, he says.

Then he hikes up his pant leg and reveals the mole. He knows she can remove it in seconds with an electric loop excision cautery unit, but he wonders if, instead, she wouldn't mind carving it out with an old-fashioned scalpel.

Garrett shudders under the rush of topical lidocaine. It makes him feel like part of his body is already gone. He asks if he can keep the flesh, and if the request grosses her out she doesn't show it. She tells him it should go to pathology for testing.

But we can do a second mole if you really want.

How about the other leg, he says. For symmetry.

She drops the morsel into a Formalin bottle, which he then places in the freezer.

* * *

She wants to subvert the systems that make food impossible. Pick one, she says. Anything. I'll show you evidence that links overconsumption and underconsumption to mirroring late-stage metabolic disorders.

With a bashfulness he hopes she finds endearing, Garrett admits to a childhood quirk of salvaging the cheesy pepperonis off his pizza and tossing the crust. Once upon a time, he ate nothing but dry hamburger patties and boiled hot dogs with ketchup. If two kinds of food on his plate ever came into contact, he'd refuse to eat. Anything resembling the animal it came from was intolerable.

All of this changed at sixteen when friends dared him to swallow a live beetle and he popped it into his mouth without hesitation. Felt its little legs wriggle all the way down. Later, he lay awake wondering if it was still alive in his stomach, imagining its dissolution, dreaming sacred mysteries out of the consumption of the totality of a body. As if the heart molecules of a beetle might merge with his own. Liver to his liver. Brain to his brain. In the morning, Garrett discovered an insatiable appetite. He longed for all foods spicy, slimy, ugly or exotic. He devoured snails, sea urchins, amphibians and various internal organs. Hungering only for flavours he did not understand.

When my waistline ballooned, he says, I signed up for dance.

But the harder he worked, the more he ate. Around that time, his sister – who cut a pathological fixation for sucking ice cubes with a chronic hair-chewing habit – hacked up her first trichobezoar. A few years later, they would remove a five-pounder during an emergency C-section.

I was desperate to look at it, Garrett says. Writhing in sick florescence, hot on the chrome tray, brown and knotted, moulded into the shape of her stomach. Alien-brained. Inverted. The inside outside.

* * *

Shortly before their first kiss, Myra takes Garrett to an underground jazz club. Nautical-themed, almost enough room for a three-piece band. Only one couple at a time on the dance floor. They crouch in the corner beside a heavy oak cask. Something in the way the music lights up her eyes makes him aware for the first time of how previous generations must have lived in worlds no less vibrant than his own, perceiving themselves as the sole guardians of time's edge, clutching at effervescent futures with desperate, unsteady hands.

The music is a little too loud. They have a few too many drinks. They don't go home together. They don't realise they've fallen in love.

* * *

During an evening of casual conversation, Myra mentions that personal saliva is the best thing for cleaning one's own blood stains. The concept gives him a little electric thrill. Self-sufficiency in the DNA. Twisted splines swirling back on themselves in holistic self-reference. Remedies unlocked by embedded chemical combinations.

It leads him to the suspicion that a single drop of blood with a bowl of so-called soup purchased from a so-called food provider might act as a kind of inoculant against the evils inherent in the product. He knows this is probably magical thinking, but it comforts him, which he figures might at least reduce stress levels and boost his immune system. All truths lie along the same tangled chain. So it becomes his custom to carry a special sewing needle tucked into the spine of his wallet.

* * *

Throughout their budding romance, Garrett and Myra rarely shop for food. She introduces him to freeganism and the complexities of the global food conspiracy. She knows when and where to find perfectly edible produce and other goods that supermarkets throw away. They stock up on bread, cheese, and meat abandoned for no better reason than its loss of marketable lustre. They launch a website so others can benefit from their surplus and they organise guerrilla gardening operations in half a dozen city parks. They host late night chats concerning the sinister impacts of FDA policy and the rise of GMOs.

He tells her about the time he was thirteen and his mother asked him to clean uneaten food out of the fridge to make room for fresh groceries. Half gallon of milk, bruised apples, hardening bread and cheese, two pounds of pecked-at chicken wings. His conscience ached. He imagined the faces of starving children as if all the world's hunger circulated inside him. At the dinner table, he collapsed into a lump of depression and refused to eat.

Finish your goddamned plate, his father had said.

We waste too much.

So you're wasting more?

Myra touches his hand. She explains how over-consumption drives up demand and contributes to rising food prices. Another way the poor get poorer. Garrett pictures invisible ripples radiating across a global economic web, penetrating into the heart of foreign markets – micro-dependencies sensitive even to the food he'd kept his mother from buying those many years before. That night he lies down to enjoy a full uninterrupted eight hours of sleep for the first time in as long as he can remember.

He loves the sound of her voice and will sit for hours while she describes physiological curiosities and new medical procedures. She reciprocates with enthusiastic support for his passions.

Your talent springs from a lack of comprehension, she tells him one evening.

Is that a compliment? he says.

Other dancers rely on rational systems and the vocabulary of movement, but you seem to stumble intuitively along a path of least resistance.

I mean, it doesn't *sound* like a compliment.

It's like your limbs flow naturally to points of rest along some invisible grid.

He resonates with the observation. It is unfathomable to others because it is unfathomable to him. He doesn't know how to dance. He only knows where his body is and where it needs to end up.

But you manage to get it there without disrupting the music, she says. Like you slip through the gaps between notes.

When Garrett is selected for a collaboration on the Harris Stage, he begins a routine of preparing for rehearsals by taking a razor to the epidermis of his heel, toes, and the balls of his feet. Thin strips, nicks off the angles. He sculpts himself for maximum fluidity. Micro-adjustments, never quite deep enough to bleed. Like peeling the rind off an orange.

Reintegration follows – the simpler task by far, though he knows few would feel the same.

Within days, Garrett begins to experience movement in ways he never imagined possible. He can feel his body redistribute the molecules of consumed flesh, patching them efficiently back into former coordinates with fresh and perfect form. But his performance at Harris does not receive as admirable a judgement as he'd hoped. It's a failure he can't quite let go. He does not follow up on an acceptance letter from Joffrey. Instead, he swims upstream against student debt and resigns himself to life as a gift shop clerk and occasional private dance instructor. Myra encourages him to continue pursuing his art, but he puts on a smile and tells her there's more to dance than performance and there's more to life than dance.

Instead, he starts attending regional city rallies on weekends to protest against the use of hormones in dairy products and the unethical treatment of animals. He is torn between the impact of climate change on agriculture and the dangers of entrusting world food production to globalization. He obsesses endlessly over obesity, the food crisis, the corn wasted on oil, the gallon of water it costs to grow a single almond.

By now, Garrett has fully ritualized the consumption of his flesh. He has learned how to administer the anesthesia, perform the incisions, and suture the wound. Once a month he mixes a single excision with homemade chicken broth and free-range meat from a farm he has personally vetted. He eats it all and does not know which bite is him.

When Myra announces her pregnancy, they spend a full day in tears and conversation. They realize that they want this child no less than if they'd planned it all along. Aries if it's a boy, Annabelle if it's a girl. He prepares his soup, and this time he can tell what's what. Feels the flesh on his tongue. As it slides down his throat, he imagines it dissolving into a whirlpool of enzymes. The body knows its own. He prays he will be a good father.

* * *

He stares at random items in the grocery store and considers their ethical, fiscal, and nutritional dimensions – all of which fill him with horror. He grows inward and contemplative and agonises over his paternal future. He meditates and sits in stillness. His relationship with hunger takes a dramatic turn where the gradient between peckishness and starvation collapses, and he wakes up in the middle of the night desperate to eat but too weak to cook. He thinks he is dying. He thinks he is immortal. He dreams of splitting concrete and liberating latent gardens along the highways, of entangling corporate headquarters in vines, and planting fruit trees on a million suburban lawns.

More than anything, he enjoys putting hands or lips against the skin of her stomach to feel those muffled turns and kicks. He lies with his head on her lap for hours, flipping through books on nutrition, anatomy, cellular biology or genetics. He reads stories in which the microscopic or otherwise invisible seep into scientific theory by way of myth or intuition. When Myra falls asleep, he whispers new knowledge to their unborn child.

James Watson's model for the double helix came to him while dreaming of a spiral staircase, he says. And did you know a 19th century chemist's structural hypothesis for the carcinogenic petrochemical benzene was inspired by a vision of the Midgard Serpent?

This is Jörmungandr, second born of the trickster god. He encircles the earth, nibbling his own tail, savouring himself, strangling the world tighter and tighter by degrees. Ancient stories predict that when this monster's jaw slackens and loses hold of his tail, it will spark a war to destroy the gods. Thor shall bruise his skull, and he shall crush Thor's heel. Benzene occurs naturally in crude oil, he whispers, a liquid echo of ancient life pressed to pulp by time. Smeared and scorched. Encircling the earth. Strangling it by degrees.

* * *

When Annabelle is born, Garrett experiences waves of joy and terror, terror that feels like joy, and intervals of delicate awe. His love for Myra grows gentler, even as their bond intensifies. For the first time, hunger feels natural, and he no longer dwells on its shape or shadow. The new parents waver between bliss and exhaustion. They marvel at how accessible contentment has become. Myra speaks less about toppling the food industry and eases her workload at the clinic to part time. Before Annabelle is even a year old, they start talking homeschool.

The girl grows so fast that Garrett can no longer entirely connect with the emotional reality of a time before she existed. A week after her first steps, she starts biting her fingernails. It reminds Garrett of his sister, and he freaks out a little. Myra assures him it's just a phase. Probably even beneficial – exposing her body to new germs. Same with the nose picking. A cocktail of filtered bacteria. Nature's inoculation.

Annabelle the toddler babbles on and on. She turns what she sees into characters, what she experiences into stories. Garrett dances with her in the living room. She mimics his steps with startling precision. When she scrapes her knee, he kisses it better. The magic works, staunches her tears, brings on a smile.

They are cautious with her diet. Myra prohibits sugar and gluten. Eventually they cut out red meat. One night around the dinner table, Annabelle asks why.

In certain parts of the world, Garrett says, it's impossible to raise animals for food. So they eat insects.

Annabelle squirms, but her squirms shed sparks of delight.

Bug legs are like fingers, she says. I want to be a butterfly.

First you have to be a caterpillar, Myra says.

Caterpillers sleep inside a croon and grow wings.

Only after they turn into soup, Garrett says.

Soup!?

Yep. They break into tiny pieces in their cocoons and all their insides get shuffled around. That's how change happens.

The next day, he catches her in the yard crushing bugs. He runs to her, fearful that she means to eat them, but she's only stroking their broken bodies with a leaf. Fat tears on her cheeks, calm eyes. I'll bring them back to life, she proclaims. Garrett encourages these enchantments as if she might just pull it off.

* * *

He never knew someone so ill could be so happy.

My body is clumsy on the inside, she says. So it keeps breaking myself.

She laughs at this, and Garrett hates himself for laughing along.

The doctors assure them their daughter's condition is an autosomal recessive disorder caused by a random mutation pairing. There was nothing they could have done to prevent it other than not having a child. But having a child didn't guarantee the disease, either. It all came down to bad luck.

Two months into late-stage treatments, Myra catches Garrett scraping epidermal flakes off their sleeping daughter's bare shoulders, carrying the accumulation downstairs to the kitchen, and mixing it in with the next day's medicinal milkshake.

It seems to demand every ounce of her willpower not to scream. He explains himself in religious terms.

I believe, he says, that this will heal her.

During conversation it comes out that he has been consuming tiny bites of himself ever since they met – that this was, in a way, *why* they met. Even the chunk of flesh she'd carved from his body on day one, he had later cooked and eaten. She tells him his secrets weave too tangled a thread, especially when he is willing to involve their daughter. He begs her to hear him out. She waits for him to explain, but he's unable to put it into words. Her disgust is palpable. How can I trust you if you won't talk to me? But his feeling is that she simply can't stand the thought of it and will never be able to look at him the same way again. He grows resentful, withdrawn. The silence eviscerates. Both walk out of the room. Later they agree to stay together for the sake of Annabelle's health and happiness, even though Myra starts sleeping on a small collapsible cot in her study.

For the next several months, the little girl weathers her treatments and pain with unwavering confidence that everything is going to turn out okay.

If I die, she asks on her sixth birthday, will it be beautiful?

What can a parent say…

And it is beautiful. How horrified Garrett is made by this awareness. In the end, she does not suffer but slips away like a trickling stream. He can find nowhere to hide but a dry silence. Myra becomes fury itself. She shatters all objects she can reach against the floor and the walls. Garrett hardly notices. His ears have turned to cotton. He stares at the little body between them, transfixed by the pale ripeness of her cooling skin. Still soft, he thinks, like a moth. Only later, standing over her grave, does his body cripple in profusions of guilt and despair. He dances there for a while. A few strange steps she'd come up with to make him laugh. He does not recognise the fracture when it appears. He arches his spine, trying to fold every inch of flesh backward around his hips so he might flatten his palms on the grass and melt into the earth.

* * *

Myra moves out. Garrett doubles his teaching hours to keep up with the bills. The following months leave few traces of memory. Then, on the one-year anniversary of Annabelle's death, he prepares a bouillon cube out of his own flesh. He boils strips from his thighs to a reduction and dehydrates the remains. Yet he no longer craves eternal life or even physical vigour and robust health. In his dreams he makes his way through labyrinths toward the omphalos, where he is swallowed down a river of bile and expelled back into his own body. He wakes in a cold sweat. His legs are mottled and scarred. He despises them and he hungers for them.

* * *

A car clips him while he crosses the street. He walks away with a hairline fracture just below the hip. He can't decide whether or not he did it on purpose.

He takes every reasonable precaution before attempting to remove the leg. He applies primary and backup proximal tourniquets and keeps multiple hemostats on hand. After copious amounts of ketamine and bupivacaine, he severs parallel flaps of his thigh with a Langenbeck blade and peels flesh from bone. Before taking up the saw, he phones Myra. Despite clamping, tourniquets, and intravenous fluids, he's certain that if she doesn't arrive in time, he won't make it. As consciousness takes flight, he decides he doesn't mind either way – only that his stomach aches and wishes he'd eaten.

She finds him surprisingly stable. A note on the table begs her not to call an ambulance. Stop the bleeding, administer post-op procedures, but don't drive him to the hospital. Just wait for him to wake up.

Is this some kind of penance?

I killed her.

We killed her. Us. One gene apiece. Self-destruction baked into the design. Why is your leg in a cooler?

I'm hungry.

I'll cook.

She doesn't leave him again, but her caution is evident. She brings groceries from the market, everything organic, sourced and verified. She keeps an eye out for infection, but his body seems determined to recover. After regaining strength, he hops into the kitchen to butcher the leg and file its cuts in the freezer. She watches without comment.

* * *

Explain it to me, she says. Tell me everything this time.

She's sabotaged the kitchen so he can't cook without help. The wheelchair alone keeps him fairly confined and well-behaved.

It's a mystery, he tells her.

Not good enough, she says.

The body is only one small part of a far grander machine. True sensation distributes itself throughout space and time.

I don't know what that means.

I've figured out how to live forever.

No, you haven't. You almost died.

That was before.

This is stupid.

It started out as inoculation.

Against yourself?

Against everything else.

She squeezes her eyelids and pinches the bridge of her nose.

When Xeno was a baby boy he stopped halfway to his mother's arms, and there he saw his own death for the first time.

Okay, so I guess the pills are kicking in?

Let me eat, he says.

She stands up and walks to the door.

I'm going out.

* * *

He does not expect her to help him. It's too much to ask anyone. Too much to ask himself. How would it even work? One can only get so far before sheer feasibility reaches its limit. Could he wire himself into a web of life support? a Dialysis Machine? Extracorporeal Lungs? What would be last to go? He imagines a digestive tract encased in glass with a mouth on top. A floating ghost aching to complete the circle. It's absurd. No words for it. No way to ask.

But she already knows. The same way he already knows what she is saying yes to. Hanging there between their eyes, the real story.

It's a bright Sunday afternoon. He stares out the window. She pretends to read a magazine.

Okay, she says. On one condition.

* * *

Myra wheels a white board into the living room. The felt-tip squiggles and squeaks.

Logistically, this is our best plan, she tells him. It will get you as close as possible, as near as I can figure.

Okay, he says.

Cancel your students. The surgeon I work with pays more than enough.

Okay.

I've scheduled everything on this calendar.

Six months.

Yes.

It's too slow.

Your body needs time to heal between sessions.

Okay.

Shall we go to bed?

* * *

It's their first time since Annabelle was alive. The atmosphere is electric. His hair burns. Her skin melts over him. She kisses the stump where his leg used to be. You're beautiful, she says. He submerges his fingers in her hair and imagines them gone. Everything aligned on a molecular level. They lay back on cool, damp sheets and watch the moonrise through the window. Is it waxing or waning?

She reaches for his hand, lifts a finger to her lips and kisses a knuckle, nibbles the tip.

Can't you save these for last? she asks.

* * *

She installs the necessary equipment in a spare room. There's the adjustable operating table, a high-powered cautery machine, and portable basin with Betadine pump. She bolts 150,000 lux of pure white light to the ceiling. Lying on the table are various scalpels, hemostats, scissors, clamps, sponges, spreaders, pick-ups, bone saws, sutures, and staples.

He makes all the legal arrangements. The just-in-cases. Though he'd rather start with the whole arm, she convinces him to take it slow. The immune system can only handle so much. He leaves the middle finger of his left hand in a crock pot until the flesh peels off the bone. She refuses to stick around for any of the cooking or the eating.

His moods stagger from day to day. He's keen on smashing plates when he grows impatient. Myra finds him trying to take a bite out of his unpartitioned bicep. She won't stand for it, forces him to promise never again or she's out. He breaks down. He wishes he could make her understand. She says he doesn't have to explain. She tells him she's pregnant.

It's Annabelle, he says. Returning to take my place. You are the waxing moon and I the meniscus. Soon I shall be one with the enveloping night.

* * *

She peels a sock off his remaining foot.

That's how it feels, he says.

Like getting undressed?

Like loosening a tie or shoelaces, like unstrapping a belt that's too tight.

She leans over the back of the couch and watches the gutter drizzle.

He suggests they move on to another finger.

Our plan says we stick with the torso this week, she counters.

How about a rib?

We'll shave a couple strips from your flank.

Lovely.

* * *

Should be long gone by now, he thinks. Always some reason to adjust the schedule. Excuses about the pregnancy or his white count. You have to trust me, she says. By her third trimester, he's down to one arm and half a leg. The remainder of his body is an archipelago of flesh. He demands a piece from within. A kidney perhaps. Threatens to do it himself. She relents. Just one, we can't afford dialysis. Afterward she tells him she needs space and books a hotel room for the night. Before leaving the house, he overhears her whispering to the roundness of her belly.

You're not Annabelle, she says. You are brand new. A miracle like the world has never seen. Listen, darling. I need your help. I need you to do something for me.

The next morning, she comes home to find him passed out on the floor with a bottle of whiskey.

I thought you were dead, she tells him later. For a fraction of a second I was grateful.

He nods. Says how strong he feels, how far from gone.

I'm hungry, he says. I'm going to live forever.

He takes her by the arm. Finger and thumb make a circlet. Three tender nubs against her skin.

He says she'll betray him.

Never, she swears.

You'll have me wheeled off, locked away.

This house is a crime scene, she says.

The rest of the leg next, he insists. I'm done with legs.

* * *

Finally, he accepts the fact that he won't finish the job. The human body simply doesn't work that way, and he knows it. He's always known. So which cruel god burdened him with the desire? He pictures himself down to ribcage and spine. There are devices well beyond their budget. An artificial heart was always a pipe dream.

He regrets never tasting an eye, and wonders if he might squeeze one in at the end.

He'll do it while she's at the hospital. No better alibi. His affairs are in order. He considers his last meal.

But when she goes into labor, all his careful plans unravel. He winds up in the ambulance with her, clinging to her hand. Fine, it's fine, you're fine, everything's fine. He'll get a taxi home and do it tonight. While she's sedated.

Both of them are wheeled into ER. A nurse thinks he's a patient. From outside the labor room he hears Myra scream. He imagines them cutting the baby out, then diving back in for various organs. Incisions around each leg. Twisting off her limbs. Stretched out on the table. Five doctors, one at each apex of a pentagram, pulling her to pieces.

He hears an infant cry. He isn't exactly sure how he ended up in the room. A nurse places the swaddled girl between his arm and chest. Her eyes folded shut. The beak of her lip worming up and down. So light he has to hold on to keep her from floating away.

You tricked me, he mutters to Myra, who is fast asleep.

He hopes his daughter's eyes are deep and blue and wide like the sea.

This will be a good life, he thinks.

He touches her nose. Her tiny mouth opening and closing. He puts the tip of a pinky between her lips. She snips it clean off with a single bite. He didn't know newborns came with teeth. Such an active child. Climbing up his chest, groping for the dangling fruit of his ear. Nibble, chomp, chew. She's going after all the parts he missed, growing like a balloon as she slurps the skin off his bones, quarries an eye and feeds it back to him. No, a cherry tomato. He's just gone blind. A long time coming, to be fair. Then a biscuit, softened with tea. Soup from a spoon. My child, my child, how old have I become? She sings him the songs he sang to her when she was young. His heart is full simply because she is alive. And we are all immortal, he thinks, so long as we stay a little hungry. He focuses on his breath, feels his body wasting away. The world tilts on its axis as grandchildren crawl over him, beginning where he ends, taking repose in his empty spaces, eating their fill, driving their hands into the gaps of his flesh and pulling out whatever they need, as if he were a stream and they were his sheep.

The Thing Adored

Hanako Senzoku

While they waited to take the stage, Mikami let Yunjoo fix her hair, unexpectedly swirling around her in the passing breeze. Never mind about the sheet music. They laughed about whose idea it had been to hold a string ensemble concert outdoors, though who could predict the weather? Yunjoo looked eagle-eyed over the crowd, pointing out a certain boy she had a crush on, noting his jet-black hair, semi-long and tucked into a tiny ponytail and his long eyelashes, scolding Mikami for looking in an obvious way. There were other boys there, and which one had come to see Mikami, and which one did she like in return, didn't it seem strange that Hiroki was there since he was supposed to be at practice.

Mikami thought that Yunjoo didn't understand a girl's need for secrets. She remembered when she was eight, and she had a crush on a boy and her friend did as well, and they agreed not to fight, and to accept if he liked either of them, which was dumb and possibly the most peaceful total-war she had ever engaged in. So she gave up.

'I'm thinking about Vivaldi.'

Yunjoo ignored that. 'You need to understand love before you graduate, or it will be too late.' What Yunjoo said might have made sense except that they were already seniors and her focus would be on exams for the next six months. In fact, the grade head had gone so far as to suggest anyone with a boyfriend or girlfriend should break up if they were serious about study. Besides, you'd have to be blind not to notice how people started avoiding couples. Love had a predictable shape. A story that hadn't changed in a thousand years.

Afraid to say so and spoil Yunjoo's mood, Mikami asked her not to hold her disinterest against her. Her personality just wasn't like that. According to a dubious online personality survey, Mikami was the type that pondered on the truths of the world. She didn't think that she was destined to be a genius or anything, but she wasn't lying when she'd said Vivaldi interested her more than a small crowd of sporty boys. They were performing from the Four Seasons. Vivaldi's summer shaped itself around her, humid and blustery with the threat of a storm coming.

Mikami had attended a Shinto kindergarten, which wasn't an altogether uncommon thing, particularly for families that had lived many generations in the same town. She played on the grounds and was encouraged to make friends with the trees and stones. Great old pines and cedars dressed in thick braided ropes, preserved and inhabited by gods. She'd wanted to know where they went when she was looking and why they weren't showing themselves, wary with a five-year-old's suspicion of being tricked. Her teacher had told her to touch the tree bark. That was the reason. If she saw them straight up, she'd be completely captured and the experience of them would be like air. To be felt, they had to come across as if they were just wood. She had to give it to him, even though it wasn't much of an explanation, it stuck with her. Probably a trick. She was fairly certain of a godless world.

Yunjoo dug an elbow into her shoulder blade. Before she could protest, Mikami saw that Hiroki was standing before her, having broken uninvited into the circle of performers. At first, Mikami took his flushed cheeks for embarrassment, the same embarrassment she was being gobbled up by as an accessory to his trespass, but this appraisal was adjusted when she noted his panting. He held out a page of sheet music. Vivaldi's Concerto No. 2 in G minor.

'What is that?' Mikami asked. Yunjoo's elbow had hardened her into a white marble block.

In oafish amazement, he was about to answer that it was her sheet music, but then he noticed that she was indicating the outline of a footprint stamped over most of the right score. Just to prove he was sorry, he tried smoothing out the page against his chest.

'Hand it over,' Mikami said. She was grateful for the score, but there was something infuriating about the scene, the spectacle of him standing there, kicked-in baseball fetch instinct yielding a grandstanding moment that she wanted no part of.

'You should take more care,' he said, leaving before she could vent her displeasure. What did he know about Vivaldi other than the glee of chasing it down in the wind with his clumsy foot? Yunjoo lapped up the whole scene, smiling with satisfaction.

A week after she turned eighteen, Mikami ran into Hiroki in Shinjuku, on the metal staircase of an exam prep school for a prestigious music college. More accurately, she was run into by him as he tripped up the steps and fell into her. Automatic apologies were followed by noises of surprise, leading onto explanations, standing outside in the hot sun on that staircase.

Hiroki was wearing a white gauze eyepatch over his right eye. He was getting corrective surgery, one eye first, then the other. He felt the need to explain this because people had assumed cosmetic surgery, a double-folded eyelid. Some people rushed out to get cosmetic surgery the minute they turned eighteen. The timing couldn't have been worse, because it meant an end to baseball. Without depth perception, he couldn't catch.

She helped him up the stairs, slinging her violin on her back. Later, she would realize it was the first time she had held a boy's hand since her father passed away. At the time, she was so confused by his presence she did not notice. When she asked him whether he played an instrument, he confirmed that he did. The prep cram school had a high standard, and she couldn't believe it. Not this dark-tanned baseballer. He didn't have an instrument with him.

She asked him what instrument he played. He asked her whether she was serious about going to music college. She didn't particularly want to study music – she had always regarded the violin as a life-long hobby she never outgrew. A constant. She would apply to music college as a safety, as an option she pretended she would be happy to take. She wondered if it was the same with him.

'Don't change the subject,' she said instead, self-consciously taking back her hand, feeling an urge to shake the heat out of it.

He slid open the door to the cram school and, lowering his voice, said the harp.

When Mikami arrived at school, the hallways shaped themselves differently around her, the cadence of every voice clear. She appreciated people with an odd sense of regret. For six years she had filtered people out, designating most of them empty vessels who revealed so little about themselves because there was so little to reveal – but wasn't it possible, likely even, that they were complex and charming and filled with things that would amaze her? Hiroki was one example. She didn't know anything about him. When she walked up staircases, she found herself closing one eye. Yunjoo noticed the change in her demeanor. Mikami said it was probably the new hairband she as wearing. She was the same Mikami.

Throughout the morning, it got worse. Looking at Hiroki pleased her, though she had no idea why. Watching him knock his pencil off the desk and reach down blindly to pick it up meant something. Meaning swept her up. She thought about her own hands, how the fingers on her left were longer than the right because of years of violin exercises. She waited almost the whole day for chance to meet her half-way and contrive a slightly plausible reason to be near him out of earshot of others and asked him if he wanted to eat lunch together the following weekend before her music lesson and he agreed. When she insisted it be at a small hole in the wall udon place she knew, he didn't argue.

He arrived a little late to the udon shop, looking nervous, passing it off as not knowing how to find the place. They went inside and ordered. Mikami had decided on the strategy to make him confess everything he knew about music, thinking maybe that would satisfy her curiosity. While they waited for the noodles, she began her cross-examination, feeling ever so anxious, putting it down to the way his bandaged eye meant that she could only look at the uncovered one in a way that felt too much like a fixation.

Hiroki was reluctant at first, embarrassed, he said, because most people understood the harp to be the province of white gown wearing girls, which was not the case. Why the harp? Was it his choice? In a way. A five-year=old asked by his music teacher what his favorite shape was – a triangle. His teacher congratulated him on his choice of the harp, which he still didn't know what one was except that it was triangle shaped. Anyway, he was glad. The music of the harp was healthy for the soul. It was an old instrument, thousands of years old. Was it difficult to play with one eye covered, Mikami wanted to know, thinking about the baseball and the pencil, the lack of depth perception. No, not particularly.

'If I just turn my head more often when I play, I get a good enough sense, even playing the upper octaves. Same with you, I bet. You know by instinct.'

Yes. And with the comparison made, it became their next pastime to compare schedules, examinations and techniques, and then other things. She discovered that he had grown up close to near, and how strange it was that their paths hadn't crossed.

'If you hadn't stepped on my Vivaldi, I never would have known you existed,' she grinned.

'That's not how I remember it,' he grinned back.

'Anyway, what did you think of the concert?'

He told her he thought her playing was good. She liked that. That he had been listening.

'But it might have been a tad too perfect.'

'I'm sorry, did you say *too*?' She enjoyed that, too. Playing with him.

'I like it when a note is struck wrong sometimes. Not the wrong note. Just struck wrong. It gives a sense there is something there outside the execution. Have you ever tried closing one eye?'

'You're pissing me off now.'

The lunch had gone well, in the most unpredictable ways, and as they stood to part outside, she felt the air around her electrified with meaning and it took only a moment to realize he was going to kiss her. Would she have let him kiss her lips, out on the public street? She started to rise on the balls of her feet, but he took her hand instead, and turned it to catch the bright summer light, so that it glowed milk white. And he kissed there, the inside of her wrist.

Then, releasing her hand from that somewhat clumsy and unexpected embrace, he smiled and told her he was running late, that he'd see her later, leaving her confused to the point of despair out there on the street, still raised slightly on the balls of her feet.

Mikami had her own busy life, of course, but from that afternoon at the udon shop, she entered into what she referred to Yunjoo as a happy obsession. She found herself frequently returning in her imagination to the past. She replayed the way he had tilted her wrist in the light, wondering why he had done it. It had pleased her to see the way he was admiring her, to see herself as beautiful through his eyes, that strip of flesh so white it seemed to be glowing.

Yunjoo found her tedious and repetitive, and would sit stiffly listening, cautious when she got near the topic of Hiroki, even though Mikami believed she permitted herself the same self-deprecating irony as she always had before. She had never been able to imagine herself being the cute, clumsy damsel in distress in the silly romantic manga, and she still couldn't. Then what had changed? For one thing, all meaning seemed to trace back to him. Say, if he were huddled over his phone, she felt the same hypnotizing power of its light, not even knowing whether he was checking a baseball score or texting a friend. When he played the harp for her, she was reminded of her false assumptions, and of her own history with the violin. Then, when she praised his playing, he didn't seem impressed with her.

'I just think it's weird to love your own art. If I ever thought I had got a piece right, I'd have to throw the whole thing in and never touch an instrument again.' Besides, there were other things he would rather do, brushing his thumb delicately across her cheek. It seemed natural to submit. He had such an insightful way of looking at music. It reminded her of a story she had studied in world history, Pygmalion, about a man who falls in love with his sculpture. She thought about the precision she had always striven for in her violin playing with a sense of regret. She felt flustered, as though her life had been upturned, but then stabilized by the meaning he brought to it. I love him, she wrote on a page of her journal, as a simple statement of fact, reading it back to herself many times.

In the fall, Mikami sat the entrance examination for a music conservatory. She still had her heart set on studying law or letters, but the plan was to cover every eventuality. Preparing for the exam had become less suffocating, more funny-on-purpose alongside her harpist boyfriend. Yes, he was her boyfriend, publicly, and no longer a mystery. If it ever was.

But on the day of the exam, she couldn't find Hiroki. He wasn't replying to texts and she had even tried dialing. They had sat the theory exam and all that remained was the audition. All the candidates were to wait in an anteroom until called in. Mikami paced outside the building, splashing loudly through puddles she didn't notice. In one hand, she clutched the small woven good luck charm her mother had received after donating to the local shrine, and in her other she held her phone.

'I'm outside the building and I'm having a panic attack,' she said.

'Why are you outside? Go in. Easy as pie.' Yunjoo sounded amused, as if it was a relief that something for once wasn't about *him*.

'He's not here. I don't know what to do.'

Yunjoo sighed and told her she was crazy. 'Do you see that? I'm starting to think you have seriously lost the plot. Go inside and play your fiddle.'

She hung up. Mikami permitted herself one more turn, back and forth in the cold drizzle, and went inside to sit her audition.

Later, when she tracked Hiroki down, he turned to her calmly, as if nothing had happened and asked her how her audition had gone.

How had it gone?

'Fine. I guess it went fine. I struck a few notes wrong, so you would have approved. Where were you? Did something happen?'

He looked at her with a confused expression. 'No, I told you I wasn't taking the audition.'

For one outraged moment, she almost let him have it. He had done no such thing, and the fact that he would claim to – well, it made no sense. Maybe he had? He must have, what else would explain it? He meant so much to her. That intense meaning had acquired the power to turn back time and transmute reality. She felt a sense of wonder at that, and an excited sense of doom.

It wasn't long after the audition that they broke up. He broke them up. When he did, Mikami felt as though she had been ejected out of the universe. Cut off from all meaning. What was it he'd said? Things were going *too* well. How was she supposed to make sense of that? It could only have been a lie. To spare her feelings. There obviously must have been something wrong. Nothing wrong can't be something wrong. It was ridiculous. And then there was the comment about the stories.

They were taking a walk to clear their heads after a session where they had both actually got a lot of study done. It had snowed in Tokyo, enough to lay. They piled on warm clothes but left their gloves behind.

Snow silence and the velvet crunch of their footsteps provided wonder to them as they wandered aimlessly through the streets they had both grown up in. Occasionally, one would share a memory. They ended up at the local shrine, the place where Mikami's mother had obtained her charm, and the kindergarten she had attended. The grounds were deserted. White frosting lay over the stone lanterns and the carved lion-dogs acting as guardians.

They stood before each other, breathing on each other's hands, and to Mikami, the moment could not have been conjured better in her dreams. Everything beautiful in the world seemed to emanate from their center. 'I feel so alive,' she said.

That was when he said they had to break up. Her head swayed with a sudden flush of heat, she couldn't swallow, couldn't breathe. She must have misheard. He was talking, trying to *explain*, and through the static of shock she had to concentrate to hear.

He had placed his gloveless hand on one of the large stones in the shrine garden. He wanted to feel the texture of the stone, he was saying. No, he *had* to feel the texture of the stone or he wouldn't feel anything at all. So that was that. And she remembered her own past, and she supposed he had attended this very same school and kept it a secret. Not that it mattered. He'd rather she be a stone than alive, alive, alive. That was how it had to happen. In one big bang, he was gone and he was everywhere.

The Watch Case

Hanako Senzoku

A mystery out of all proportion served itself up on the day I got my braces adjusted. My parents had decided on an orthodontist in central Tokyo, though we lived almost an hour away. After the appointment, I found out my train card had no charge, that I had no cash on me and that my cell battery was flat. Such an unlikely set of events, for a while I couldn't see any reason that I shouldn't burst into tears as I played out how many small decisions had lined up to get me into such a mess.

I must have walked myself to Hibiya Park and taken a seat on a bench, absent from the life of the park going on so matter of fact around me. How would I get home? I could get a terribly expensive taxi and have the driver wait while I ran inside and got money. But why, was the question. That didn't seem fair. I could jump the gate at the station. Maybe if I explained my situation, the station manager might pity me. I found myself trying to explain bad luck to a guy next to me on the bench. How the conversation got started I couldn't say but if I was to guess, I was almost talking to myself and then, he would have spoken back as if one of my questions had been put to him. I didn't pay him much attention, wrapped up in myself. As a result, I was caught flatfooted when he stood up and handed me a five-thousand yen note. I held onto the note dumb as what felt like every trouble life contained was whisked away.

The boy, embarrassed, was already walking away. He had performed the gesture in an awkward, non-negotiable way, and before I knew it, I'd let him go.

Later, I went over what I could remember. Suppose he'd been there to walk one of the dogs sniffing the lawn. But that hadn't been the case. He'd indicated one of the surrounding high-rises, I thought. Another thing I'd failed to notice until after the fact was how nice-looking he was.

I decided I would return that money and thank him for his kindness.

The only person I wasn't too embarrassed to tell about it was a girl named Towa.

September last year, I'd visited Towa's apartment for the first and only time. She'd been going through a rough patch after her mother had caught her father cheating with a floozy in Nagoya. It wasn't the first time he'd been caught. On the previous occasions her parents had stayed together for the sake of the family. The betrayal still stung, Towa confided almost soundlessly, as if it was the last time she would let it. Living at her apartment was Towa and her sister, her mother and her deadbeat father who would return from Nagoya on weekends to a frosty reception.

I wasn't prepared for what I found when I got to her bedroom. For one thing, it was enormous by Tokyo standards. But what astonished me was the walls, covered in fine line drawings mistaken at first for a pattern, but revealed as row after row of hand drawn cityscape.

When I asked her about it, she shrugged as if to suggest I had asked a childish question. It was a view from the Yamanote Line facing outward. It was Tokyo, meticulously sketched. Her parents encouraged her – she would be an architect, they probably thought. Twice a month she went out on the Yamanote and walked the track until she found an apartment or parking lot she could get high up on. Rooves were easy to break onto, she said too casually. She would break out a sketch pad and digital camera and get to work.

I spent an hour looking at that drawing. Some places were especially detailed. There was a magnifying glass on an articulated arm that she could roll around the room. I managed to locate her apartment at head-height, extending up from Gotanda, and used the magnifying glass to look at it. The curtains and the balcony plants were right. I told her my address and hunted for it, but it was only a vaguely sketched skyline.

I thought again how unlikely that my parents would tolerate such an eccentric project, let alone encourage it, jealous of her license or possibly her guts.

We hung out, and I listened to her try to reconcile her skirt-chasing father. Then I went home, and that was the only time I'd visited her. Every now and then at school, I wanted to ask her about the drawing – it was the strangest thing about that day – but I could never bring myself to. The topic was too unrelated a non-sequitur, too forced a question to deserve an honest answer, and anyway, I was sure she was still at it, working away at her drawing as if it was a favorite book she could read forever.

When I told Towa about the guy and the five-thousand yen, she said some judgmental things that made me want to give it up entirely.

'Why didn't you just go back to the orthodontist and call someone?'

'Because...I didn't think of that at the time. I don't know why.'

'It's irresponsible of you not to ask his name and let him get away without finding out how you could repay him.'

'I know that. You're making me feel stupid, thanks. I was in shock. Who does that?'

'Five thousand yen is more than you need to ride a train.'

'Maybe it was all he had.'

A series of questions that made me feel as though there was something about me or my story that didn't measure up, and a pause to laugh at how only I could find myself in such a situation.

'I wanted to ask you to help find him.'

'How would I do that?'

'I'm glad you asked. I've given it thought. The only way to find him is by going back to Hibiya. He probably lives around there. Maybe he goes to a cram school. And I remembered you said you sketch, which is basically watching.'

'What do you need me for? You just sit there. Take a camera. People think you're a train spotter.'

'I figured – it's just, I also thought, since you're going out anyway...'

'You want company.'

'When you put it like that, it could be anyone.'

Her vision shifted, projecting back into her bedroom, looking for Hibiya.

'I could keep you company while you draw.'

Her pupils shrank back around me. 'Okay.'

'Okay?' I hadn't intended to let on how important it was. Obsession on my part had never shown itself before.

'Do you even remember what he looks like?' she asked.

I was confident I would recognize him, his mannerisms must have been familiar to me to begin with, as though we'd known each other since we were small children.

'I start early. Seven at the station. Dress boyish, a cap or hoodie. Less chance creeps will bother us. Bring gloves for climbing over fences. Put your eyebrows down. Sometimes the right place is over a fence. Charge your phone and put money in your wallet.'

I took the train to Ginza and walked to Hibiya under a silver fall sky, the streets wet and reflective. Towa arrived five minutes late in a long coat and a white baseball cap. She made me show her the bench where the boy had given me five-thousand yen but quickly decided it wouldn't do, giving me a look of mild disapproval that I would ever choose such a bench to sit at.

Bordering the park was a view of the Midtown Shopping Center and the Imperial Hotel, interesting subjects to draw, but she took us north to a view of the bench that looked south at a row of non-descript commercial buildings where she unpacked her things at an identical bench.

For the first hour the park was quiet. People walked dogs. It was a fancy area, so the dogs were fancy breeds. Occasional joggers puffed past a group of elderly people doing tai chi.

Though I don't like nosy people, from time to time I peeked at how her drawing was coming along. She worked in pencil, outlining the geometric skyline and the garden pathway. At some point, she began aggressively rubbing out her lines and redrawing them from a perspective ten or twenty meters higher than we sat.

I talked to her about drawing, though she didn't seem to be particularly interested. Such a plain and obvious thing wasn't worth talking about. When did she start to draw? The same time as everyone else, as though what she did was an extension of crayon faces. It was a hobby she didn't grow out of – the way people play video games or take ballet lessons or practice the violin.

'Nobody draws a city on their walls,' I said, wanting there to have been an acknowledgement of that.

'So, what?' she shrugged. 'That him?'

Whenever a young guy walked through the park, she'd point him out. After a while, it turned into a code for pointing out nice-looking boys. I'd ask her sometimes. 'He could be,' she'd answer, 'in my dreams.' Sometimes an oddish person came through, prompting the question and we'd giggle at our power to pass our own judgements.

My mum had packed two lunches with cookies, potato chips and thermoses of iced coffee. At ten o'clock I broke out a picnic sheet. Towa reacted with surprised gratitude, putting down her notebook.

'The light is too bright on the glass,' she said.

Since it was too early for lunch, we had cookies and iced coffee. I asked for an update on her father. Looking back, it was random of her to share that story about her dad, uncommon in Tokyo to dismantle the barrier between public and private like that.

Nothing had changed with her family life. Her father carried on his romantic life in Nagoya, returning to Tokyo most weekends to a family dinner.

'Your mum and sister are good?' I was careful not to ask her what she thought.

She shrugged. 'Not good. It just is. No point making ourselves upset all the time. Every now and then sparks fly, attitudes are made known.'

'Is that why you're not doing so good at study?'

My school published the class ranks, and I couldn't help but notice Towa had gradually fallen near the bottom.

'I don't turn in homework. I have better things to do. They should teach in class.'

'That's not a normal take.'

'So, what. That him?'

I looked but nobody was there.

I asked if I could flick through her notebook, careful to dust crumbs off my fingers. Recent sketches from somewhere north – Nippori, maybe – preserved billboard architecture, shaded awnings of a bead shop next to a woodblock print fabric seller, old potted plants that somebody watered.

I wanted to know why with her talent she drew the city. 'Not people or fashion or comics or flowers.'

'You don't need a reason to do something or not do something,' she said, confiscating the book. 'It's a city. Me in every way but how I am. Everything I could be. You should ride the loop if you want to know.'

It takes about an hour to ride the loop. I wondered how many times she'd done it, and about the implication that she rode the loop the same way, say, clockwise. No, thank you. I thought it would drive me crazy to know the city that well. Then more foot traffic, and I had to stretch my eyes open to sharpen my concentration.

'Why this particular guy?' Towa asked, back at sketching.

'I don't know. I don't remember ever being saved before. Don't laugh. By fate or by kindness. I should have known it was just some meaningless guy who got freaked out.'

'Then why are you here?'

'What if he doesn't come?' Was it possible that I'd wasted the entire morning? I was full of misery. There ought to have been an acknowledgement.

'He is supposed to. Look, a brand new five-thousand yen note from the bank. A card would have been too much, don't you think?'

'You could come back tomorrow. And the next day.'

'The next day is school.'

She shrugged. It annoyed me, that satisfied shrug, suggesting I'd already been given five-thousand yen by a stranger out of the blue, disregarding that every future presence withheld would be an absence felt more keenly. I wished I could retrieve my right to suffer and complain about indifference, to be stranded in the middle of Tokyo.

'When he shows up, I'll give him a piece of my mind,' I said crossly.

Midafternoon, the warm weather turned us out of our coats, where we tried on each other's sunscreen.

'Your drawing is really good.' I regretted my word choice. Her drawing was more than good. She would later shrink it down and detail it through her magnifying glass onto her wall, looking out from an imaginary Yamanote loop high above the horizon. What would happen to the sketch? I asked her if I could have it. She bit her lip and said, 'I'll think about it.'

At three o'clock, the high-rises cut long cello streaks of shade over us as we neared the same time I'd been there, a week earlier. I was at the edge of exhaustion, onlooker to an entire day's worth of park tenants, and not a single candidate. The absolute assurance I sought continued to elude me and only actively looking at where he had temporarily sat solved my unease.

'We have to go,' Towa said. 'The light is no good.'

She was right, but I couldn't bear it. What if when I looked away I missed what came next? No reprimand came from her as I sat another ten minutes, hearing transmitted across the still dusk air the distant rumble of the Yamanote as the city wound itself down.

At Hibiya subway I was myself again. Smiling and joking as I slid the crisp five thousand yen note into the train ticket machine.

'Your dad at home this weekend?' I asked her as we paused at the ticket gate to say goodbye.

'Maybe.' We hugged and touched our hands together, and I marched through the turnstile. 'Either way, he's there,' she said.

On the subway, when I went through my things to check that I had everything, I found that Towa had snuck a gift to me. I gasped when I saw it was her drawing, roughly torn out. It brought tears to my eyes. There, on the park bench in the center of her masterpiece, she had included a figure waiting, and it was him, exactly as I remember it.

Flash Fiction

First Steps in Probability

Susan Wigmore

We're kicking fag packets down the alley behind Tanners Lane and I let you win because I want to tell you I love you, there in the scrubby weeds and litter and dog-piss stink of it, and I do. Love you, Chrissy O'Connor. I love you.

You lean in as if to hug me but instead do that daft tripping thing your dad does and run off laughing. I brush grit from my knees. Your hair is so dark it shines blue like a magpie's wing. Prove it, you say, when I catch up, your hand already on the Merry Widow's gate. You push it open. Strung across the yard is a washing line with its straggle of clothes.

A pair of knickers, you say. I dare you.

We know she's home. We can hear her singing.

There's ivy on the fence, huge shovel leaves, veins yellow and fine. There's a tartan peg-bag and tights the colour of toffee, and look, there's my hand snatching the Widow's knickers. See the pegs fly! See my pumping heart flow in my veins, Chrissy O'Connor!

You're by the bin at the town end of the alley where your dad meets his girlfriends. The knickers are saggy and grey. I'll push them through old Harry's letterbox, I say. That'll set tongues wagging.

Silly cow, you say, and run across the road.

We do star-jumps at each other, cars jammed between us, and you hug me when I reach you, my mouth deep in your magpie hair. The thought of kissing you makes me gasp. Your bag slips from your shoulder and you push us both away. In your hand, the Widow's knickers filched from my pocket. I watch as you chuck them in a skip. Your slow smile. The thrill of it all –

Dynamics

Barbara P Tarrant

I catch Ma reading a book, *Don't Be A Victim*, while she skins a piece of hake.

Does that mean, I say, *you're going to stop doing the martyr thing*?

Leave your mother alone, booms Da from the front room.

It's unbearable here since the brother and sister moved out.

DINNER!

Ma puts my plate down. Melting butter runs off the hake through the peas and celery but doesn't penetrate the tough skin of the baked potato. Da gets salmon because he's the breadwinner.

Did you do that thing, Da says, itching for a row–*the thing you were supposed to do this morning, yesterday even*?

My fork hovers over the white flaky fish —

I will do it, I say, *in my own time*.

Da's eyes bulge. He calls me a cheeky wagon. Ma slams her plate down accusing us of sabotaging her dinner after all the effort she's put in. I point out the victimhood in that statement and she accuses me of sarcasm and agism. I'm thrown, so is Da – victimhood is a new one on him. I've blown up another dinner-time with my carry-on.

Meanwhile, I move my plate slightly to the right to balance a still-life composition that's forming within a circle shadow thrown from the light above. I take my phone and snap – for my portfolio – my ticket out of here.

ENOUGH, my aggrieved Ma cries, trying to grab my phone.

What did we say about phones at the dinner-table? Parrots Da.

While the pink salmon yields under Da's angry fork, I remove me and my dinner from the table, slam the plate down on the draining board – and the fragile buttery glaze cracks, Vermeer-like, on the surface of the untouched hake, peas and celery. It's a gift. A nod from the universe.

Because it is Impossible and Yet

Emma Goldman-Sherman

A girl became a tree, and even as a tree, they fucked her, scraped her bark slap off. Afterwards alone, she became a laundromat full of lost socks spinning. A bakelite radio locked in her throat snapped on one Sunday morning's church, and from her mouth floated curses.

She prayed the organ play to drown her out, grateful for the wheezing sounds of disbelief, self-righteous coughs as they covered the ears of their kids. The men insisted she leave as pity ran like piss on poured concrete staining the velvet kneelers. The ladies implied she be grateful she's alive, should sing of hope, but none rose to help. But heaven listened as children listed toward the bright sun beyond the open door.

She made herself a traveling suit but remained rooted as her cambium cried against the suggested penance. She tried to craft an apology. About to hand it over, she happened to notice the hand of the man ready to read what she wrote. So white, so smooth, but beneath his nails, she eyed the ragged truth: rude remnants of bark —

Gripping her plea, she ran. Ripping the paper to ribbons, stripping off her apron, she sang herself back to the mendable memory, able now to recall the faces of all the men counting tithes in the sacristy, erect in the stone-sculpted rectory where she'd started to turn herself from truth to tree.

Then she knew she lived no longer rooted or wrecked; with the means of protection; that a girl can survive as an unmated sock; that a heart can be hocked and bide decades without purchase; that the organ hides sin with what sounds like searching to rend it unseen, but the heart remains waiting within. The heart waits within.

The Hunger Wall

Mark Bowsher

He's been watching *Great Art Explained* on YouTube again. Says we should spend some time appreciating the Rothko on the wall. It's his turn to cook tonight. S'ok. Not hungry yet.

~

This is pretty chill actually. Forgot we had that print – think he bought it. It's his turn to cook.

~

God. We've been staring at it for like 10 mins now. I'm getting wine.

~

We didn't speak for a whole min. Staring at the Rothko, silent, drinking wine. omfg we're wankers now.

~

He's said 'negative space' like 4 times in the last min. It's his turn to cook.

~

I've suggested takeout. He's offloading Rothko's wiki on me. There's a pack of cheese n onion on the side. Hate cheese n onion. Might give it a shot.

~

He's talked for an entire min, don't think I heard a word. More Rothko wiki. Perhaps I could kill him with a coaster. That possible? His turn to cook.

~

Fuck. He's asked me for my opinion. Said something. Hasn't landed well. Oh god, I'm being interrogated re. the validity of whatever the fuck I just said. The hammer on the side is nearer than the cheese n onion.

~

Hammer would be messy. God you'd really have to mean it. Can't be arsed. Been looking down at the hammer for too long. He's staring at me. There's a solo chopstick on the table for some reason. Would that work?

~

It worked. Fuck. Bit messy. Quiet now. Wonder if you can eat human? Incognito tab.

~

Ugh. Bit of a faff. Need a saw. Too many recipes with marinades. Getting Papa Johns.

~

Your order is being prepared.

~

Your order is being prepared.

~

Your order is being prepared.

~

Bit of blood on the Rothko. Quite like it now. Less negative space.

~

Your order is being prepared. ffs.

No!

Patricia Newbery

To the man who told me what I was like as a child, although he wasn't there.

To the man who showed me how to eat an orange, because I was eating one wrong.

To the man who said the walnuts in the salad were stale.

To the man who was always late when we met and said I was unreasonable if I complained.

To the man who said he corrected me out of love.

To the man who sneered at the gift I'd hunted for and didn't take it with him when he left.

To the man who sometimes listened when I spoke and, after a pause, said, 'I already knew that'.

To the man who smirked when I said I was too busy to translate his report and didn't take it with him when he left.

To the man who said I was aggressive on the rare occasions I objected to the way he went on.

To the man who scoffed when I told him to be careful what he said to journalists during the Arab Spring.

To the man who went to Europe for ten days and was refused entry to Egypt when he returned.

To the man who says he misses me and is sure I miss him, even if I won't say so when he asks.

To the man who's been living in Italy these past few years and has asked me repeatedly to visit him.

I See Jesus in My Fevered Dream on Quay Street in Galway

Linda Nemec Foster

He looks surprisingly cool and hep, with sunglasses tinted dark blue and a cell phone encased in a hard plastic Superman cover. But his clothes still look like he came from central casting circa 1956 Cecil B. DeMille – or the statue of the Sacred Heart in my dead mother-in-law's bedroom. You know (or you should, you doubting agnostics): the white tunic, the red cloak, the long brown hair parted perfectly in the middle, the heart superimposed on his chest with flames leaping out from its top like lava and a crown of thorns encircling it like barbed wire. That guy. What I don't expect is his casual smile and totally chill attitude. He's late for this party in a small flat in Galway on Quay Street and wants to know, "Where's the food?" Answer: it's a buffet spread in the kitchen towards the back, down the hall. I thought he'd already know that – since he's God and all. But he shows no omniscience, no omnipotence. He's not here to change water into Merlot, to feed all the guests from a package of water crackers and a couple of plates of sushi (I told you he was hep). He's done with showing off. He's done with pleasing his mother. He's just here for the party – whether he's invited or not. Meanwhile, I'm burning with as many questions as a cast of thousands in a Biblical epic. "Oh, those are so last millennium," he says as he sips his white wine and looks nonchalant. I look for the nearest exit. Take my questions with me.

Witness Statement

Molly Underwood

The devil? I saw him twice in my life – only twice. First time was walking down the street not far from Green Park, very residential area, lovely area, really done up since I was a kid. And there was this sort of – well, he was so much younger than I thought he'd be. Funny how we have these ideas in our head. And he was kicking litter – I remember he was kicking these cans down the street where they'd fallen from black bins. Probably foxes. And he – there was something quite awkward about him, actually. Long arms, long legs, like an insect, or a fawn.

I'm thinking: there's really nothing to be scared of here, basically the guy is harmless, a big kid, and he's kicking these – sort of straggling past these rows of houses that obviously aren't his, obviously this was not where he lived, most of the time. And he's going nowhere, I realise. And he gets close, and there's something in his eyes that puts me – well, just right on edge. Big eyes, fawn-like, these very unusual eyes, and they're quite unfocused, like he's been drinking all day. And he doesn't even look at me. Looks right past me. I remember he was carrying a Tesco bag, and that really caught me! That really – there was something so human about it. A Tesco bag!

I did think about stopping him, asking him anything – *where have you been? Is there heat in the old soil, still? What grows amongst the ruins?*

I didn't do it, of course. No point. He was so sort of purposeless, loping along, headed away down the street – and I just watched him go. I couldn't have stopped him if I wanted to.

Anyway – that was the first time.

The Full Package

Martin Daly

The package had arrived unexpectedly. It bore no return address. I pondered its contents as I ate breakfast. Finished eating, I laid it upon the cleared kitchen table.

I recognized him immediately – a self-portrait. Even after the passage of 30-odd years, he was inimitable, if older, and I felt an immediate urge to sit, or to run or have a drink – something! I placed the painting face down on the table and felt a modicum of calm return, albeit still shaken.

This called for tea, rather than alcohol. Safer, I decided. As I sat, warming mug in hand, memories began to resurface. Hadn't all of this been over for years, now? Hadn't there been enough pain and damage, with scars – both physical and emotional – to prove it?

I examined the picture again and noticed the unmistakable arrogant signature on a lower corner. Yes, I thought, the bastard's still the same.

There was more of a chill in the air this early autumn evening, and I decided a fire was appropriate. The phone rang as I prepared the woodstove. I recognized his voice.

"Hi," he said. "Did you get the package?"

"Oh yes," I replied. "I got the full package – a long time ago."

"I need to tidy up some loose ends," he said.

"That makes two of us," I replied, and hung up.

The painted canvas burned with a curious flame. The empty frame burned more slowly, drawing smoke-wrapped scars up the metal flue.

The Story of Our Beautiful, Smiling Family in Twenty-One Chapters

Kurtis Burton

Chapter I. Our Beautiful Home in the Woods
Your father didn't make it.

Chapter II. Our Beautiful, Smiling Family
Your father didn't make it.

Chapter III. The Toy Soldier for Your Birthday
Your father didn't make it.

Chapter IV. Hours After the Discarded Wrapping Was Gone
Your father didn't make it.

Chapter V. The Beautiful Blue Ringing Your Eye
"My father didn't make it."

Chapter VI. The Salving Apology
Your father didn't make it.

Chapter VII. The Sentence You Would Not Forgive but Would Have Saved You
Your father didn't make it.

Chapter VIII. Eye Contact on the Way Out the Door
You didn't make it.

Chapter IX. The Effort to Dial 10 Digits
You didn't make it.

Chapter X. Your Beautiful Home in the Woods
You didn't make it.

Chapter XI. Your Beautiful, Smiling Family
You didn't make it.

Chapter XII. The Gift Card for Your Daughter's Birthday
You didn't make it.

Chapter XIII. Time For Unwrapping
You didn't make it.

Chapter XIV. Your Daughter's Beautiful, Darker Eye
"You didn't make it."

Chapter XV. The Sentence She Would Not Forgive but Might Have Granted Peace
You didn't make it.

Chapter XVI. Eye Contact on the Way Out the Door
Your daughter didn't make it.

Chapter XVII. The Call from the Hospital
"Your father didn't make it."

Chapter XVIII. The Effort to Dial 10 Digits
You made it.

Chapter XIX. The Decision to Pick Up Despite Everything
Your daughter made it.

Chapter XX. Her Beautiful, Smiling Family
Your daughter made it.

Chapter XXI. Our Beautiful Family's Mistake
Your daughter didn't make it.

He Who Dares Wyn Jones

Ian Johnson

Wyn Jones and I loved to banter.

'I'm half Welsh and half English,' he said.

'Oh yeah,' I said, 'which half of you is Welsh?'

He sucked hard on his roll-up and blew out a grey spectre into the cold March air.

'The half I left in Afghanistan.'

I stood up behind his chair and wheeled him into physio for yet another battle.

Short Memoirs

My Mother's Daughter

Anneke Bender

1.
In the picture, my mother and I are walking in the Grand Canyon holding hands. That summer, she worked at the Lawrence Livermore Lab and we had driven across the country to get there, halfway in a bright orange VW bus, halfway in a Corolla hatchback called *Blusie* after the old bus "swallowed a valve." My mother, the biologist, always claimed the best way to study nature was to talk to creatures. I was taken with Native Americans the whole trip, looking at cave dwellings and bright turquoise in silver bell caps. We would stop at trinket stores and I wanted each tiny thing, each stone and bracelet, flute and arrowhead. I imagined living in a cave, tucked in by a fire. Back then my mother called me by the nickname *Nic-A-Lee* and brushed my hair into pigtails, and I can hardly write these words.

2.
My mother and I walked in the Grand Canyon holding hands, my hair in pigtails and my lanky string-bean legs brushing their bell bottoms together as we travelled down the dusty path. She was a scientist and worked all summer at a lab in California while my dad watched us during the day. We got there in the back of Blusie, camping the whole route in a cross-country family adventure. Blusie's windshield shattered once pulling into a gas station for cheap gas, because my dad saw the sign at the last minute and turned on a dime. He was always looking for the cheapest gas.

3.
My mother and I walked in the Grand Canyon, my hand in hers, her hand in mine, her bright smile that was always there shining in the sun. We went into the canyon for a bit. Not all the way down, just enough to get our feet dusty. Just enough to put footprints along the path, the way

Native Americans put footprints on the same land a long time ago. We had driven there from our home in Atlanta – my brother, my mom, my dad, and me. The long, slow hours passed while my brother and I played 20 questions and looked for license plates from Alaska. The first question my mom always asked after we set up our tent each night was: "Do you want to go explore?" She was always so kind, pushing my brother and I to be curious, to find adventure. She is still kind.

When you are young, you see only the moment; when you are older, you see a story strung together, a line weaving through years during which everything shifts, the slow tide. Glass, in the end, settles downward. It is so strange, is it not, to sit where you are now and see what you were then? A day in the Grand Canyon, my mother holding my hand as we walked the trail. Who took that picture? Surely my dad. Maybe he and my brother were walking ahead, and he turned back for a moment, his thick hands lifting the viewfinder to his eye. My hand lifts to his and together we turn the dial, focus the image until it sharpens the lines memory has frayed. Her kindness – this is the picture.

* * *

That world – my early life – was crafted for me by my parents. They taught my brother and me about Gandhi and Martin Luther King, about my Mennonite father's side and how my mother used to be a nun. It was perhaps my mother's kindness that drew her to the Catholic Church, caused her to don the nun's habit. She had a stunning beauty, but never cared much for it; cared, instead, for a hidden mysticism she seemed certain was drifting in the air between us all.

Hold each other in the light.

Ask your guides.

Listen to your dreams.

These phrases were woven into the patterns of my childhood, as ever present as *because I said so* might have been in another family. They were her answer to any manner of problem, never mind that a child has little concept of dream interpretation and even less of what a "guide" might be. Later, trying to explain my childhood to others, I would stumble, unable to translate the messages my mother gave me into a language anyone else would understand. *When I had problems, she took me to psychics. It wasn't as weird as it sounds.* Except that maybe it was? My childhood lacked practical education. I was unschooled in how to match my shirt with my pants – ran around with iron-on superhero jerseys and wild, bright print "culottes" – but was drawn into an invisible magic buzzing around the world of creatures. My mother incited constant engagement with these unseen forces and, strangely – because I was not raised in a church – a deep belief in god.

She used to wake me up whispering "bluuuuuberrrrry paaaancaaakes" in my ear, and I knew I would be arriving late to school. We would sit in Mr. P's Diner long into the morning hours, drinking orange juice and sopping a doughy, buttery short stack in syrup out of a plastic bottle. My mother never cared if I showed up for school, or if I followed rules. If anyone around us adopted a serious tone, she would glance at me sideways with a twinkle in her eye, as if we were renegades in our own special universe. She was taught as a child never to jump on beds, so she encouraged my brother and me to leap around on our mattresses as often and as wildly as we wanted. To this day, I grow bored with people who try to be excessively good, unable to erase the image of my mother rolling her eyes from the back of my mind. The sugary platitudes of the American South didn't work on her, and she taught me to cringe at that sweet taste in my mouth, too.

* * *

It all seems so obvious in retrospect – that she would be my mother, that I would belong to her. She always said that when I was born, she recognized me.

In another picture, we are carrying a pot of water together and it is obvious in the way we are both smiling that I am a wanted child. This was a wind at my back that followed me through my early days, the fact of her affection for me. When did that affection change? It didn't, I can see now; it has been a constant. It was me, not her, who changed.

The inner-city school where I came of age was filled with the complications of post-integration, a colliding of cultures, unspoken histories of trauma laid out in our varied skin colors. Underneath these daily trials, I lived with a strange awareness of loss and loneliness, a struggle to contain deeper uncertainties. I was haunted by the thought that my parents would die. I was conscious of the fears of others and how they hid them. When I was told about my Mennonite grandmother Esther – her sensitivities and insecurities – I recognized myself in her ways, as if some invisible familial defect was passed on to me and I was not quite strong enough for the world.

Even now I can see my mother's eyes as she watched me labor under the weight of my ruminations. It was still too early for me to know how her trusting nature and stubborn positivity had blinded her to things – how she swept what she didn't like under a magical rug. My cousin used to marvel at it: "I don't know how she does it – you try to pin her down and she just slides off topic." It was still too early for me to know the benefits of simple instruction in the ways of the world, and how I would need to get that from somewhere else.

In an effort to solve the spiraling trouble in her heart and mine, my mother formed a hybrid spirituality. She often quoted a line from a poem with tears in her eyes: *Oh world, I cannot hold thee close enough.* She pasted together a version of things from books and gurus and 1,000 cassette tapes from a channeled being named Lazarus. *You create your own reality.* She took me to see mediums, plied me with crystals left on my bedside table, and stacked books with guided meditations around my room.

As I hit my 20s – trying to press the gas pedal on a stuttering life – my mother and I landed together most mornings at a neighborhood bagel shop. We each got an iced tea with one packet of Sweet'N Low and a toasted onion bagel with cream cheese. I can't remember what we talked and laughed about, but we talked and laughed for hours. It was sitting at our corner table one day when she said she didn't want me to tell her my troubles anymore. *I only want to talk about good things*. This was the moment, sitting over iced tea and bagels – the moment she kicked me from the nest. We were too wound up with each other, and she was so afraid of my troubles, even as I worked hard to smooth them over.

So I stopped.

As we finished our breakfast, my mother and I finished something else: she had completed her job raising me. She had taught me what she could and the rest would need to come from the world. Her trust in the world faltered only when it came to me. Our relationship shifted and we would never be close in the same way again. I made my way forward, and began to craft my own hybrid philosophy, an approach more fact-based, emotional, dark, and tenacious than hers.

* * *

When I was in my 30s, my mom and I took a trip to her hometown of Ashley, North Dakota, stopping along the way to visit her old convent in Rochester, Minnesota. My mother's Catholic history is a thing I sometimes share as a fun fact about myself. *I was raised by an ex-nun*, I say, and people laugh, asking if she left the convent for my father, which she didn't. I tell the story about how she had to peel bananas with a knife and fork. *I guess the church worried what might happen if a nun got her hands on a banana.*

Sleeping for a night in the motherhouse, I felt a strange and easy peace drifting through the marble hallways. We ate dinner in the large cafeteria where my mother once accused herself of her sins, the ways nuns are required to do. One day when the mother general was out of town, someone stood up and jokingly accused herself of *being a jellybean*, a story recounted to me as I sat with a group of holy sisters, my mother's friends from before I was born. They were a smashingly good time. I learned that nuns like to get away with things, stealing bottles of whiskey from the fathers and smoking cigarettes in the back woods. They slyly winked at me between stories.

I finally understood how hard it must have been for my mother, lying awake in the convent, realizing she no longer believed in the Church but not yet having the courage to leave. I realized she left this life and these women in stages, almost precisely the way she is leaving me now. My mother and I are both careful, take our time with choices; we are not inclined to leave precious things behind.

As we drove from the motherhouse towards Ashley, we passed signs for a Corn Palace. It was one of those roadside attractions that rise up, iconic, while driving along a flat, endless highway. We got off and followed a maze of roads, realizing it was farther than we had imagined and wondering if it would, in the end, be worth it. As we got closer, we noticed a lot of people. *This Corn Palace is a pretty big deal*, I thought. We had to park several blocks away. Lining the sidewalk were booths selling buttons, posters, and t-shirts. As I looked down, I thought South Dakota must have a strange and strong affection for Barack Obama, because his face was literally on every single thing. I looked up and saw a huge red, white, and blue sign for Obama, circa 2008. *I didn't know South Dakota was so liberal.* Far too slowly, my mom and I realized that we were headed directly into a raucous political rally.

"Mom! It's starting, like, *right now!*" I screamed. We got our tickets and walked in, both of us beaming from ear to ear. Immediately the crowd scout saw us – a mother and daughter with dazzling American smiles, full of optimism and hope – and pulled us onto the stage right behind our favored candidate. It was on that hallowed spot that I snapped a perfect picture of her: bandana in her hair, both arms lifted high to a bright sky, the sun illuminating brilliant white clouds.

This picture was taken after the time she worried about me, and before the time I worried about her. It was taken the day before I accidentally ate a tomato during the Great 2008 Tomato Salmonella Crisis and suffered a terrible fever, not knowing how I would survive the distance to a hospital. It was taken the day before my mother took over driving and immediately hit a gas pump in the gas station where we were parked. But these sufferings were trivial in the end; it is the rally I remember most.

* * *

The day my dad called to say we had to talk about what was happening, I wanted to cup my hand over his mouth. *Not yet*, I thought. *Don't say it aloud just yet*. It was a move directly out of my mother's playbook: if we close our eyes and hold our tongue, what we fear cannot find us. I was going to see a play my friend was in and continued on to the theater in a daze. While everyone danced onstage, I clenched my teeth, but tears burst from my eyes – my eyelids could not hold them. I blustered apologies and left at intermission.

My mom was eventually diagnosed with mild cognitive dysfunction at a "memory clinic." These words put a thin, polished veneer over a reality that feels impossibly dark. I sat with my dad as he tried to explain to the doctor how she had become obsessed with *the other side*. I jumped in as translator, the way I have learned to do with my parents, explaining that my mother had become obsessed with books about near-death experiences. Ignoring the topic entirely, the doctor reported she had done fairly well on the tests but was showing some issues. As I sat in that antiseptic room, I realized that no help was coming – not from the doctor, not from the tests, not from a pill. I hopelessly wanted someone to understand and spoke carefully:

She tells the same stories. She talks about how the last person in the town where she grew up just died, frozen in his barn. She talks about wandering the prairies of North Dakota with her friend Bonnie, listening to the meadowlark sing. She thinks she has always been Catholic. She sits at the dinner table and drifts and I have to go looking for her, trying to pull her back with jabs and taunts – I tell her that her hair looks terrible, and she sticks out her tongue at me and we laugh, and for a moment she is there with me, and then she is gone drifting again, and I can't find her, and where is my mom going? Do your tests show that? Is that mild? How can that be mild?

* * *

My mom became a painter after she was a biologist. She painted during the period between her work life and when her memory problems reached a point where she could not paint anymore. How many possible lives are sacrificed along our chosen path? One of my mother's was the life of a painter. She created the most beautiful watercolors in a prolific flurry of creativity that marked much of her 60s and 70s. They are soft, dreamy landscapes that open a seam to the unseen world – a world filled with water, creatures, sky, and always the bright and distant circle that could be a sun or could be a moon.

These paintings are my threshold. Looking at them, I can see most directly. But I cannot think how to finish those sentences: The threshold to what? What is it I see? My mother's creativity happened as a series of surprises, thoroughly unplanned. She would watch the paint and how it swirled, move it with her brush, help it along. It was a conversation, the colors speaking to her in the same way creatures used to – the same conversation she has had her whole life, letting the world in and feeling where it wanted to take her. It is the same way I write, watching words as they craft themselves into meanings I could never predict, words that help me, that have always helped me along my way. Inside this endless give and take – our small story mixing with the rest of life – lies the whole mystery. My mother taught me this? I taught my mother? We taught each other, life taught us both. When I look at her paintings, I see myself.

Our hybrid philosophies are different, of course. Maybe if we had a religion – if she had raised me in the Catholic Church or my father had remained a Mennonite – maybe then we would have had a common language, agreed more. But that isn't how we are, my mother and I – we prefer to leave things unsaid, floating in paint, drifting in the unseen, outside the box of rules. Besides, we need our differences: her life belongs to her and mine belongs to me. In a way, I'm so glad she had the courage to kick me from the nest when the time was right.

When friends ask me how my mother is doing now, I never know what to say. How do I explain how I sit with her, how I listen to the story of the meadowlarks and we talk about those beautiful birds, their mournful song, the longing it makes us feel? She tears up and repeats that line from the poem: *Oh world, I cannot hold thee close enough.*

Should we talk about where you will live if something happens to dad, I ask? She rolls her eyes, skilled, as always, at shifting the conversation away from things she doesn't like. *Sometimes late at night, I realize something has changed,* she says. Death lurks like an angel between us, where he always has. Somehow through the length of our deep connection – my heart weaving into hers – we have always known we would have to say goodbye. I don't say the thing I suspect: she is doing this for me. She is saying goodbye slowly, letting go in pieces, backing out of the room in small steps so that my heart won't break all at once.

In one of her paintings, two great blue herons stand side by side. There is golden light everywhere. One is firmly planted in the world; the other's eyes gaze to the sky, to the horizon, to the beyond. I stare at the painting where it lives on my wall.

When you go, I will hold you in the light, I will ask my guides, I will listen to my dreams, I think. You taught me well.

The Dead on Street View

Nuala Roche

We now know that memories are not fixed or frozen, like Proust's jars of preserves in a larder, but are transformed, disassembled, reassembled, and recategorized with every act of recollection.

— Oliver Sacks, neurologist and writer, from his book *Hallucinations*.

In 2019 when clearing out the family home, after my father moved to a nursing home, I took notes that informed this writing. Words or phrases surface and repeat, patterns emerge. Gatch is one word that resonates in my family recollections. Gatch, as in how someone carries themselves, the way they walk. But it is more than an individual's movement, it is an embodiment of attitude, a life's experience. A distinct way of moving the body through space.

From foclóir.ie:

NOUN, extravagant gesture, *geáitse*

'He turned with a flourish,' *Chas sé agus é ag déanamh geáitsí.*

My word-by-word, linear translation from the Irish: 'he turned and he making an extravagant gesture.'

From Bernard Share's Slanguage – a dictionary of Irish slang (1997):

gatch, gache [Ir. *geáitse*, affected manner] ... swagger. Antics.

Share's earliest example incorporates an instrument or tool in the swagger: 1866 Patrick Kennedy, *Legendary Fictions of the Irish Celts*: 'she sent him to Bunclody to buy a billhook to cut the furze. When he was coming back he kep' cutting gaaches [sic] with it round his head ...'

This speaks of a time of physical relationships with different tools and implements provoking different daily movements; a three-pronged pitchfork, known as a prong in some places; the spade just for digging drills; an iron-handled bucket; butter paddles; darning needles; carded wool. The tools that influenced the gatch of a person.

I recognise the particular bend in my son's neck as he leans into his mobile phone screen: Snapchat conversation. He has interpreted his friend's gurning selfie and pulls a commedia dell'arte sad-face in reply. Snaps it. This back and forth continues for about ten minutes. I am bemused by the visual Morse code that has evolved between them and slightly concerned at his forward-neck posture. Then reminded of the shock of a finger poke between my shoulders and the admonishment to stand up straight by my father – my father before the stroke. With his recovery came the slipper-shuffle and curved shoulders hunched over the walking frame. I recognise the (new) gatch of him from a quite a distance in the nursing home corridor.

* * *

I visit my father's home where he lived alone for the most part, since my mother died. The house feels booby-trapped. Its walls tick and crackle in the strange autumn heat. I pick my way through the bare rooms, as if they are trip-wired. Are there messages to decode in the stacks of decorative tiles on the kitchen windowsill, explanations in the boxes of newspapers that span seven decades, day piled upon day?

I circle the living room, empty save for greasy cushions and thin woollen blankets heaped in the centre. Time is wind-milling around me.

My three siblings have already taken what they want to keep; what remains is for the auction house, the charity shop and the dump. I will hire a van, drive to the house, load up twenty-five boxes of family ephemera and haul them to my home seventy miles away. Boxes of photographs, tools, everyday objects, a walking jacket with sleeves that crook at the elbows from years of daily wear. I store the boxes and the jacket in the attic, like the flying lark in Aristophanes' play *The Birds*, entombing her dead father's body in the back of her head. In her song *The Birds*, informed by the play, Laurie Anderson intones:

'And this was the beginning of memory.'

It goes on: circling empty rooms, driving back and forth, hauling crates, furrowing the old ground again. After the final house trips I recall the hydrangea bush planted, no *transplanted*, from another home in 1987 by my mother, who lived for only seven more years. Had she told me to put a two pence coin in the roots, so that the flowers would bloom blue?

A copper coin cannot change the pH of soil and now that I have recalled it once, the memory is overwritten with her saying it and disputing it. I can't recall with certainty. In my mind's eye the hydrangea flowers toggle between pink, white and blue. Who knows which attic box will yield photographs of this house exterior and that bush? I cheat, take the shortcut and look it up on Google Street View.

I first learn about Street View in 2009 when my sister's boyfriend gets a job cycling the early morning streets of Dublin on a Street View Trike. Picture a trike like a cargo bike but instead of children in back, it is mounted with a camera rig; the camera automatically takes panoramic images as the operator pedals.

Out of the blue my brother emails from California saying that the grandparents' Wexford homestead 'is looking pretty overgrown, neglected.' He's been doing drive-bys of the farmhouse on Street View.

Following his instructions I open Google Maps, find my house, drag the yellow figure named Pegman and drop it on my street. From inside my house I stand outside my house.

I scroll on to John Street Lower, Upper, over the bridge. The streets are deserted. Swoosh, forward on the arrow, along Rose Inn Street. Swish onto High Street, past cars. Clusters of people.

I whoosh past a side-street, catch a glimpse of an interaction. Click & rotate, zoom in: two adolescent boys in school uniform; one, with elbow angled to ward off blows, head tucked into shoulder. The other boy's arm raised, fist clenched, torso leaning in. A blow in motion.

Farther up the street, zoom in, three more boys in the same uniform, hands in pockets, mid-stride. But the discreet glance over the shoulder. They are watching too. It feels voyeuristic but I keep looking, tapping, zooming.

If any of these boys was my son, despite the pixelated face smudging, I would know him; his stance, the outline of his hair. I would recognise the gatch of him.

I screenshot the scene, save it with filename StreetViewPrivacy01.

Google offers the '*Report a Problem'* feature on Street View. I do nothing about it.

In 2014 Street View introduced a new feature. Click the clock icon on the top left of screen to view historical images; 2012 is about as far back as it goes in Ireland, with sporadic coverage from 2009. I find niche uses for this feature, join Twitter conversations where I glean tips and hints for locating departed loved ones on Street View.

A Scottish user links to his YouTube film about searching for his deceased Nan in historical images (from 2012) outside her terraced home, long since sold on and renovated by new owners. But he swears that is her in the ground floor window, sat in her reading chair. He crowd-sources opinions – 'yes, that is a person reading.' 'No mate, that's the shadow of a tree branch.'

The Victorians took post-mortem portraits to memorialise the dead but Street View images are 'found portraits,' people going about their daily business, unposed. Their faces are blurred with a digital thumbprint, to protect their privacy but if this were your loved one would you not recognise them? The shoulder slope as they crouch over the flowerbed. The leg thrust forward, mid-stride. The arm swing. The heel strike. The hip tilt. You wouldn't mistake the gatch of them.

Three years after I screenshot the schoolboys I revisit the scene. The image I saved is gone. In its place is the moment before the engagement: the unsuspecting boy, shoulders slouched, hands in pockets, the moment before he pivots and raises his arm defensively.

The other boy? The aggressor? Foot poised to step onto the path, shoulders set: the moment before the fist-clench and thrust.

Did someone *Report a Problem*? Or was it an algorithm updating the timeline, shifting bits, interpolating images, and falling on random frames?

Memory is mutable.

I learn to swivel the Street View frame 180 degrees when the image captures the approach of a person; once the camera has passed them by most people look back over their shoulder. Why wouldn't they? They have been passed by a strange-looking tricycle, or car, with a dodecahedral camera array mounted on top. Swoosh past. Swivel 180 degrees for the reverse view. I play with the angles, toggling back and forth. This is familiar and satisfying to me, as a former film editor.

The look back would be insignificant, fleeting, if the person were alive. But after a death it is filled with portent, meaning. The look back feels unresolved. My regret that they had no opportunity to meet their death, to make peace with it? Or is it my secret wish that the person in the process of dying is saying, 'Yes, I am leaving. I'm ready but I just wanted to take one last look at you.'

In Ovid's *The Metamorphoses* Orpheus is granted his beloved dead wife's return from the Underworld with one condition: that he should not look back as they leave the Underworld. His look back – *metuens avidusque videndi/ flexit amans oculos* – is variously translated as 'eager of seeing her/ the lover turned his eyes' and 'longed to look at her/ ... he glanced behind him.' Google Translate offers 'fearing and eager to see/ he bends his loving eyes.'

I scour neighbourhoods on Street View, working my way through the twenty-six addresses listed on my Garda Vetting form. In suburban Cork I find a familiar figure. It is April 20__ on Street View's historical clock. There he is, tipping away at the flowerbed, bending down to pick up something. Or he is rising, on his way back up again?

This is the man whose terminally-ill wife had confessed to me harrowing stories of his violence in the house after he had been moved to a care home. Fifty-five years of terror behind this facade. The mystery is solved and there is no one to share it with, and why would I share that?

Inside the house was carpeted and hushed, almost cosy. A chintzy tissue-box holder from Ibiza on a credenza in the hallway, an ironic gift from one of the grown-up children. While she spoke I wondered at the homes I had visited where every solid thing was covered, wrapped or draped; antimacassars, draught excluders, rugs under kitchen tables, lined curtains, drying mats on the sink – absorbing sounds, preventing breakages when tables are knocked over or swept aside in an outburst. Mother, why all the tchotchkes?

On Street View I zoom in on the first-floor bedroom window. A ripple of a childhood feeling; the thrill-shiver of discovering something horrific or worse, inexplicable. The window blind is at half-mast, matching the window blind on the ground floor. Immaculate. That is how neighbours would describe the house and garden.

Immaculate.

This is the bedroom window where G____ had perched outside on the sill, biding her time; when she would leap into the hedge below as her husband pounded the locked door with a garden fork. Once she had gestured casually to this implement on our way through the back garden, 'He has green fingers,' she said, 'that's the fork he used to bust down the bedroom door.' Had the sight of a late middle-aged woman perched on a first-floor windowsill not seemed odd?

A neighbouring woman passing by the house had shouted up, 'I hope you're not cleaning those windows G___,' and G___ had replied laughing, 'I'm just getting some air.'

The next morning, on inspecting where she would have landed had she jumped, G___ discovered that the box hedge disguised a border fence forged with iron pikes, a fence forgotten after the manicured hedge grew over it.

Each way lay an impaling.

* * *

Before Street View, I worked as an assistant editor on feature films in Canada, in the days of separate magnetic tape. Before digital. When a word or a line was cut out, it was labelled and hung from a hook on a trim-bin. Sentences were this long (hip-width) or this long (the assistant editor's wingspan). You could feel the weight of a ten-minute conversation in one reel in a film can. On 35mm film, 1 foot = 16 frames = 0.66 of a second.

I could literally take your breath away. Unspool a hip-width of tape. Halve it. Huh. Huh. A breath was tangible, it could be held in your hand like a bird. Fluffed lines – too slow, too fast, faltering – spooled downwards into the soft denim or canvas bin that held the off-cuts.

While actors delivered variations on dialogue, take after take according to director's instructions, in the cutting room the intention, the delivery itself could be changed. Create hesitancy, some uncertainty by inserting extra spacing (clear or white) between words – and on the second audio track set a strip of Room Tone ('silence' from the location of the original recording) to cover the cuts. Seamless.

Spooling is another word that surfaces in my notes, it is as likely that my subconscious has latched onto it and pounces on any opportunity to offer it up. Its circular shape. Sounds, stories and words spool. The winding hands of sean-nós singers.

From my earliest working life sounds and words have had a physical quality, outside of the body. As a school-leaver apprentice to wildlife filmmaker Eamon de Buitléar, I listened to hours and hours of field recordings on a reel-to-reel player. The round and roundness of the sound of a hot summer's day on blanket bog, meadow pipit, seashore, cliff, kittiwake. The Shannon callows. Corncrake. What delighted me more than the living creatures was rolling these words around my mouth. New words. New rhythms.

We are each editors of family narratives: receiving stories, rejecting parts, omitting people, cutting a line here and there, even putting words into people's mouths. I hear stories third-hand, forget to write them down and at family gatherings offer my best recollection and compare to others' versions, tracking the changes.

Take 1.

Recall in your own words, your aunt's words:

'We visited Leitrim to find out more about father's people. That bitch Nora has the information but she won't give it to us. As we walked up the main street in Drumshanbo – his people were from Sunnaghmore – a woman was squinting at us and as we got closer she pointed to me and said, You're one of the Mahons. I asked her did I look like them, no she said, I knew by the gatch of you.

Recall in your own words, your aunt recalling <u>her</u> mother recalling <u>her</u> aunt's words – these are, after a fashion, your great grand-aunt's words – on a visit home from America, circa nineteen hundred and twenty:

'For all I seen and done in Colorado, I wouldn't have all the tea in China ...'

Recall your aunt's words, recently, about her own life:

'I'd like to have known what I could have been.'

Take 2.

County Clare.

Summer holidays at Granny's where my unmarried aunt lived, I would climb the stairs to the landing where the busted chaise-longue and bookshelf made a nook. Laying on the floor as an adolescent plucking the spines of the books – my aunt's books – 'cos books and fags and drinks with ice were her thing but most especially, books were her thing. She particularly revered John McGahern.

In a documentary film about his life McGahern reports the head of the teachers' union met with him after the banning of his first book in 1963 and said, 'If it was just d'oul book we could have done something for you. But then you had to go and marry a foreign woman. What were you thinking, to marry a foreign one when there's thousands of Irish women with their tongues hanging out for husbands?'

That last image. Where do you go with that?

On one side of the upstairs landing was Granny's bedroom: a long dark room, one window to the street at the front, another to the yard at the back. Satin eiderdown, bolster pillows, teeth in a mug.

Opposite was the aunt's bedroom: door ajar, Nina Ricci perfumed air, the floor carpeted with blouses, half-slips, discarded nylons, so much man-made fibre in the '80s, clothes that squeaked when wrung out after a sink-wash. The orange spines of my aunt's paperbacks, dog-eared pages that smelled of Carroll's Number 1.

At 13, at my granny's, I discovered *The Country Girls* and devoured it in one go, falling into the pages as the light time-lapsed to a mauve dusk.

I knew the people in this book. The language. The bow-way. Nuns. Damp clothes. Men's things. Baba's bouldness. I was astonished that people and places I knew or heard tell of, could be in a book.

Three steps down from the landing there was the bathroom, its dimpled glass-pane door offering some privacy but not enough. I could make out shadows, the gatch of them as they wiped, washed or un-did and re-did under-things. Copper rivulets leaking from the taps. Badedas. Chestnut. Silky. Green. Bath water.

Down the rest of the stairs and into the hallway: a Pye briefcase portable record player, spinning a 45. Its cover has a built-in speaker so it is propped against the wall. My aunt is dancing, fag in one hand, glass in the other, Scholl sandals sliding on the lino. She is dancing around the record player, singing along with Rod Stewart, ice clinking.

Her tongue wasn't hanging out for a husband.

She spotted *The Country Girls* in my hand, 'You're reading that one?'

McGahern could mine his life for stories, for fictions – my aunt swore she recognised a doorman in a McGahern short story from her days frequenting Dublin's Metropole dance hall – but on O'Brien she was cooler. A bit full of herself? The mouth-full accent. She was another Clare woman, older than my aunt by ten years. Was O'Brien the one who had gotten away?

Ten years later my friend and I share a flat off Dorset Street, both of us working in the emerging independent film sector. Her boyfriend, a freelance cameraman, has been contracted to film an interview in London. It is before mobile phones so he has given our landline as his contact number.

We get home from work, press play on the little white Phillips answering machine laying on the hallway floor. The tiny tape spools, beeps and plays. A voice announces itself into our flat, smooth as, gliding the sine waves of analogue tape:

'Hello Liam, this is Edna O' Brien.'

Double double-take. Our heads shoot out of our respective bedroom doors.

'I'm looking forward to meeting you tomorrow *(bird-pause)* in the Groucho Club.'

I whisper *'Baba.'*

I imagine her voice coming down the line from a London Victorian three-storey house, Edna perched against a telephone table in the hallway, the long coil of the telephone cord winding about her calves, fag in one hand, ice-clinking glass in the other.

Recall in your own words, your aunt's words:

'I'd like to have known what I could've been.'

On Street View I swizz past Granny's house (timestamped 2009) and round the corner onto the quay road. At the entrance to the bow-way the wrought iron gates gleam in the summer sunshine. I rotate the image. The timestamp jumps to 2012. A blurred woman leans against the gable end, in conversation with a grey-haired man.

The woman stands with one sneakered foot in front of the other and for a moment I see my aunt in her pose, in the outline of her short ash-blonde hair. I pass them by and look back, tweaking the angle until I confirm that the gatch of this woman is all wrong: it is not my aunt. I do not know this woman. Someone who knows her would recognise the gatch of her.

* * *

"The dead are always looking down on us," Billy Collins writes in his poem, *The Dead*. I wrote a poem in response, *The Dead on Street View:*

On Street View
The dead are always looking back at us,
The dead are still gardening:
Weeding paths, deadheading tulips—
walking hand in hand, or pushing a pram.
Stepping into the porch, out of the car,
walking home from the shop,
milk & paper or dog leash in hand—
Sometimes there is just a blur where the dog should be.
On Street View
The dead are hiding behind hedges—
Isn't that Grandad's cap/sombrero/fedora/touk?
I swivel and cut to the reverse
for the dead are always looking back at us.

Escape Van

Sabine Casparie

Sitting in a creaky foldout chair, the soles of my feet touching the hot, brown grass, I watched my husband set up the tent and thought about death, the cool, crisp release of it. Even though we were on holiday, it had been another hard day; the days were all so heavy lately that it felt like they were stacked up on my chest like rocks.

We had arrived at the Denver airport from London the night before and picked up the campervan from a company called *Escape*. Each van was spray-painted in bright, thick dabs of colour – animals and plants and mountains and desert. I had to admit that I had felt something at the sight of it, a little pang of excitement, or maybe it was hope. That someone had come up with that imaginative plan, to paint the vans like artworks in a museum.

The campground in the Rocky Mountains was on a slope amidst dark green furs, with no running water and a pit toilet that smelled putrid and dry. The children didn't mind. They were chasing each other on the open field, their hair still tangled and pasted to their heads from the long flight. Lilly had just turned six, and was still in awe of her eight-year-old brother Matthew. I watched them and wondered how long the infatuation would last. I had always wanted to have an older brother, or maybe I had just wanted someone to show me how it was done. Life.

* * *

The trip would do me the world of good, according to my psychiatrist. It was hard to place him: quintessential Englishman – pleated grey suit and wavy grey hair – but then also he was an eccentric with a thick silver bracelet and matching necklace. This was a good thing – my psychiatrist not so much another human being, as a symbol; the progress of medicine assembled in one moving vessel, dripping one medication after another, waiting for the one that would stick.

They all sounded promising enough. Citalopram contained an element of vitality in its upward-ending sound, but it had done nothing for me but a fast, restless heartbeat. Mirtazapine had made me fall sleep, its elongated vowels like the lullaby of a sweet old bedside nurse. And yet I would still wake up every morning at 4am, only to notice that the night nurse had left. Seroquel was really bad. It carried the pledge of something fast, something clinical, but it had left me like a zombie, dizzy with the faintest sound or movement. And then there was good old Lithium, tested widely over so many years, its chemical substance not much more than a salty hit washing over my arteries. Levels that were too high had the danger of bringing me into a toxic stupor, so my husband had to feed me a tablet every night from his secret stack. Quite romantic if you think of it, my husband the doctor and I the patient, but if anything could be further from my mind it was romance. And anything else having to do with physical attraction for that matter, the pills leaving me like a motionless doll.

Recently a new mix had entered the playing field. A psychiatrist in California had discovered that if you combined Mirtazapine, a nor-adrenaline enhancer, with Venlafaxine, an SSRI, it could cause rapid improvements for otherwise treatment-resistant patients. That was what I was now, treatment-resistant. It sounded better than exhausted, disillusioned mother. It sounded like there was an illness, which in turn meant there was a plan. So I packed a compartment of my rucksack with the boxes of pills. When I Googled the combination it was described as 'California Rocket Fuel', which sounded like a party drug and immediately left me feeling a little bit lighter.

* * *

My husband had finished setting up the tent. From my chair I watched the children run to it with shrieks of excitement, nestling their soft little bodies into the folds of the polyester, making bulky shapes in the thin, green fabric. I felt a smile pulling at the corners of my lips. It was a sensation I hadn't experienced for such a long time that it almost felt brand new.

'Can we have s' mores?'

Lilly's face appeared at the bottom of the zipped-up front. Her cheeks always turned bright red when she was concentrating – it had taken her a while to find the opening. Lilly had read about s' mores in her school back in London – Charlie and Lola were eating them when they camped out in their garden, in a tent made of a colourful quilt. Lilly looked at me and hesitated.

'Mum, you look happy?' she said and it was the question mark that sliced right through my heart.

* * *

I woke up the next morning to slivers of light. I couldn't remember the last time that had happened and it briefly disoriented me. There was some movement above my head, where my husband and Matthew were sleeping, in a tent that folded out of the campervan like a shark fin. Lilly and I were in the belly, on thick cushions as soft as clouds. I peeled away the purple curtain of my small side window, which framed a snowy mountain top against a baby-blue background. It was true then, what they said about America's big skies. I had only ever been to New York, where the sky clashed with tall blocks of steel and glass, and only slivers of it were visible when you looked up: thin air and solid mass in a duel for space.

Usually the first thing I thought upon waking was that this could be the last day. Eight months ago it almost had been. It had been a cold December morning and I had awakened at 4am, like clockwork. Struggling with a deep depression, not sleeping for months on end, I had at once felt an absolute clarity about what I had to do. Walking upstairs to the kitchen as if in a dream, I had grabbed the bar stool, trying not to make too much noise when I carried it down the stairs and placed it in the guestroom of our garden maisonette. When we had moved into the apartment earlier that year, our builder had convinced us to install an old Victorian laundry rack, three wooden slacks connected by ropes. It was an odd but quirky detail, to have a laundry rack just like the Victorian family would have had when they lived in this house a hundred years ago. Had they ever been tempted by it?

It was a lacklustre attempt, especially from a perfectionist like me. Or depending how you look at it, a brilliant attempt: just enough to fry my husband's heart with fear, but not too much to abandon the burning flames of being alive. Deep down I had wanted to be helped, but my broken brain had simply not allowed me the language.

* * *

Now in Colorado, when the rest of the family woke up, my husband made a breakfast of fried eggs and bacon on the van's small cooker. I sipped my instant coffee. Half a day and there were so many tasks, cooking and washing and making beds and packing up the van. My husband took care of all of these, and it soothed me to watch him. Some campers walked up to us, their faces smiling. *Who painted your van? It's awesome!*

I let my husband do the talking, listening to the American vowels dragging out the words. Then a different sound, from inside the van.

'Muuuuummmm! You packed the wrong leggiiiiiings! I need the stripy ones!'

I twisted on the picnic bench. Packing my own clothes had been a chore, let alone choosing the children's. These tasks were no longer automatic since my brain had been rewired, constantly looping in on itself.

My husband's calm voice released me. 'Darling, we are going to drive for eight hours through Wyoming. Wyoming is America's least populated state. I don't think anyone will notice your leggings. Buckle up!'

At eleven we were on the road again, heading for Cody, a small town at the edge of Yellowstone National Park.

The trip took eight hours. Dry, empty fields swished by so that eventually they became just smudges of yellow, sometimes interrupted by a lonely cow. I didn't realise the world could be this empty. The children were asleep sometimes, at other times they counted red cars or houses or cows, but nothing added up here in Wyoming, so they reverted to counting their sweets.

'This doesn't look like America,' Matthew belted out.

Did anything ever look like it was supposed to? Why do we keep making up pictures in our mind, little balloons, bright and secure? And just like that, the dark thoughts re-appeared. They bounced against my window, though with less force than usual, as if muffled by the nothingness outside.

You are a bad mother
You are nothing more than a mother
Why didn't you do better?
Study art history like you always wanted to
You have wasted your life

A road sign pointed to an Indian reservation called Wind River. I picked up the guidebook my husband had brought and opened the chapter on the history of the Native Americans. The letters crowded my mind, became blurry, so all I could read was the box at the bottom, describing the tribes. Crows, Shoshone, Cheyenne, Arapaho – I whispered the names slowly, let them get carried away by the loud whirring of the camper van's engine and the slurring melody of country music coming from the radio.

Shame settled in the dark pit of my stomach like a mould. I loathed myself, for my sad act of surrender. For the chemicals that ran through my veins, keeping me here in a half-life. Why was it so hard to talk about giving up? Was it easier if the fight had been heroic? Was there ever triumph in mental despair? Suicide is not something that happens to you, but something that lives inside you, in the capricious grids of thousands of cells, in the stormy rivers of your synapses.

* * *

Whatever the exact form of the suicide attempt, from there it's all protocol. You are admitted to a psychiatric hospital. You stay for a few weeks. You discover that psychiatric hospitals don't cure you; that all they do is keep you safe from yourself for a while, suspended in a limbo of nurses and pills and the tortured screams of other patients. Then they send you back into the world, drugged sufficiently to bear it, sedated just enough so that your body does not want to do anything at all, not even die. You get a bi-weekly ticket to group therapy, where you do not talk, because what is there to say? You are a privileged woman who has everything – a beautiful home, a happy marriage, two adorable children.

But one subtle thing will change. You are from now on a person who has been suicidal. You are now the person who has tried, however shameful and lousy the attempt, to leave this world for another one. That wish to escape – no, an urge really, that's what it was – doesn't magically disappear, but in some twisted way, now that you have been found out, now that your husband and your friends have discovered the secret compartment in your mind, ironically your disappearing trick can never materialise again. Because now you carry the burden of betraying the ones you hold dearest in your life. Now your death is on their watch. So all that is left is the veil of depression, hiding you from yourself.

* * *

Yellowstone Park is its own small universe: pristine lakes glittering indigo in the afternoon sunlight, hot water jetting upwards from the dry cracked earth, with a force older than life. On our way to the campsite, there was a traffic jam and we spotted a mother bear with two cubs crossing the road, entirely oblivious of the clicking cameras. We saw herds of buffalo everywhere grazing the light green meadows.

'Look who's here, too,' my husband said, reversing into the concrete strip of our designated camping site. A buffalo was spread out over the cold stone, its prehistoric head bent over its chunky legs, like some giant furry dog. The campsite guardian simply shrugged his shoulders and said there was nothing we could do, so we went for a drink in Lake Yellowstone Hotel, a wood-slatted building with a temple entrance, the way only Americans could mix and match the world. Sipping hot tea from china cups, I thought how it was strangely satisfying having to accommodate this animal, to bow to his ancientry in these pre-historic lands.

'If we get a dog, maybe we should name it Cody,' I said out of nowhere. My husband's face snapped sideways. I returned his gaze with questioning eyes.

'You haven't talked about the future for so long,' he said, in a low voice so the children wouldn't hear. He grabbed my arm and held it for a very long time, until darkness settled and we headed back to our campsite, now buffalo-free.

* * *

The Buffalo Museum of the West was quiet when we arrived the next morning. The children ran straight to the educational video about the bears. They were particularly mesmerised by the instructions on using bear spray, the pending attack of a grizzly re-animated like a trailer for the latest Marvel movie. I walked on ahead, towards the dark atmospheric rooms of the Plains Indian Museum.

The Plains Indians, who were here before the settlers came, lived a nomadic life, said the opening text, sustained by the herds of buffalo who grazed the hills of Wyoming. Indian peoples used almost every part of the buffalo: for food, clothing, tools or shelter. The buffalo was not merely a source of life; it was a companion, a spiritual partner. Canvas-like leather hides, sewn by women with sinew and decorated by men with natural pigments, showed intricate scenes of hunters, their spears aligned with the manes of their horses, moving diagonally up, like a string of musical notes. The soft texture of the leather, held up by a few pins, enhanced the ochres and crimsons like the colours of a spectacular sunset. Each detail exquisitely rendered, the minutiae of a life that was full and fulfilled.

Why had I never come across artworks like these? Western art was always rushing forward, pulled forcefully into the discourse of progress. Perfect classical bodies. The ideal dimensions of a Renaissance church. Da Vinci's perspective like a divine intervention. Abstraction hailed as the triumph of mankind. Yet here was an art made out of the sunset of an existence, and it moved me more than anything had before.

I snapped back into the present, the sharp giggles of the children like crickets high on sugar. They had found the equivalent of their campsite tent, a replica of an Indian tipi. It was lit up by a dome that featured a glittering sky.

'Can we go to the Buffalo Bill rooms now?' Matthew asked. They were already gone, hop-skipping to the cowboy adventure, the other story that was fast and fun.

* * *

On the fourth day we took a walking tour to Lost Lake with a guide. Walking had felt like a chore back in London, but here my legs seemed lighter, as if carried by the promise of those blue open skies. The peppery, minty smell of pines greeted us when we stepped out of the guide's 4x4. Starting at the side of a petrified tree, a fossilised redwood trunk about three meters high, the trail wound its way upwards, past widely separated Douglas firs allowing a peek back to the valley. An hour later we reached a small stream.

'Look here,' our guide said, 'and tell me what you see.'

I peeked down into the clear blue water. It took me a moment to discern the shapes. Hundreds of terracotta-coloured fish crowding beneath the surface.

'Cool! Fish!' Matthew shouted, before pulling his sister's sleeve to play *It*.

I hesitated and looked at the guide.

'They are swimming against the current?'

'It's breeding season,' he explained. 'Once a year, these trout swim upstream, back to the place where they were born. They carry the scent of birth deep in their minds and when they mature, they instinctively follow it back.'

'Amazing,' my husband said, before catching up with the children. 'Who's hungry for lunch?!'

The guide followed behind, but I couldn't move. I couldn't stop staring at these small, shiny creatures, their tails flapping furiously behind their elegant, scaly bodies. Guided by instinct to do what was right.

* * *

The skies remained cloudy that night at the campground. Maybe the stars were cherishing their moment of reprieve from the constant demand to shine and glitter. But when I woke up in the early hours of the morning to relieve myself, I opened the van's door to millions of stars. Moments later, another click of the handle, a soft thud when the door fell back into its place. My husband walked up behind me, putting his arms around my waist. I nestled my face against the smoothness of his chest.

'I want to do it,' I said quietly, my words floating away over the wooded campground like a mantra.

'Do what?' my husband whispered.

I could go back to university. I could study art history. I was handed the world and would no longer waste it. It would be hard, like the trout at Lost Lake, swimming up a stream. But wasn't that what life was, swimming against the stream, until you could lay your eggs in a safe place?

I took my husband's hand and looked into his soft, brown eyes, the eyes that understood everything. They were wet and shiny against the dark blue night.

'Life,' I said.

We both stood there for a while, looking up at the brilliant darkness, trying to decipher what was written in the sky. So many messages, light-wired from the past. My husband pointed at a falling star, but I missed it. I had already turned my back to enter the warm safety of our *Escape* van, to catch a wink of sleep.

A Brown Night

Thelma McGough

'Do it. Do it! Just do it!'

Ears in action, I hear the commotion.

My little sister and I share a bed. With care, I sneak out from under the blanket so as not to wake her. Not allowed a candle or a bedside light, I feel my way in the dark. With a sense of foreboding, I creep down the stairs, one at a time, clinging to the wooden bannister. I step only on the outside painted edges to avoid creak alert. I don't want them to hear me, to know I am awake.

Finally, my feet jolt on the freezing tiles of the small square hall. My toes scrunch up, tight. To stop the shivers, I cross my arms and tuck my hands under my armpits – havens of heat. A keen draught wafts through a gap beneath the front door, biting my ankles. My teeth clatter. The month is August, I should be warm, but fear makes for cold.

Behind the living room door, voices are raised. Loud. More than two, not just Mum and Dad's, there's a third voice – a man's. I hear bangs, grunts, and scuffles, then a screech from my mother. A rip. What can be going on? I can't bear to just listen, I must *see* – though I know I'll get into trouble. I grip the brass knob with two hands, turning it as slowly as possible until the door opens. Success! Daring to step inside, I sneak a brief peek but just at that moment, a towering stranger flings my dad across the room. He lands on his back in front of me, bashing the door, which rebounds in my face, cracking my nose. It stings. My eyes water. I check for blood.

Desperate, I try again to get into the room; this time I make it. I can smell cigarettes and beer. The settee has shifted and the armchair is upside down. My mother bawls at me, "Get out of here!" Struggling to his feet, Dad lurches at his attacker but it's an uneven contest. A punch to his mouth knocks him back to the floor, he's losing the fight, and I sense he is also losing my mother – she is supporting the opposition, standing close beside the tall man. There are four of us in the room; we are all white-faced. Frightened, I cry, and yell, "Stop it. Stop it!" at all three of them, but at no one in particular.

My mother shouts, "Shut up! Go back to bed."

The man throws another fist at my dad, turns to my mother, and says, "I'm going. Are you coming with me?"

Scared she might agree, I block the doorway to the hall. They push past me and out the front door leaving it wide open and my father flat out on the living room floor – defeated – in anguish. His face contorts; he winces as he tries to catch his breath. Unsteady, he clambers to his feet, by which time they're down the path and out the gate. We stand in the hallway at the open door; our neighbours' curtains are closed, their houses quiet – everyone in bed. And we watch as Mum continues to walk away without so much as a glance of concern in our direction.

"Go after her, Thelly," Dad pleads. "Quick! Bring her back."

"I can't, Dad. I'm only in me knickers and I've got no shoes on."

"Quick, run Thelly, or she'll never come back. Do it. Do it! Just do it!"

"Dad, Dad! DA-A-AD!" Hysterical now, jumping up and down like a terrible two in a tantrum, not a sensible nine-and-three-quarter-year-old. "Get her. Get her! You go and get her, Dad."

"She won't come back for me," he cries.

And I know, as a knowing child does, that he's right.

"Mu-u-Ummm … MUM! MU-U-UM!" I scream as I continue to jump up and down on our doorstep, afraid to venture down the path in case anyone should see me in my knickers. Terrified she's abandoning us; I howl and yell as loud as I can as she begins to disappear along the crescent. Already she's two doors away, outside Mrs Milburn's – our school cleaner. Now she's four doors away. She breezes past the Sherlocks' who have the best front garden in the street. Oh, Jesus, she's up to the house where the man lives who puts his hand up my skirt. I lose sight. It's dark, the gas lamp has gone out in the next streetlight, though I can still hear her high heels clattering on the pavement. There she is, I can see her again – she's outside the house at the very end where the

Roman Catholics live, it's all lit up by an electric lamp. Mum doesn't stop. She turns left, behind the high wall built down one side of the Murphys' front garden, then vanishes into the alleyway under the two red-brick-covered arches. The alleyway where our gang play hopscotch when we want to get out of the rain. The 'Arches' lead to the main road, to buses, to tramcars, and beyond.

The stranger had his arm around her the whole time.

Mum's gone – all because I wasn't brave enough to run out and stop her. Dad tells me to shut the front door. I close it, and we stand in the dark hall for a minute. I'm trembling. Shocked. Distressed. Confused. Trying to make sense of what I've witnessed. How to understand? We sob, moan, and slobber, our cheeks wet, hot, stuck together with snot and tears. Clinging each to the other, arms entangled, one body, one pain, one fear…

"She'll never come back. She'll never come back." Dad has only one phrase.

I'm frightened. Frightened from watching the fight. Frightened Dad is right – Mum has gone for good. I can't stop myself from shaking. I'm worried his loud whingeing will wake my little brother and sister, so I calm myself down and try to soothe him. "I'll look after you, Dad." I lead him to the leatherette armchair, which usually sits to the left of the hearth; it's been knocked aside in the fight and has landed upside down across the room in the centre of the bay window. With difficulty I turn it back over and straighten it as best I can, though it's hugely heavy, and I feel weak.

Dad collapses onto the velvet seat cushion. Leaning on his elbow, he supports his head in the palm of his hand. Tears run off the side of his face, dripping onto the brown leatherette chair arm, making a splat, splat, splat sound. A crimson clot of dried blood stains the right-hand corner of his mouth, spreading outward across his face – the maze of dried cracks mimicking a jigsaw puzzle. Under his chin, his normally pristine starched collar has been yanked from its brass-collar stud and flaps awry above his Adam's apple. Perfectly formed red dots stain the curved front edges. Halfway down his chest hangs his tightly knotted tie held together by a mere thread. Directly down the centre of his split bottom lip, a stream of fresh blood flows down the chasm that's opened between two swollen mounds of wet, purple flesh. For a second it reminds me of the diagram in my school geography book of a tributary setting its course through the mountains. He looks a bloody mess – I must try and think of ways I can make him feel better.

The stranger had looked younger, stronger, and do I dare think it? more handsome than my dad. He had a full head of wavy black hair slicked back with Brylcreem, and his black eyebrows looked solid and bushy. He reminded me of my mother's favourite film star, Robert Taylor. I saw him yank my father across the floor by his jacket, I heard the rip. The torn lapel hangs forlorn, limp, folded forward onto itself as a flower snatched from its root.

"I'll mend your jacket, Dad," I say, wanting to put some heart back into him. Aren't I top of the class at needlework? Even so, it's clear that my very bestest of tiny stitches will show. The jacket is ruined, it's part of a suit, a 'demob suit' I've heard it called – a brown pinstripe suit.

Was everything brown that night? The wardrobe, the blanket on the bed I share with my sister, paint on the living room doors, the linoleum on the floor, tiles in the grate, the sideboard, and the three-piece suite. Yes. I remember right. Outside, the sky on that warm summer night seemed brown as well. I do remember correctly.

In the kitchen, I wet the rag dishcloth in the deep stone sink, take down the towel from its wooden roller behind the kitchen door, and go back to the living room. As I gently begin to wipe the mess from Dad's face, lines of spittle – delicate as the threads of a spider's web – trail from the corner of his mouth when I lift the cloth away. Caked to his cheek is what looks like a brown map of Australia. My mind wanders... On the giant revolving globe in the corner of my classroom, Australia is red. "Everything you see that's red is *our* Empire," Miss Webber told us. "It belongs to Great Britain. King George VI is the crowned head." India is red too. "Ignore that," we're told, "because we've now lost India." Lost? Where? What does she mean? How can you lose something that size? A sudden wail ends my daydream.

"She'll never come back."

"Please stop crying, Dad." He doesn't hear me. He won't stop.

Witnessing big men fight and watching my mother march purposefully off into the night without so much as a hug or a wave, is fearful enough, but the stuff of real terror is watching a grown man cry, especially my father. My organs are doing the conga inside my skinny white stomach – I'm scared they might soon spill out of my bum, and I'm at panic stations in case I poo myself. On the verge of hysterics, strange voices come into my head, shouting commands:

Calm down!

Control. Take control!

What's going on? Stop frightening me. Go away.

Dad continues blubbing. Every attempt to cajole him doesn't work, and failure saps the strength I need to keep me from sobbing along with him. The 'other' voices come back, issuing instructions:

Use the wet cloth, wash, wipe, and pat dry.

Take the edge of the towel and straighten his eyebrows.

Stroke his forehead.

Whisper to him.

"It's okay, Dad, you've got me."

Why is this not enough? Little girls never understand why Dad prefers Mum, anyway. Make him a cup of tea – that's the answer. "Our Thelly could make us a pot of tea when she was only three," my parents proudly boast to the world. He won't drink it. I sit on his knee and hold on to him tight, afraid to move until my rigid arms ache. Freezing cold. No fire in the grate. Bare feet. Naked, except for my navy-blue cotton knickers.

On the mantelpiece, the alarm clock with the luminous green dial shows the little finger has moved past 2, the big finger sits on 6. Silence outside the house. Misery inside.

Calmer now, Dad begs me to go back to bed; he assures me he'll be all right: "I'll be up soon myself." I slide back in beside my sleeping sister. All is quiet in my little brother's room. And I wait. I wait because I *know.*

Over the past months, along with the little lumps developing under my liberty-bodice, I've sprouted powerful antennae, invisible of course – my very own early warning system. Danger – I can sense it a mile off. Smell it. Hear it. Feel it coming. I *know.* It frightens me: knowing. Not that I'm a spiritual child; everything must be tangible, visible, to be believed. I paint with precise, hard edges, and, according to my teacher, I do the neatest cutting-out, better than all my classmates. Order pleases me. Fantasy does not. I don't believe in ghosts, fairies, or the supernatural, but this isn't natural – sensing things out of nowhere. Often, I want to be wrong, but I never am.

Knowing: when it is safe to sleep. Knowing: the nights to be alert, stay awake and listen out for raised voices. Aware of times I must creep downstairs to eavesdrop. Sit on the bottom step, feet like blocks of ice on the Cardinal-Red quarry tiles, clutching my knees tight to stop them from shivering – not from the cold, but from fear of what might happen. Nothing, nothing, will stop nausea. If only I could be sick, I'd have an excuse to go in and they'd have to stop. Vomit rarely arrives to rescue me. It is my entire fault. I've heard:

"Thelly wants new shoes."

"Thelly wants a new frock."

"Thelly wants more paints."

I don't want anything – only the rows to stop.

"You don't love her as much as the other two."

"Yes, I do."

"She loves me more than she loves you."

"Let's ask her then, come on? Now. Let's ask her who she loves best?"

I do not know. What will I say? Quick, dash back upstairs, shout from the top, "I'm not feeling very well." Turn it on. Start crying. Be too sick to answer. It works because at times such as these, the arguments stop, and Dad sits on the edge of the bed, scratching my back, slowly, rhythmically, until I fall asleep. Or Mum comes, strokes my hair, and sings me her special medley:

I'm forever blowing bubbles.

Pretty bubbles in the air…

I wonder who's kissing her now.

I wonder who's teaching her how.

I wonder who's looking into her eyes.

Telling lies…

Oh, my darling, oh my darling,

Oh, my darling Clementine. Gone forever, lost forever…

At last, my favourite:

Daisy, Daisy, give me your answer do.

I'm half-crazy all for the love of you.

It won't be a stylish marriage.

I can't afford a carriage.

But you'll look sweet.

Upon the seat

Of a bicycle made for two.

Finally, a happy ending. I tandem off to sleep with Clark Gable pedalling protectively behind me.

I don't have long to wait this night – though I can't work out what's happening. Noises downstairs that aren't familiar. Not the rattle of dishes on the wooden draining board or coal being brought in from the yard. Not the ping of the pantry door? Yes! Got it! Dad is closing the windows; first the back kitchen one, now the little one in the bay at the front. They've been opened to let in a summer breeze – a tornado tore through instead. I hear him bolting the back kitchen door, he's been outside to the lav, that's it. That horrible, cold dark lavatory that stinks every morning of my mother's first cigarette. Never any toilet paper, always the Liverpool Echo torn into squares to fit the wooden box fixed to the back of the Forest-Green door. I hate it, not because the newspaper is hard – which it is – but because it leaves black ink marks between my legs off the newsprint.

More unusual sounds: the heavy bathroom doors banging together – two narrow, wooden ones leading off the kitchen. Green doors: Eau de Nil. I hear him next at the door to the stairs. Is he coming up at last? No. He seems to rattle it on its hinges – checking it's shut. Now the door from the living room to the kitchen, he's *definitely* closing that one. I can tell, it doesn't fit properly and makes a sound like a fart when the air is forced out between the two ill-fitting edges.

No more noises. Absolute silence. Perhaps he's fallen asleep in the chair? Maybe he's thinking? Crying quietly? Why doesn't he come up the stairs to bed?

Oh, flip, I can hear the weird voices again, telling me what to do:

Close your eyes! Go asleep!

I mustn't. I daresn't.

My antennae are on red alert; something is wrong I *know*!

I creep downstairs to listen closer. Don't tread on that one, it creaks. Keep to the edges. Hang on to the bannister. Nothing – not even an itsy-bitsy sound. Thelly, have you noticed how you can hear better in the dark, I ask myself. Yes, but I can hear nowt. My stomach is churning. My heart is banging, I'm scared stiff it might burst through my chest any second. What to do? I'm confused. I can't hear myself think. Crazy voices butt in again – I can't tell if one is mine.

Stop! Wait!

For how long?

A bit longer.

I'm shivering.

It's summer!

Stop shaking!

I can't, I'm frightened to bits.

Call him.

"Da-ad?"

He'll tell you off for getting up.

"Da-aad?"

I reach the bottom of the stairs and turn the brass knob on the living room door without making a sound. It won't budge.

Turn around, bang it with your bum! a bossy voice tells me.

It gives an inch. Why is there a towel wedged underneath? With an extra bang of my bottom, I can squeeze through an open gap into the room where the fight took place. The light is still on. That's strange – dirty washing from the bathroom floor is bunched all along the windowsill; it wasn't there earlier. The armchair is empty. The velvet cushion has gone. Dad's jacket is folded on the floor in front of the hearth; on top, sits his tie and bloodstained collar. I glance at the clock on the mantelpiece, the big hand has moved to 9 – it's a quarter to three. Have I ever been up this late before? I can't remember. "Da-a-AD?" He must be in the back kitchen. But we don't usually close the door from the living room to the… I cannot open it. Nothing is happening.

The mithering voices come back.

Push harder!

I am. It's jammed, there's a tea towel stuck underneath it. Why?

Turn around. Bang it with your bottom!

What's going on?

It's okay, it's working.

Why are you crying?

Stop it. Shut up. Open it!

"DAD! DA-A-AD!!!"

I see his feet first. His shoes: brown leather brogues, laces undone. Brown woollen socks, held up with narrow elastic garters, above which are strips of his white hairy calves. Chocolate-brown pinstripe legs lie stretched flat on the terracotta quarry tiles. His fly is unbuttoned: grey buttons that do not match. One of the little leather straps that fasten his braces to his trousers is unbuttoned too – like a catapult adrift from its wooden handle. His crumpled shirttail is hanging out. Oh no. No! I can't see his head! The open oven door blocks my view.

I stop seeing.

A sense more powerful suddenly overwhelms me. Smell. An intense, pungent, tidal wave hits. Whooosh! Travelling right up my nostrils, filling my lungs, and expanding my chest – my tiny, dainty, pointy chest. I gag, I'm choking! On impulse, I cup the palm of my hand over my nose and mouth. I stop thinking. Stop reasoning. Smell it. Hear it hiss. See it – all the gas taps on, and Dad's head, leaden on the velvet cushion right inside the gas oven. Eyes closed. Mouth open. Brown cushion. Brown stove.

No need to be told, 'Just do it!' Instincts kick in.

Shut off the gas taps. Unbolt the doors. Open all the windows and drive a draught through the house. Fill a cup with water; throw it on his face. Clutch his wrist; lift his arm. Pull.

With two hands, girl!!

Drag him out …

Prop him up.

Grab the cushion.

I kneel, holding his head on the cushion in my lap. Slapping his cheeks, I repeat, "Dad, please wake up… Dad, please, wake up…" over and over. His face rolls toward me, his eyes open a smidge. Like in a silly game we used to play, I swipe his nose with mine, back and forth. My face hovers above his, "Look at me, Dad. Look at me," I plead. I don't have tears; they've stopped of their own accord, or else my eye tanks have run out of water. "Dad, can you hear me?" There's a slight *ckckckckckcksssssss* from his throat before the chest hairs sticking out of his open collarless shirt, rise in an almighty heave as he takes in air.

Awful, is the sound that follows – like the sound of a balloon filled with air, untied, and let fly. Disgusting is the smell. But my dad is alive! Both my knees hurt from bearing the weight of him. I need to shift; we both need to shift. Darkness is dwindling. Soon, daylight will bounce through the windows, charging my five-year-old little brother into action. I'll need to tidy the place up before then – get rid of the dirty washing strewn around and put the wire shelves back inside the oven. Shut the door.

Rousing Dad is an ordeal. We struggle, his legs are weak but by leaning on me for support, he manages to wobble back to his chair. There – the teacher never taught you that one. Top of the class in lifesaving! No book prizes this time.

"Leave me. Leave me. Why didn't you leave me?" Dad has a new phrase now. I don't dare leave him, wracked with dread that he might try again and make me an orphan if Mum doesn't come back.

In the following days, I spurn trips to the swing-park, and instead, swing on our front garden gate. Not that Dad has the energy for much. It might be the effects of the gas: dangerous stuff, that coal gas. A couple of months ago, after police battered down the front door of a house down our road, I'd watched a man being carried out to an ambulance on a stretcher, covered in a red blanket, only his mousey, greased hair poked out. He was dead. "It's illegal to kill yourself, y'know," I overheard one of our neighbours tell another.

I've rescued my father and saved our family from shame. But Dad isn't grateful. For days, he simply sits flopped in the same armchair, in the same pose, his pallor as grey as his eyes, whimpering pitifully. Inconsolable. He wears the same wrinkled white shirt and doesn't bother to attach a fresh collar. Each day, the bristles on his face get longer and blacker but he makes no effort to shave. His bruised eye-sockets change colour: purple... green... then a waxy yellow. Occasionally, he snores.

Not once does a word pass his broken lips. He refuses the cups of tea and jam butties I make – not with words but by the loll of his head from side to side.

We, kids, fend for ourselves. I filch coins from Dad's trouser pockets and send my seven-year-old sister to buy bread. My little brother will only eat tinned condensed milk, which he steals without asking from the slate slab inside the larder. He spoons it straight from the can. I'm unable to keep food down, though I yearn for the comforting taste of powdered eggs – the kind we had before the war ended.

School is closed for the summer holidays. I encourage my brother and sister to go to the park and tell them they're allowed to play out for as long as they want – while I stand guard at the end of our path. If they know anything, they do not say, nor do I ask.

And never do I tell.

Secrecy weighs heavier with each passing year. Vigilance is an ever-present companion.

Anxiety loiters – borne from fear I inherited my dad's suicide genes. In fragile moments I wait for them to pounce.

I am thirty-seven years old before my dying grandmother confides, the man whom I'd saved aged nine, was not my biological father. My genes run free of frailty.

The autocratic voices stay squatting in my head, awaiting eviction.

Death by Overwork

James Scoles

When I wait more than a few minutes on the platform it's either a suicide or an earthquake; Japanese trains don't break down or travel late. The delays are one of the few times I speak with my fellow commuters: we do the cigarette shuffle, discuss the weather or baseball. My Japanese isn't great but I've gained a decent vocabulary; I know what people are talking about, and it helps to know when to toss in the odd comment, nod or shrug.

"Seibu Lions, eh?" I say.

"*So desu ne,*" the businessman beside me says, and we shake our heads.

Japan Rail never gives the reason for the delay if it's bad, and I can't tell by the look of the commuters as the Express arrives for the frenetic passenger exchange and my two-minute shot to Kanda Station. They're late and aggressive and the morning crowd always has an edge to it at the core of Tokyo. Pushing and shoving, active low elbows in the daily assault by millions on the downtown.

I walk slowly down the busy, wide sidewalk, let the crowd surge around me on my three-block stroll into work. With a great salary and free apartment, I'm the English teacher's equivalent of a high-end polisher. My clients call from their offices or overseas trips, from Ginza to Guatemala. My job's golden, but I've been the minion in the grunt-work of teaching, proving myself over three previous sojourns overseas. I now give excellent English speakers a good finish – over the telephone.

"Good morning, Mr. Okada."

"Good morning, Jack. Did you receive my paper?"

I adjust my headset, open the folder to his smiling 8x10 photo. "Yes. It's disturbing."

"You learn a lot from editing our work."

"I don't have to work on the periphery of pharmaceutical research to know the fine line between drugs and death. Did you read the newspaper article I sent you?"

The jovial Mr. Okada, a specialist in their agricultural division, is my favourite. It kills me that he's being transferred to Australia to sell hormones and drugs to giant farms.

"Yes. How you say … *disturbing.* So many suicide by train."

"Nearly every day, somewhere in Japan."

"I can't wait for Sydney."

We have to be absolutely pressed and polished from head to toe, but our 45-hour weeks are nothing compared to what Japanese workers are responsible for. Even with a North American businessman I wouldn't jump into a suicide discussion – we're actually told to *let clients do their free-thinking at home* – but I know Mr. Okada can handle it.

"You can feel so much stress."

"Surely there's a better way to deal with it than diving in front of a train." I'm their vacation from a very ordered, high-pressure world; I try to keep things loose and organic.

"*Mmm.* Suicide with train not so common, *nowadays.* Family must pay fine."

"How much?"

"One million yen, each minute train is late."

"Are you serious?"

"*Mmm.* How you say, *no kidding.*"

"Comes down to efficiency."

"Suicide under slow train is rare. Unless crazy … or guilty," he says. "You take Chuo Line?"

"I only had to travel the morning Chuo once, before seeking a gentler route. I take the Sobu Line to Ochanomizu, then the Chuo to Kanda."

"Why? Sobu Line so slow."

"The morning Sobu Line starts at Nakano Station. I get there early and get a seat. The JR guys don't use sticks to pack us in."

He laughs. "You love to reading."

"I love to read. I don't mind the morning commutes, the luxury that a train ride is."

"Chuo Line is *Suicide Line.*"

"The abject morning congestion and suicide rate are why I don't take it. It's not worth the eight minutes saved. On the way home, it's a different story."

"A different story. I like that."

"We're out of here before the six o'clock rush."

"By the way, what is *abject?*"

"Miserable."

"Ah… my company is maybe *abject*."

"Really?"

"A different story."

* * *

We discuss the suicide article – emotionless, but poignant – throughout the week.

"You can't disgrace your company. That is worst. Then your family and neighbour."

Though 80 percent of train-suicides are businessmen, the article tells stories of a teenager with musical ambitions and a retired schoolmaster. Unable to live up to the expectations of his father – a 40-year company man – the teenager dives into a rush-hour train, guitar in hand. The schoolmaster – after five women come forward with stories of abuse – walks to the edge of a platform on his final night of freedom and bows, before falling backward into the train in a final gesture of guilt.

"He was still alive after first set of wheels pass."

I shake my head. "Some go for drama and spectacle, others aim to create little mess."

Some people have tackled jumpers to safety, and the article does mention a few horribly maimed 'survivors.' But rarely is the train unable to do the job.

"I would not choose a slow train, no matter what. *Shinkansen*, maybe."

"It's really about outside pressure and pride. How about you?"

"Because I'm married and have family, my situation is different," he says. "It's worse for single men and managers. They must work *all* overtime, like Accounting and Finance… these colleagues have lots of stress, but bigger bonus."

"I would kill my company long before myself."

"Nobody from my company ever commit suicide. Or kill company," he adds, laughing.

"How about *karoshi?*"

'Mmm. You mean *death by overwork*?"

"I've read about people who drop dead at work or on the commute. Their bodies simply shut up."

"Maybe one person here die from *karoshi*."

"But nobody has committed suicide because of work? Do you ever see people who look like they might be on the edge?"

"*Mmm*, every day. But I see no suicide. How you say, *thank god*."

"You're Buddhist."

"Exactly. How about you?"

"I see a woman every morning on my train. She always gets on hurriedly, just before the train leaves. She's pretty, but pain-faced. Like she's sitting on a ledge. In all directions."

"Maybe she is afraid of train."

"She stares straight ahead for the three stops to Shinjuku and then dashes head-down into the throng. Immaculately dressed and trembling." I think of her worried beauty, and what I wrote in the margin of my book: *Like a birch sapling in spring: vulnerable, slim, elegant. Nervous.*

"She's on edge."

"Only a couple times I haven't seen her. Then I imagine her dashing down the platform."

"Do you see her at other places?"

"Never. Not in the streets or the station... not on the commute home, either."

"Maybe she hate her company."

"Or life." I don't tell him it's as if she's missing a different piece each day, like something forgotten and constantly searched for, an emptiness clawing around inside.

"We will be hopeful. By the way, Jack..." he says, and when Mr. Okada clears his throat to lower his voice, I know it's something good. "Have you heard of *Ubi Sato?*"

"Odd first name."

"*Mmm*. She is famous. No, *in*famous."

"Nice. How so?"

"She dove into train and became *unconscious.* Somehow, train pass over."

"Really?"

"*Mmm*. Train miss her. How you say... *it was miracle*. When she wake up, she have *amnesia*."

"She forgot the dive?"

"Ubi Sato forget everything."

"Why did she try to kill herself?"

"She forget that also."

* * *

I take my seat beside her. She's extremely shy at first but so am I. We tread awkwardly through our first communication: a stilted, but sweet beginning.

All that matters is we begin.

I learn over our first walk that she learned English from the radio, plays piano and like me hates karaoke and listens to bluegrass. Our gentle talk, Suntory whisky and my bootleg collection of The Bad Livers takes us deep into our first night.

She teaches me two Japanese dishes and we wander Tokyo Castle, spend an evening in Yoyogi Koen. We share favourite places, discover new spaces together in our massive city. We learn each other and our lesser secrets.

Our first love is made to candles burning and Junior Brown's *Long Walk Back*. I am under her as she hovers just above; that's our position, the way our bodies together ask for and understand pleasure. She tastes like new grass and melted butter; we talk of the wind outside between songs.

Our two becomes three nights a week, as we find favourite ways to learn from and lean upon each other. We earn and share whole new vocabularies, a mixed salad of new words and fragile passion.

On our first earthquake together we speak of true love. Then after glasses of warm sake and one grown cold, she spills her heavy secret, the sorrowful thing she carries in her haunted, worried gaze.

Her shadow like a different, dark season: the monsoon I saw waiting, but couldn't chase away.

* * *

It's a depressing sort of wet. A warm and sticky May evening in the rain.

One of the things Darryl and I agree upon is that a few drinks make our commute much more pleasurable. It also gives us a chance for the practical application of our Japanese language skills with the delightful serving personnel at our favourite Izakaya, where we practice ordering whisky, draft beer and a dozen little plates of everything from sashimi to fries. And by the time we're ready it's after eight and the wet day looks much better in darkness.

"There's something so right about being a little drunk in the rain on a night-train," I say, dangling from the loops of our evening train car with little leaning room.

After Ochanomizu, the Chuo Line takes the outside track and picks up steam, ripping due west through the local Sobu stations. Well shy of Shinjuku we come to a sudden, abrupt stop: between us and the end of the Yotsuya local platform is a waiting Chuo that shouldn't be. The commuters look a little more stunned and emotionless than usual.

Everything looks and feels utterly different. Like just after an earthquake.

Our car turns immediately hot and sticky and the old-school fans kick in loud. When I slide open a window I see the blue uniform of a Japan Rail worker on his knees between the trains, reaching for something. He stands, shifting his weight, trembling. A woman's watch dangles from shaking fingers, shimmers like a foreign and precious thing.

"The Japanese are so polite they stop the train to pick up a watch," Darryl says, but I'm immediately ill as we realize the situation. "Wait… we got a jumper!"

As six jogging JR emergency personnel and a stretcher travel down the space between trains, the chatter and curiosity quake down our car at the same velocity.

"Yuck, here come the pieces…" Darryl continues his half-hammered play-by-play.

"Darryl, *shut up*."

"Holy shit, oh fuck, it's a leg!"

"*Shut the fuck up, Darryl.*"

"*That's* cauterization, folks."

I know I'm in trouble, my body half-curled away, sweating a thin, cold fear. I feel an echo inside, an opening-up. I try to breathe deeply but start hyperventilating. The JR workers finish their recovery, but just as they hustle away the covered stretcher tilts, then slips from their hands, and her parts spill out onto the crushed rock. In a single quick glance: nothing of innards or blood, just clean-sliced human chunks tumbling. I glimpse a leg and a torso and then what begins haunting me immediately: her face.

"Daijobu?"

I wake up to the xenophobic face of a businessman: an apologetic, gracious yet freaked-out gaze. Loosening my tie and watch, he knows how to deal with strokes and heart attacks the same way we know what to do for people choking or on fire. Everyone's moved aside in our commuter cattle-car.

"Yoroshiku. Thanks," I stammer. Still stunned, grateful but bathed in cold sweat while Darryl stands dumb. "Everything gone?"

"Yeah, even the train," Darryl says, looking on from the side. "No blood or guts, man."

Our train begins to roll.

"You fainted, eh?" Darryl smirks. "You were dead weight, man."

* * *

We get off the train at Shinjuku and Darryl's excited: he sees this as an amazing opportunity to get hammered together, fast-feeding coins into the beer-machine. "Really shook you up, eh?"

We stand guzzling Asahi Super-Dry and smoking. I'm still stunned, but it's soothing to watch the masses rush around us.

"I can't go anywhere for a while."

"You're shaking like shit."

When the congestion finally dies down, we take another for the Chuo, two stops past Nakano to an Izakaya in west-Koenji. Darryl gets quickly loaded and I decide to go no further than a walk with convenience-store beers back to the station.

"*C'mon*, nightcap. We still haven't toasted the dead."

"Darryl… I need to be alone and for you to fuck off."

He lurches into me, offering final bad-breath advice: "You gotta just forget about shit like this."

Escaping from Darryl, I get home to my trailer-like second-floor earthquake shack and quickly strip myself clean of my costume and tie, pour myself a tall, noisy vodka-grapefruit and toss some cushions below my only window and crumble.

"To you and me." I raise a toast. "Erased of everything sweet and sacred… like a night raked bare of her stars by a city you'd think had a soul."

I imagine her thin frame sitting perfectly, dressed immaculately. Leaning against me, before the empty sky, concealing, resting upon her secret.

"I could have saved you, my fragile, commuter-angel. Did you have family? Did you escape something? What's your secret?"

I take a long sip, before sending the ice into a good, musical circle.

"To a city that steals even the freckles of night."

Prone, sweaty drunk, half-splayed out on the tatami under the fan keeping cool. Sipping my dripping drink under the clear night without stars. Flipping through pages of my journal.

"To a city of twenty million, less one."

The first time I saw her, and every time after, I always smiled but never got a smile back. Maybe I tried too hard; if she was a full-on xenophobe, my efforts to wake her smile may have contributed to her demise; that on top of everything else in her life, she was persecuted by a *gaijin* on the morning commute.

"My next newspaper lesson: *Woman Troubled by Foreigner?*"

It makes me question my decision to leave the silence and peace of the small town near Mount Fuji, which is breath-taking no matter how often you see it, let alone all day, every day. I was meant to love the countryside and for a while thought the little town was perfect, until it drove me a little insane.

"To living in the innocent Mount Fuji sticks, well south of this empty sky." Now I crave those big starry night skies, and an actual apartment, not the miniature-tin-can version.

"To an electricity I can't get enough of."

But Tokyo's electric, ancient energy requires sacrifice, and periodically spits out tragedy.

* * *

My mother taught me how to live a little longer each day by being truly present. Because when you really listen to and observe your world, you not only learn and live more, you form bonds and relationships. With a month each year spent on my commute alone, the least I could do was give myself over to wonder. Slow down to enjoy the daily exodus from my Self.

My over-attention to the world around me, however, breaks me. Leaves me a listless ghost left drifting through each moment because of the one bond I didn't make.

* * *

The day after I'm still numb. On the way into work my local stops in the tunnel where it happened. I can't stop thinking of her. Work is a complete mess but at least keeps me focused. The commute home with Darryl is brutal, but we have beers.

Middle of the night I wake up wound tight, sweaty, rattled, shaken from awful dreams I can't remember; I drink myself back to sleep.

Next day I decide on my commute to pay homage. I get off in Shinjuku and walk to the tracks. I convince myself it wasn't her and spend a half-hour wandering around hopeful. Then I start crying, wondering how many minutes she delayed the train, the millions of Yen her family had to pay.

Everything is happening quick around me and I'm in the way.

Later in the day I consider how much of a delay I could afford, and if I'd impress my company by having the cash on me. I imagine going for drama: dressing in vintage and taking an old valise of unpublished poems, manuscripts and money.

Each day I become more dedicated, devoted to her, promising myself not if but *when* I see her I will ask her out and soon after marry her.

Each night the dreams get more and more real, become a nasty game played in my head with the troubling images I saw for two seconds on the train tracks. All of them half-lucid and ridiculous, too, black and white, out of sequence, featuring clothed body chunks. Not ripped but neatly sliced: hiking in a forest, I find two parts ill-attached and go scavenging; in another, while swimming in a friend's pool I discover a key piece of her to a previous puzzle; at the post office I casually collect a parcel of her parts.

The dreams are all I have left of her; I'm custodian, caretaker of the pieces of memory, that which remains.

* * *

Saturday I walk Shinjuku Station platforms for hours, hoping to turn up more than only the memory of her face. In every direction and both sides of the tracks, in the rain and wandering dazed under an umbrella in hot and humid, thick weather. I explore Shinjuku's narrow streets praying, begging to discover her safe. To find out what I saw was wrong, that although I did see a sliced-up human, I didn't know it.

I look for anything in the English, even the Japanese newspapers; I desperately want her to become a miracle, my Ubi Sato. But like her body, her story appears swept up and filed away.

Sunday I can't stop fussing, mostly to keep from hacking out too many dark, rambling poems and journal entries. All day I sip along to my CDs, each offering its soundtrack to consumption. All afternoon I reorganize everything in my apartment to gospel music. For hours I sift and sort, write and wander.

By the middle of night, my world is upended, dusted and I'm sufficiently drunk enough to sleep, and maybe miss the body-part dreams.

* * *

Hungover and shaky as hell on Monday, I pick up a *Chu-hi* and my favourite 'genki-drink' to level things off. One's a jacked-up mimosa and the other is pure pharmaceutical rocket fuel, including liquid nicotine.

At noon I send a rambling email to my folks from Kinkos, telling them about everything except my plans to marry the dead girl I love. When my mother calls I step onto the fire escape.

"I can tell you're really sad," my mother says. "These things we're not made to see."

I start crying, light a cigarette, and grip the rail. "I'm fine. It was *intense*, Mom."

"Could you take some time off?"

"In Japan your own death is the only excuse for missing work. Even that must be officially verified. Plus we're not allowed to talk about or have problems. They beat us."

My mother laughs, then gets serious. "Grandpa worked for CN Rail. He saw a young man take his life. Told us it was the most silent moment you could imagine. Like birth. Think about that."

I do, and when Dr. Kodama and Fujita-san cancel, I excuse myself from the office. My stroll takes me past several beer machines. I know a few on the way back will keep Darryl quiet.

* * *

Completely surrounded by wide, busy streets and dozens of skyscrapers, I find my slice of peace. Along with Aoyama Cemetery and Yoyogi Park, the Imperial Palace is among the most peaceful places in Tokyo. I love the ancient moat, roomy pathways of crushed rock twisting throughout the expansive grounds around the stately old castle where the emperor and his family still live.

The castle remains beautifully huge and imposing, something that says: *Just in case you forgot, this was* Edo*, motherfuckers.*

I thought my favourite tree in Tokyo was a bonsai, then a gingko, but it's a simple Asian pine, old-and-super-gnarly. Like it's been shaken by history into a whole new species sprouting big dripping hairdos of soft, deep-green leaves.

I lean back and sigh, a bit worried about the developing disaster of my body-part dreams, and pray things'll dissipate. I'm aware it's post-traumatic stress, and like a tsunami, the threat always remains.

I can't believe I knew her.

I crack another beer and think: they aren't really nightmares, because I like them right up until her cartoonish remains slip in. I stare at the Imperial Palace and imagine a scene of concubines, before finally drifting off for a much-needed nap against my Asian pine.

There's only one thing I can do.

* * *

When the big one comes, our two-storey tin building is designed to give just enough time for those below to get the hell out before we shake on down. My apartment emergency kit comes with a coil of thick rope, a hardhat, heavy-duty flashlight and for some reason a pair of zip-up white overalls. The suit's tight, but if I stay fairly crouched, it works. I uncoil the heavy rope and though I'm tempted, I know the young family in the slightly-larger tin box below me might not find my rappelling into their garden particularly amusing.

I pour two tall vodka-grapefruits and take a seat for a nightcap with my client. I withdraw Mr. Okada's folder from my briefcase and pin his 8x10 photograph to the wall next to my mirror.

I finish his drink before calling him in Sydney. "Mr. Okada," I smile wildly at his photo, and then into my mirror. "How's Oz?"

"*Mmm*. Very friendly. And you?"

"I only role play in teaching when I'm in costume and alone."

"What are you … talking about?"

"A little after-work project I'll claim overtime for. My tickle-trunk's full of liquor tonight."

"What is *tickle-trunk?*"

"A different story, Mr. Okada. You should see my get-up."

"Get *up?*"

"My costume. Anyways, why I'm calling … Mr. Okada, do you remember the woman I told you about … on my commute?"

"The woman on edge."

"Three weeks after you left, she killed herself."

"Oh my god. It is *terrible*. Are you certain?"

"She's gone … I saw it. On the Chuo Line."

"*Mmm*. So sorry, Jack."

"I wish she was my Ubi Sato …" I finally smile into the mirror. "The commuter who carried her sorrow …" I break down, so long needing to talk to the one person who knew about her.

"*Mmm*. So sorry."

I light a cigarette, gather myself. Give my drink a good swirl with a deep, sad frown. I stare at Mr. Okada, tears in my eyes. "I knew… I could tell she was worked over. Stripped of choice. So fragile … carrying her grief-case. We never spoke. Now it's what she *wasn't* that troubles me. I just want a single story of who I'll never know. Christ, I've imagined our love story."

"Sorry, Jack."

"You know, I don't think what happened was suicide. Not *jisatsu* … but *karoshi*. Not a coming or going, but something birthed … from the borderlands of escape."

"*Mmm*. She had no choice."

"A shadow among the millions of people in Tokyo and I think I could've saved her." Mr. Okada's expression in the photograph seems to change just slightly. "What haunts me most about everything was the pure relief in her face … so calm and peaceful. Mr. Okada, she was finally smiling."

Speaking of Love

Kathryn Phelan

Between what is said and not meant,
and what is meant and not said,
most of love is lost.
Kahlil Gibran

He grew up throwing punches in a north Limerick housing estate. Normally to protect his brother or his friends, he says. Not like he would go looking for it. Kids from 25 years ago, he still remembers as pussies because they ran away. The word sounds strange on his lips. A scratch in the varnish. For a moment, he's a boy with a smashed-up fist, looking around to find himself alone, trying to stand his ground.

Threading his fingers through the hole in the knee of my jeans, he says, You're a hot tamale. I say WHAT? He looks up and asks, Do people not say that in Michigan? I say, People don't say that anywhere. He laughs.

The first time he kisses me, I shock myself by ducking my head. I think we should be friends, I say. It's not true. It's an emergency handbrake. No one is convinced, least of all my body, which presses up against him before I pull back. This keeps happening – an impulse and a recovery. I feel chaotic, in violation of myself. My hands are in his hair and his face is close to mine when he says, lightly, I'm about to not give you a choice. It should frighten or offend me but it's the perfect thing to say. This is what I need: someone who will disregard what isn't true about me. Who will let me have what I want, by force if necessary.

I notice the gold necklace on the bedside table and do not mention it.

I tell him I'm going to Mexico City for Day of the Dead. He says maybe he could come. I shrug and say sure, like it's the most natural thing in the world for someone you barely know to join your two-week holiday in another hemisphere.

In the morning, he is quiet, withdrawn. He starts asking what time I have to be into work so I put on my clothes and he walks me to the door. He has to uncross his arms for me to hug him. The sudden coldness disorients me. I hop on my bike and he yells something from the doorway, but I don't hear him. It would be ridiculous to go back and make him repeat it, but there's a part of me that considers it. A part that would insist on more words.

His mom died when he was young. He tells me how she taught her classes in Irish before Limerick had a Gaelscoil, how everyone loved her, how no one knew what to say. I wonder if this is why he wants to come to Mexico – to see a culture that looks death in the eye. Not like Ireland. Death here is quiet; the dead stay buried. I tell him that in some Mexican villages, families spend the whole night in the cemetery. Some dig up the bones of their ancestors and scrub them clean. I'm not sure I could do that, he says. We'll stick to the face-painting so, I say. And dancing, he says, and would we go to the parade? Sure, I say, we can do everything.

The owner of the necklace. An ex-girlfriend. Who has two sons, whose toys still clutter his front room. Every time he mentions these kids, he says Her-sons-not-my-sons, as though I might have forgotten. It's delicate, because the boys regard him as a father figure. It's delicate, because she still stays over sometimes. If the necklace doesn't move, she knows there's nothing to worry about – no girls like me. I say, That doesn't sound super healthy. He says Yeah. It's delicate.

He tells me he is an electrician too. In addition to being an engineer. Did he not mention it? He's not up to the latest qualifications, but he wired his own house, his brother's. I am terrified by how attracted I feel to this information.

Pulling his shirt over his head, he says, I'm going to pretend I'm American and it's not a big deal to sleep with somebody. I have no idea how to take this. Is this what he thinks Americans do, what I am doing? I say, Hang on, you don't have to pretend you're American! But by then it's too late. His hand finds my neck and he presses down just a little, to see how I will respond, and how I respond is that I like it, this filament of violence, being fucked by a boy who grew up fighting.

I feel giddy, he says. Why do I feel so giddy with you?

The more I think about it, him coming to Mexico is a reckless idea. But it's one I'll take like a shot, chase with lime. I find myself imagining it – dancing bachata, parades of catrinas and calaveras, getting drunk on mezcal and facing what is difficult, surrounded by music and fragrant orange flowers, far from gold necklaces and Ireland's rainy skies.

He mentions going to counselling with a huffy laugh, like Oh-isn't-it-ridiculous. His counsellor keeps asking if he thinks he deserves to be happy. After a moment I say, Well do you? He says, Think I deserve to be happy? I nod. He's quiet for a moment before saying Yeah, yes, yeah, I do.

One weekend, I almost give up. Seventy-two hours without a message. The absurdity of it, the desperation like a biological craving in my body. His silence feels conspicuous, another shock of cold, so I plan my next message: *Things seem complicated, let's leave it*, but I don't send anything. When he finally responds, it's with an apology. Been a stressful few days. Low on energy. How are you? How are things? How are you fixed for a pint later?

He doesn't tell his family he loves them. Not his brother or his dad. His nieces and nephew cry when he leaves, and he jostles their little shoulders and tells them to buck up. It's the best thing he can do for them. As he tells me this, he moves his hand over my shoulder with exquisite gentleness. My hair falls into my face and he tucks it behind my ear. Maybe I should tell them, he says. Maybe I'll say it next time.

I look up his mom's obituary. Why? I don't know. To see. I'm ashamed to admit I could spend nights rolling around in his bed but still google the most important thing that happened to him. Anyway, the 72 hours he went quiet. It was the anniversary of her death. You know what I wished – that he would have told me. That I could have stood beside him in that particular fight.

Leaving my apartment one morning, he hears the neighbours in the hall and whispers, Should I wait? I nod. But even when they've gone, he keeps kissing me. These are nice kisses, he says, like a proclamation. I start to laugh but recover it. They are, I agree. He nods like we've established something. It is so endearing. I've been feigning indifference about him coming to Mexico but I tell him my stance is no longer ambivalent; I do want him to come, and he says he's happy with that, and he looks like he's trying not to smile, and he hugs me hard, for longer than I expect, before he leaves. He says he'll book tickets this week. Leave right after work on the Friday.

None of the men in my life are fighters. They're academics, diplomats. If someone tried to punch my ex-boyfriend, he'd talk them down with tact and composure. They'd end up shaking hands. My dad is a pacifist. His dad the same. I don't think people like this should be called pussies. I think there's dignity in de-escalation and the skills required to achieve it. And yet. How madly I find myself drawn to this Limerick lad who, if backed into a corner, would swing.

He wears a baseball cap to dinner, where he tells me about presenting to 150 people at a conference and the possibility of being made manager. He stars out swear words in his texts but punched a guy in Flannery's last Christmas. He rides a €6,000 bike but does the kinds of tricks on it that you only learn if you grew up thinking you'd never own a €6,000 bike. What I'm trying to say is that I don't understand how someone who calls me a hot tamale, who says These are nice kisses, could be the same person who forces his hand against my clavicle, and it has slightly ruined me.

I think I'm just shy, he says.
Not always, I say.
Not always, he agrees.
It's confusing, I say.
For me too, he says.

How strong is this beer? he says, looking down at it. He has been talking about his mom. How he and his brother never got any help. They went to school, joined sports, got into scrapes. They bucked up. What else could they do? The world had jostled their little shoulders. Really, he says, they probably should have had some support. In retrospect like. Some counselling or whatever. Someone to check on them. She got sick in November and was gone in May. It's a big thing to have happen.

Things he likes about me: my Michigan accent. How I like to travel. That I use the odd word in Irish, my *cúpla focal* of his family tongue. How I ask questions. My hair in a ponytail. That I work hard at friendships. That I run faster than he does. How tightly I hug. How even though things are complicated, I always think we should keep trying.

One evening at his, he picks up his guitar and plays a song he wrote. I tell him it's lovely. He says it needs lyrics and asks if I'll write them. When I say yes, he gives a surprised little laugh. Writing is my job, I say, as though it's a professional matter. I ask what the song is about, and he says: Em, I guess most songs would be about my mam.

When his mom was dying. They were all there – his brother, his dad. Not talking about it. Finally he said, Mam, you know we love you, right? He said it – he made himself say it – he had to say it. Put the three words that mattered in the middle of a sentence, like a disguise, a secret delivery. But even then, he worried what his brother would think. If he'd call him soft later.

On the phone one night, I ask my dad about his pacifism. He tells me he was bullied in school. Pushed down the stairs, the top of his head cracked open with a rock. You never fought back? I ask. I didn't think that was the right way to behave, he tells me. Still don't? I ask. He thinks for a moment. No, he says, but that's only for me. If someone was hurting you or your sisters, boy, I'd release the pain hounds from hell! I'm not sure I know what that means, I say. You get the idea, though, he says, and I tell him I do. It's about what you'll fight for, he says, even though I already said I understood.

Things I like about him: how he calls out the best lyrics in songs. How he's proud of his Irish language, easy with it, insists on the fada. He drives to Thurles every week to babysit his nieces and nephew. He has read almost all of the books on his shelves. He makes me laugh. He punctuates emojis like they're complete sentences. All the old fellas in the pub know his name, come over to say hi, smile at me.

He says: I don't want it to become meaningless. To say I love you. I don't want it to be something you just say every day.

We are talking about Day of the Dead – how in Mexico they say the only real death is when no one remembers you. You set out the favourite snacks of the person you loved, beer and clementines and pan de muerto, and believe they will come home. In ancient Ireland, lament took form through keening, that eerie, hollow wail of pain that came up against the church for being too pagan and unrestrained. He asks about death in the Midwest and I tell him our farming traditions: topsoil from your own land carted in the loader of a tractor to a tiny rural cemetery, so the earth you covered covers you, and he nods. Grief is not meant to be quiet, we agree. It's meant to be keened and unburied and scrubbed clean and churned around like fresh topsoil. But if you ask me, love is not meant to be quiet either. It's also something that should be sung.

Tonight, even though we have bikes, we walk. We spill out of the yellowy pub into the clear night air, and without agreeing it, push the bikes along the pavement and talk the two miles home. I say, I'm still trying to work you out. He says, I'm trying to work myself out too.

He says: It has caught me off-guard, liking you. I just. I was not expecting it.

He found a song about Michigan and is learning it on the guitar for me. I think about this when he goes quiet for another 72 hours. I think about how he sent me photos from the train, held my face in his hands, told me I am changing things for him. I think about the lyrics I've written but not shown him. I think about his body, my arms pinned above my head, the times he went cold. I think about what it means that the gold necklace is still on his bedside table.

He's not coming to Mexico. A few reasons, he says. Too complicated to explain. Life is getting in the way. I say yes, fine, don't worry. It's not what I mean to say. It's not what I mean. For weeks I will tamp down the mad desire to cycle back to his doorway and insist on more words. I want him to know there is more than one way to be a pussy. There is more than one way to run.

Of many things I have no clear remembrance

Dani Salvadori

By the age of 30 my mother's father, Misha, had had four surnames, lived in six countries and spoke nine languages. By 35 he had settled in London and become British, his third nationality. He died when I was a child. I barely remember him.

There were many stories about Misha and his family. Not told by my mother but by my father, who loved mythologising dead members of the family. When I was young these stories were the truth. As I grew older they receded behind the veil of the horrors of mid-twentieth century Europe and the toxic end to the colonisation of the Middle East. Now I no longer know what is true and what is myth.

In summer 2022 I had to clear my mother's house as she succumbed to dementia and went to live in a care home. What was left of my grandfather's life had turned into objects to be dealt with. Some documents and photos could be kept, a few items could be sold, but most of the things were waste with no value. Clearing the house became a pilgrimage into my mother's family's past; a Grand Tour through the inanimate. They told a different story to the ones I had heard as a child.

I had few aids to navigation: a photo album; a small brown wallet containing formal documents gathered on Misha's travels; an airmail from the US, pale blue with condolences from his oldest friend; a box of books chosen on looks and not content.

The photo album showed more wealth than I had imagined – how else could a large Russian/Polish Jewish family travel from St Petersburg to the spas of Europe before the first world war? And escape the Russian revolution unscathed? I saw hope in the photos of 1920s Palestine, even a pioneer spirit, as Misha enthusiastically became part of British Mandatory Palestine and the end of the Ottoman Empire.

But in the end there was only disappointment, and even fear, etched on the faces of my grandparents, and my child mother, as they navigated life in London as World War Two approached.

§

[Cultivation]
Language was given to us to conceal our thoughts
so what is the use of history?
Begin, at the beginning
and, at the end, stop.

§

I thought about finding Misha by navigating to the places in the photo album.
Pinsk | Bad Kolberg | Cannes | Karslbad | Merano | London | Bad Elster | Petrograd | Krakow | Warsaw | Cambridge | Naples | Amalfi | Warsaw | Acre | Sebastia (Samaria) | Jerusalem | Jaffa | Aden | Baghdad | Ur of the Chaldees | Angora (Ankara) | Tel-Mond, | Anatolia | Houlgate | Damascus | Zahle (Syria) | La Zoute | Baghdad | Forte dei Marmi | Kuźnica

But as I only speak English I knew I would remain a tourist and fail to find a direction.

§

[We]
spoke a kindred language
divided into zones like a map
and in our geographical sense
dreamt in many languages.

§

[They]
held to the treasures of literature
followed the language-boundary
clung more tightly to the language
found strangeness always a misery.

§

I think the only place my mother's small family was happy was Kuźnica, the family holiday home on what is now the Poland/Belarus border. Each summer the extended family gathered there. Their last trip was in August 1939. On 31 August they left in a hurry and dashed back to London as the borders shut behind them. No one else they were on holiday with survived the Nazis. I do not know their names. In autumn 2021 Kuźnica became a place of terror once again when the Belarussian authorities dumped desperate Iraqi refugees there in the run up to the Ukraine war.

§

[Arrival/Departure]

Green lanes and black lines on the edge of the leaden beyond
low and flat, a long row of anything, everything.
The sky a quarrel of angry red lines, spiders' webs of coarse air
writhing from the ditches. On the east wind
a bitter sleet rattling on to the open marshes.
A few faces hurried to glowing, a hunt against us
through gates and dykes and spare grass.
We phantoms cried and vanished again.

§

Walking through Russell Square one lunchtime I noticed that the Wiener Holocaust Library had an exhibition of pre-1939 Jewish family photos. There were collections from many families so similar to mine. I had obviously arrived at the end of a lecture because there were a number of Chinese students in the exhibition space. I overheard a member of staff tell another that she had had to start from scratch in that morning's lecture as none of them knew anything about the Holocaust.

The biggest impact Misha has had on me is the language I speak. When I was a baby he discouraged my parents from speaking to me in languages other than English because it would mean I would learn to speak later. I suppose they believed him because he was so fluent in so many. The outcome was that each generation in my family spoke a different language: my grandparents spoke French to each other; my parents Italian and my sister and I English. I was eight before I realised that in other families everyone spoke the same language, I still remember the moment of revelation.

§

[English]
A first difficulty was to say who.
There was a language, in it lay the test.
It was the tongue of these areas
the language of families.

§

In **Economy of the Unlost** Anne Carson explores the concept of *sprachgitter* in the context of the poetry of Paul Celan – another Jew who spoke nine languages. She translates the German compound word as referring to language (sprach) and mesh or lattice (gitter).

§

[Sprachgitter]
language | mesh
language | lattice
language | grate
language | net
language | snare
language | bars

§

[Mesh]
Patriotism was warped to a
common language, in it
lay a prize-ring, a master-key
and the key of imagination.

§

[Searching]
The message which reached us
through three languages was unintelligible.

The stars were shifting
we were steering wrong.

§

Eventually I chose a selection of Misha's books in English as my guide to the poetic tour I wanted to write. When I opened them I found comfort in the familiar ex-libris labels and the few annotations and press cuttings tucked inside the front covers. I read aloud the first sentences of each book. I found echoes: but while there were beginnings there was no way to reach a conclusion.

My next act was to mine the books for *language*. Only ***Seven Pillars of Wisdom*** by TE Lawrence was available online and had sufficient mentions of the word to give me a framework for poetry. The presence of the book on my mother's shelves had always bemused me. But I did not have to search long to find out that Lawrence played both the Zionists and the Arabs for the British. It is likely that Misha would have met him.

I used my pre-PC Olivetti that I found in my mother's loft to type out my found poem on the reverse of the image plates from another of my selection: ***Carpets of Persia*** by Creasey Tattersall. The keys felt the same as they ever did.

My selection of books made little dent in the total. No one wants old books now. Even book clearance companies require detailed forms to be filled in before they will agree to take them. The books I did not take home would be recycled and turned to pulp. Only the paper had use, the words did not. Although the number of words written in the world has grown, who knows how many are read and how many wasted?

In ***Economy of the Unlost*** Anne Carson describes how the poet Simonides of Keos (556 – 467 BCE) had lived at a time when the market for words changed radically. The gift economy was overtaken by coinage and he became the first poet to charge for his writing. It leads her to ask of the process of writing: *What exactly is lost when words are wasted? And where is the human store to which such goods are gathered?*

Disposing of cultural items that no longer have the same resonance as they once did is not a new problem. In the aftermath of World War Two the spoils from the colonial excavation of Egyptian, Greek and Roman remains across the Middle East no longer seemed relevant to many museums in the UK and the US. In **Post-War Object Habits (1945-1969)** Alice Stevenson describes how Brown University's Jenks Museum in Rhode Island, USA hauled ninety-two truckloads of specimens to the University's landfill site in 1945.

I still needed to deal with the rest of the books in my mother's small suburban house. Waste management has changed but the recycling companies I paid to dispose of the contents of my mother's house filled five trucks with the remains of my parents' and grandparents' lives. The only books with any value raised £212 at auction. I still have one box of books which I will give to a friend who will turn them into artworks. Otherwise only the photo album and the tattered brown wallet remain in my sister's attic. The Wiener Holocaust Library can have them when we die, leaving others to make memorials.

§

[I]
my notebooks were full of abstract words.
Intimacy seemed shameful
unless the other could make the perfect reply
in the same language.

§

Notes

Arrival/Departure is a found poem from *Great Expectations* by Charles Dickens

Cultivation, We, They, English, Mesh, Searching, I are all found poems from *Seven Pillars of Wisdom* by T E Lawrence.

Bravo India Lima

Olivia Rana

Age five. The army stopped us at Gortmullan checkpoint. After searching the boot of my Daddy's car, they instructed him to step out onto the road. Through the open door, I could hear the scuff of their boots, and the buzz and crackle from their radios. They sounded like *The Goodies*, those soldiers, but I didn't laugh when they told Daddy to remove his shoes and stand with his hands outstretched on the roof of the car. The top of Daddy's head appeared as he bent forwards, his dark hair thick with quarry dust. I pressed myself into the back seat of our Ford Cortina and started counting.

They were going to shoot him with their long guns. Three, four, five. I wondered how I'd make it home, how long it might take me to walk the distance past Tommy Coalman's house and as far as Patterson's Cross. What would I tell Mammy? Six, seven, eight. I'd seen it on the news, bodies lying on the road covered in white sheets, the army circling around a bullet-ridden vehicle. I put my hand up against the glass, hoping Daddy might look at me. 'Bravo, India, Lima,' one of the soldiers recited out the letters from our number plate in their own strange language. Nine, ten. I braced myself, but after a pause, Daddy's shoes were shoved against his chest, and he climbed back into the car, setting the shoes on the passenger seat.

We moved past the barricades, and travelled on into the south, him manoeuvring the pedals in his stockinged feet. Only when he'd parked along the main street in the village of Ballyconnell did Daddy replace his shoes, and I could see his fingers shake as he tied the laces twice. I waited in the car as he headed into the bank, just like he did every Friday, and when he reappeared with the small plastic bags of change bunched in his arms like a baby, I started to cry. 'What are you crying for?' he asked. 'I was only gone a minute.'

The pub my father owned with his brothers was on the banks of the Woodford Canal, the water strewn with bits of rubbish dropped down from the bridge. A man drowned there once, he just walked right in on purpose, my sister told me. It was early afternoon, but the curtains in the pub were drawn so that the day disappeared. A smog sat over the bar where the few regulars were hunched over drinks, and Jim was cleaning glasses, holding them out a distance to inspect them. Everyone looked up when we came in, nodded. One of the old men insisted on repeating a trick I'd seen several times before. He swallowed his cigarette whole, parting his lips so that we could see the gaping black hole of his mouth. And then he made the cigarette reappear again between his lips, still fully lit.

'Good man Mick.' Big Padar clapped Mick on the back.

Daddy leaned over the bar and offered his packet of Benson and Hedges around to the men. They smoked a lot, and didn't say much, the television providing most of the chatter. I stood on a bar stool and poured the coins from the bank into the till, dividing them up into their little compartments with a clatter, making a real job out of it. When I was done, Jim poured me a Cidona and I sat and watched the RTE news bulletin with the rest of them. They played a clip of Johnny Logan's winning performance in the Eurovision the night before. *'What's another year to someone who's lost everything that he owns?'* he sang, the cord from the microphone draped between his fingers.

'That's a quare get-up,' Jim said, commenting on Johnny's white suit.

'Aren't you only jealous.' Big Padar laughed. 'Sure the women are mad for him.'

The news moved on to a piece about the Taoiseach Charles Haughey. He was standing outside the Dail with his hair blown upward in the wind, and then there was mention of a man shot dead on his way to work at Sir Richard Arkwright's factory in Lisnaskea. Jim turned the volume up on the television. Lisnaskea was the town where Mammy bought our groceries, and if we were good she would take us to Ferguson's sweet shop for white mice and bonbons and maybe even to the library.

'The man was shot nine times in the back of the head,' said the news reader, Anne Doyle. She had a lovely purple blouse on, with a huge bow underneath her neck.

The men shook their heads, and Big Padar said it was an awful handlin. 'They'll be after one of our lot now,' he said. 'That's how it goes.'

I thought about Daddy lying on the road at the checkpoint, of blood pouring out from underneath his head, and I thought of Ferguson's sweet shop and gumballs that could crack your teeth open.

After the news, Daddy said we'd better get home for our tea, or Mammy would think we were lost. He helped himself to a whiskey first though, before we headed back down the road. I waited for him to say something about the shoes to Jim, but Jim had moved on from cleaning the glasses to doing a crossword puzzle, his brow creased in concentration. Daddy said nothing.

Age ten. The army came to the door in the middle of the night and woke us all up. The knock made Daddy jump out of bed, thinking it was someone with news about his sick brother. We peeped through the curtains and watched Daddy standing on the cold doorstep in his pyjamas, framed by the light from the scullery. He looked like a contestant on a quiz show. My legs shook underneath me with fear, and anger too. The next day Daddy told us that it was because there was a new regiment at the checkpoint. 'They're shaky after the attack on the RUC station in Newry,' he said. I didn't understand why that had anything to do with us, and Daddy didn't have a way to explain it. 'It's just the way it is.'

The new regiment started holding up lorries ferrying sand and gravel across the border from the quarry at Knockninny, men being paid by the hour. Daddy said they were making him lose money hand over fist, and Mammy blamed them for the cracks in our ceiling, from landing Chinook helicopters in the field beyond our house. They crouched through the grass as we played ball, as my sister hung the washing on the line. Shifting and changing like shadows.

My siblings and I found remnants of their visits in our playhouses, a series of old abandoned farm buildings, lovingly pieced together with old furniture and broken crockery. We came across sachets of sugar squirreled away in crevices in the wall, and discarded cigarette butts, and we discussed what the army might have been doing there. We went over everything to see what had been misplaced in our carefully arranged spaces, and my sister was outraged that they'd broken a milk jug that had belonged to our granny. I felt embarrassed too, imagining the soldiers laughing at our attempts to set up a restaurant in an old pig shed. I no longer wanted to play house, and I hated how the army had to seep into everything we did and ruin it, like God.

Age seventeen. I was standing at the bottom of the lane waiting on the school bus to take me to Mount Lourdes Convent in Enniskillen. Every morning the driver had to make a detour across the checkpoint, to collect those children living down lanes right in the middle of the army fortification, that limbo place between north and south. The driver was asked to dismount, and a soldier walked down the aisle of the bus, gun pointed into our laps as he passed. He was a boy not much older than myself, enlisted from Sunderland or Durham before he had time to properly learn to read or write. My friend from that in-betwixt place sat beside me and we talked about everything and nothing. Crossing a landscape of security barriers and observation posts on the school route was unremarkable to us. We listened to music on our Sony Walkman, sharing mix-tapes we had put together, as she tried to educate me on Neil Young. The journey to Enniskillen took much longer than it needed to.

In between finishing school and going to college, we passed our driving tests, and my friends and I traversed the border now in borrowed cars, to The Angler's Rest, and Lizzie Buggies, then on to Farnham Nightclub in Cavan. We were a carload of girls travelling home late at night, called up to the barracks where there were sleazy comments and interrogation about who we were, soldiers circling the car like vultures. We didn't look at their faces or at one another, suddenly sober. No one could see us behind the green corrugated walls, and the fun of the night was replaced by clawing fear. We knew of girls who had been taken inside the barracks, of officers spinning them a yarn. You didn't talk about such things, for those same poor girls would be the ones in trouble. Only when the light turned green could we move on, could we be sure we were safely in the north again.

Age nineteen. I was travelling up the M1 on the Ulsterbus, marking the move away from the border, town by town: Fivemiletown, Augher, Clougher, and onwards to Belfast. The journey unhooked me from something I didn't even know I was tethered to. As a student, I lived in the heart of the Holylands, and the army was there too of course, patrolling the streets of Fitzroy Avenue and Rugby Road in armoured vehicles, but I didn't encounter them in the same way, until one day I did. I met him in a bar on Malone Road. He was from Scotland, and told me his name was Andy. He was a good-looking bloke with a broad smile and broad shoulders and he told me everything about himself, and about his sister who had died from leukemia. When he bought me another drink and leaned in to press the bottle into my hand, he kissed me. So sure of himself. 'Are you catholic?' he asked. I wanted to know why he wanted to know. 'I'm a member of the Royal Highland Fusiliers,' he told me.

'But you're Scottish,' I said.

He laughed then and I thought that the thing about the army was a joke, because off-duty soldiers didn't just drink in bars like that. Then he talked on about how he joined when he was seventeen and it was his first time stationed in Belfast. I took in the cut of him, imagined him behind a long gun, circling.

I told him I needed to go to the bathroom and squeezed my way through the throng in Botanic Inn and out into the air. On the way home, down University Square, I remembered the story about the soldiers lured to a pub in North Belfast. They were shot while they were taking a piss against the gable wall. I thought of him sitting there, waiting, but I didn't go back.

Age twenty-three. Friday 10th April and everyone was watching the news. The results of the Good Friday Referendum were being broadcast around the world, the footage shown again and again of Bertie Ahern and Tony Blair signing the agreement at Stormont. There was a sense of euphoria, even Ian Paisley cracked a smile or two. We went to Renshaw's to celebrate, and in the bar and on the streets of Belfast there was a palpable sense of positivity, a feeling that everything was going to be different.

I went to Galway with my friends. We were in The Quays pub when the barman told us that twenty-nine people had been killed in the Omagh bomb. 'One woman who died was pregnant with twins,' he said. It was thirteen weeks after the Good Friday Agreement and it felt like the world had fallen in on itself. We phoned home and bought the paper so that we could check it was really real, and then when we had a stomach full of awfulness we went back to The Quays. There was no dancing or want for fun of any kind. A sort of gloom settled over us as we drove back up the road and across the border again. The army didn't keep us waiting this time, so we got back to the north faster than we wanted to.

Age thirty. I was at the Taj Mahal with my husband, taken aback by people in saris asking for my photo. They liked my red hair and my blue eyes and asked me if I was Irish. I said I was, but it felt like pretending to be confident when I wasn't. As we drove back to Jaipur, I read on my phone how four thousand miles away in the North of Ireland John de Chastelain had announced that the IRA's last remaining weapons had been put beyond use. I tried to imagine warehouses filled with Armalite rifles, grenade launchers, and explosives, men from back roads lining up to hand their cache of weapons in. It felt implausible, like an over-ambitious action movie.

Age thirty-seven. The day after my father's funeral I found his shoes lying in the scullery. They were still coated in a fine dust of limestone. I left the house with my children and walked over to Patterson's Cross, past the orchard where my father stole apples as a boy, and on up towards the border, the road potholed from lorries. The army checkpoint at Gortmullan had been dismantled, and I tried to explain to my children what the checkpoint was like, and where it was positioned. 'It was somewhere along there,' I said, but I couldn't quite figure it out.

When I looked out over the fields, there was absolutely no trace that the army checkpoint had ever been there, like something imagined. Fields had since been returned to the farmer, army boys returned to their homes, and there was no way of telling where the north ended and the south began. It was one clear stretch of road.

For Richer, Poorer and Doritos

Cheryl Miller-Fitzgerald

"I have to split them up," I tell my little sister over the phone, as I swerve to avoid a pothole in the road. There's a long silence, and I wonder if my Bluetooth is acting up.

"You can't do that. They've been married over 20 years." Nope, it's working just fine because I hear her loud and clear.

"Really Stacey? Where has it gotten them?" For once I wish she wouldn't challenge me, like she's been doing since she was three, screaming "Push me!" from the swing long after my arms got tired.

"That doesn't matter."

"Then you can look after her the next time she gets sick," I say, gripping the steering wheel until my knuckles turn white. "I'm spending all my time taking care of her – time I don't have," and I smack the disconnect button.

I'm driving our sister Sue home from the hospital as she rummages through her handbag in the seat beside me. The road is sprinkled with lights from houses decorated for Christmas. It's been a week since she was diagnosed with pneumonia; when I brought her in she was barely conscious but trying valiantly to sing "Silent Night" through dry, chapped lips.

"You can't split us up," she says to me now in the car, and I look at her, surprised she overheard me, having forgotten she was there. I do that way too often, like she's a baby, instead of a 50-year-old woman. "Mark's my life, Cheryl," she continues in her slow, careful, medicated way. "He's good to me." She zips up her handbag, fiddles with the radio and starts singing all the words to "Janie's Got a Gun" by Aerosmith.

It's a song she knows well from her high school days, back when she nabbed all the leads in the school plays, embodying everyone from Sandy in *Grease* to Dorothy in the *Wizard of Oz* without a slip. Hours after taking her final bow she missed her cue for the first time, failing to join us for our usual post-show pizza. Instead, she sat on her bed in full stage makeup, gingham dress and red ruby slippers and said she was waiting for Joey.

"Who's Joey?" I asked her. She sat there, staring intently at nothing. "Is she acting?" Stacey whispered, and I nodded, turning away to hide my confusion.

"Who's Joey?" I asked Sue again, grabbing her by the shoulders, shaking her a little. She leaped off her bed and screamed, "Get away from me! I know he's coming!"

Our dad poked his head in the door, and like a firefighter smelling smoke, pulled me and Stacey out of the room. Within thirty minutes we watched in horror as three cops struggled to restrain my five-foot, 100-pound sister.

Hours later, at the hospital, a doctor finally appeared. I was barely 19 but knew from the way he shuffled in we weren't going to like what he had to say. "Schizophrenia," he started, and went on to use words like dendrites and synapses, anything but the word we understood – crazy. Like the man down the street from us who wore pink bunny slippers and shorts, even during the winter.

Sue was just 17; she hadn't had her first real kiss or drink; she hadn't voted or gotten her driver's license. And instead of making plans for college, she began taking "lifestyle classes" at the local mental health center, learning how to do laundry and balance a checkbook, when she wasn't learning how to distinguish between what was and wasn't real.

But my mom refused to give up on one "normal" dream for Sue – getting married.

"I don't know, Mrs. Miller," said the first of our many family therapists, Bob, a young, bearded, handsome guy who made me blush every time he looked at me. "Have you asked Susan if it's what she wants?"

My mom brushed him off with a wave of her hand and snuck a look at me – I couldn't commit to a college major, much less a man at the time. "I know what's best for her," she said.

"Seriously, Mom?" I said, rolling my eyes.

It turned out there was a huge market for young, pretty, schizophrenic women. While I was navigating the dating scene like a war field in

Sarajevo, Sue was having trouble fighting off all the guys at the center who wanted to date her. Until she met Mark, a musician and artist whose paintings were crosses between Picasso's *Starry Night* and Munch's *The Scream*. He was diagnosed with schizophrenia just as his classical piano career was taking off. He escaped into books, the more obscure the better.

"Do black holes grow or shrink?" he asked me the first time we met, and then answered his question for the next 20 minutes.

We sat down to dinner, and Sue started wolfing hers down, something she'd been doing since she got sick. "Susan!" my mother yelled, as my father turned away. Mark looked at them and placed his hand gently on Sue's back. "Slow down Sue, no one's going to take it away from you," he said.

Not long after that, Sue accepted Mark's proposal.

I don't remember much about the wedding – a low key affair at a local restaurant with immediate family and a few of Sue and Mark's friends. But I remember the vows, wondering if they shouldn't be changed given the couple's circumstances. And wondering how the marriage could even survive, given that nearly half of all marriages between mentally healthy people ended in divorce.

But breaking those marriage vows was never an option for them.

Not when things were good, as they were in the beginning. With my mom's help, the right medication and a strong mental health program, they moved into an apartment, got jobs at the local Kmart and made friends, often walking around their complex in the evening sharing cigarettes and stories, Mark's hand placed firmly on Sue's back.

And divorce wasn't an option when things got bad. Once my mom got too old to look after them they lost their way – their car died, they stopped going to work, and couldn't pay their bills. They needed supervision. It fell to me – managing my own family by then – to find them a new home.

With a small U-Haul parked outside, I stood with Sue in her nearly empty apartment, looking at the walls marked with rectangles of dark green paint where Mark's paintings used to hang, and asked her if it wasn't time to split up. I'd done my homework, consulting an underground network of people involved in housing the mentally ill; few of them had family, fewer had spouses. Finding a decent group home that accepted married couples hadn't been easy. If she were alone, I told her, I could find her a better place. "One closer to me," I say, thinking about making room for her in my own home. Her eyes light up for a second. "I could see your kids, and Bill all the time?" she asks. "Yes," I say. But she turns away.

"No," she says, carefully putting her Britney Spears CDs into a box, stopping to look through a dusty photo album that had been laying under her bed. "I'm not going anywhere without Mark." She looks me in the eye with a firmness I didn't know she possessed and turns back to the album. I want to shake her, like I did all those years ago in her bedroom and get her to listen to me. "I love this picture, Cheryl," she says, holding it up, but I brush her off with a wave of my hand.

* * *

It's been six months since she and Mark moved into the group home, and she's gotten sick regularly, but she always seems to bounce back. Just a few hours earlier when I went to pick her up from the hospital's rehab center she was playing bingo with the other residents, maybe fifty others in their 80s and 90s, gray hair and curved backs stooped over their cards. When she saw me she jumped up, and started moving through the crowd like the mayor, saying good bye to some, shaking others' hands, all the time pointing to me, introducing me. "This is my sister. She's taking me home." I thought of the high school star she used to be, and the person she could have been – a mom, leaving a book club, maybe even a real mayor, helping a town recover from a Nor'easter, or a school board member, assuring parents their kids' scores on the latest standardized test would be fair.

On our way home from the hospital we stop at Wawa to grab a sandwich and a snack. She wolfs down the sandwich as usual. Halfway to her house I see she still hasn't touched her Doritos.

"Why aren't you eating your chips?" I ask her.

She tightens her hold on them. "I'm saving them to share with Mark. They're his favorite. He's hungry at night." She giggles.

Fifteen minutes later we pull up to her house. From the outside it looks like any other ranch, albeit rundown, with an unpaved driveway and weed ravaged lawn. A huge window with a few crooked Christmas lights flanks the front, and a stream of people walk past it.

Sue opens her handbag and pulls out what she was looking for earlier – the photo album she discovered the day she was moving – and hands it to me. "Here, you'll like this," she says. She grabs her plastic bag with the Doritos and heads in, and like a returning war hero, is welcomed with hugs and kisses and slaps on the back. One man stands to the side, he's holding a book with a picture of Stephen Hawkins on it. Sue turns to him and smiles. They don't hug, but she opens her bag and lets him see inside, and he smiles back at her.

I look down at the photo album she handed me, open it and see a picture of Sue and Mark sitting next to each other at the restaurant the night of their wedding. She's wearing a simple white dress, he's in a black suit, and they are both holding up water glasses, as three other hands holding glasses are caught in the frame toasting them and their new life together.

In another picture Mark is blowing out birthday candles; in another, they are about to dig into turkey on Thanksgiving, and in still another, they are eating latkes with my mom on Hanukkah.

While I wasn't paying attention, my sister had lived a good life with Mark. Maybe it hadn't been as traditional as many, but it was all she'd known, and it was enough for her – unheard of at a time when closing the door on one relationship was as easy as swiping left.

Instead of figuring out what Sue's marriage wasn't, I needed to accept it for what it was – a bond as tight as the slim gold wedding band on her ring finger.

My Bluetooth kicks in, and I see that Stacey is trying to call me back. She's right, we can't split them up. But I decide to wait a bit before I let her know she's right.

Behind the glass, everyone disperses. Sue turns to me – knowing instinctively, like any performer, that I'm looking at her, and waves. Then she smiles at Mark again, and they both turn towards the back and walk together towards their room, Sue tightly clutching the bag of Doritos, Mark's hand placed firmly on her back.

Except for One Thing

Thomas Darlington Crancer

Three weeks.

It's Sunday night. Joan and I would eat an early dinner, drink a glass or two of homemade wine, engage in a little conversation, probably complain at least once that the weekend wasn't a day longer; figure out what to wear to work in the morning, scoop some leftovers into containers for the next day's lunch; watch a TV program from the couch, hands nonchalantly touching; climb the stairs up to our bedroom, hold each other and talk softly, make love sleepily, one of our cats watching, curious, but not surprised. We would sleep. I might wake up briefly, touch her for reassurance and doze off again. Maybe she would do the same.

We would except for one thing: Joan drove one of the cars in a head-on collision three weeks ago. Paramedics worked for half an hour to get her out of the wreck. "We are breathing for her," the doctor told me when I arrived at the emergency room. One by one threads of hope were pulled from my grasp. I held her hand as her heart stopped beating.

Altogether, six hours passed from when I was told my wife had been in a bad accident to that moment. There were x-rays and CAT scans in between, doctors and nurses compassionately delivering bad news. A doctor told me I had to okay a "do not resuscitate" order. But it never mattered. The line moved across the screen like a video game I desperately wanted to win. Then the line was flat. No more beeping.

That was just a formality, though. Consciousness probably left her in the car long before.

So I'm going up to bed alone, without even a good memory. When I think of her, I think of her puffed-up, cold body, the room filled with flowers and friends and relatives. It didn't look like her in the coffin. But that's what I remember. In order to remember Joan I have to tell stories about her out loud.

A hundred times a day I notice something I want to share with her, then I'm reminded that I can't and the sadness stabs me. There are even times when I think of seeing her, remember I can't, then say, "Then I'll phone her," and I remember I can't do that either. The regret stabs me twice.

I'm back at work. My office has a phone system that records messages if someone calls while I'm away or on another call. A red light flashes on the phone to signal that I have messages. Joan used to call me from time to time with news or an idea or to ask me what I wanted for dinner. Each time I return to my office now I find myself looking for the flashing light, hoping it's her. Now that she's gone, I realize what kind of pleasure it was to see the light, to dial up the message and hear her recorded voice, not an enormous pleasure, probably about like the pleasure a smoker gets from a cigarette, small and dependable.

The hospital, the funeral arrangements, the first few nights were worse than any nightmare I ever dreamed. Now it's a constant sadness I want to cling to as long as I can. It's what I have left of her.

Seven months.

It's been seven months. Only a couple times a week now I forget that I can't talk to her. Whole hours elapse without thinking about her.

"He's the guy whose wife was killed in a car accident." I heard a woman say it to her adult daughter when she thought I had gone. That's who I am to some people and it probably explains more about me than any other sentence one could use. Next year I'll be someone a little different. But that's who I am now.

Joan's life is all packaged up. It has a beginning and an end. It's like a story or a movie.

I wish things had been a little different – not big things, details. She gave me an elegant fountain pen for my birthday. I lost it. When I was sorting through papers after her death, I found it. I had taken it on a job interview and left it in a notebook. She had been hurt by my losing it.

When the man at the dry cleaners saw my name, he asked if I was related to Joan. I said I was her husband. He told me how much he missed her. How had she touched the life of the family that owned the dry cleaners? I wondered. I knew she had found a baby-sitter for the child of the woman who cut her hair. Her students came to her wake by the dozens and told me how she'd changed their lives.

Before people tell me how much they miss her, they apologize. They say, "I know it is nothing like the way you feel." I wish they wouldn't do that. I wish they would just feel their sorrow and tell me about it if they want to. I would miss her if I were her dry cleaner. I don't need to have my grief be bigger than anyone else's.

At times I feel okay and I wonder if this isn't too easy. Other times the despair is bottomless.

One year.

Today it's been one year. Yesterday or the day before a man on the radio said that George Burns and Gracie Allen were back together again. I knew what he meant and I envied George Burns.

Every report and every thought of death is different now than it was before. When I hear that a soldier, a crime victim, a celebrity or a condemned man has died, or I see a funeral procession or even a cemetery, the idea of death is more real and brutal than it ever was in the past. I think of the relatives who will feel for a long time what I feel.

I guess I have been living in a world all along where any of us can be transformed from a laughing, crying, hand-holding, smiling, cuddly person to a box of ashes in less than a week – the whole business, officially pronounced dead, required autopsy for those who die in automobiles in Ohio, travel arrangements for friends and relatives, religious services and burial or cremation – one week, even a couple of days left over – every one of us. Somehow I didn't really know this before and now that I do I can't work up the same enthusiasm I once had.

I walked to the church today where the mass was said for Joan a year ago. I lit a candle and asked God to take care of her.

Time is different than it used to be, not faster or slower, just different. It seems that a lot of days in the last year are missing and some minutes are as vivid as if they had been preserved.

When the funeral home called me to say I could pick up Joan's ashes a few days after the funeral, I didn't have a car. I hadn't replaced the one lost in the accident, so I was on my bicycle. I dropped by after work, put the box of ashes in my backpack, put the backpack on and peddled toward home. The sun was about to set. The afternoon was cool and tiny drops of water hung in the air. I remember the bicycle moving swiftly, the cold droplets wetting my skin and the warmth of Joan's ashes against my back. It was the only warmth I felt and it was the last warmth I have felt from her body. That moment, riding home, hangs so close to me I can reach out and touch it.

Moments from her life are that close too. I had to bring her something at work, a paper to sign, I think. She was teaching and the classroom door had a window in it. I watched her gesticulate and dash the chalk against the blackboard. She was speaking enthusiastically and waving at the board. Though her words were muffled coming through the door, her enthusiasm penetrated it easily. For a long time I watched, a child's spirit in a grown woman's body.

About two and a half years.

I lived the first two years or so wondering how life would be if those two cars had not been where they were. There had been a brief conversation about whether Joan or a co-worker would give the student a ride. It could have gone the other way. There is another path, the one my life would have taken: We would be watching the leaves change now. Now we would be swimming in the lake. I lived with one foot on the hypothetical path. Then at about two years it begins to fade. Too many things would have happened. It's hard to tell what we'd be doing. At about two years I began to let go of the other path. This letting go is difficult too. I know things I would not have known. I have pleasures I would not have felt.

Poetry

The Scene Without

"The scene" is still the same—that's what you called it,
the view from our back windows that opens in winter

like a spread scroll—the brook that runs free and full, skidding
among stones, browned meadows with their broken stems

and grasses, matted leafmold, woods stripped of cover
spilling pent up secrets, light pallid, whether bleak or tender

only you could have told. You'd still know it instantly—how you
loved the scope of it, the sheer expanse; loved even the battered,

colorless stalks, the twiggy bushes, hollow seedpods—remnants
of your care only last summer, no longer ago than that, now

unbridgeable by any quickening of spring, unimaginable by any
thought of mine. Only this morning I saw a sharp-shinned hawk

gliding overhead, ready to plunge. Before that a fox, uttering
its short, sharp yap, then loping across the yard to re-enact

the primal plot that ends in survival and abrupt extinction.
Small songbirds enact it too, gorging against the cold but not

to the point of slowing their flight from the hawk. Look there—
I want to show you the brown creeper camouflaged against

the mottled bark, until it spirals down to the base of the trunk;
the golden-crowned kinglet flitting skittishly among the bare

branches, picking at lichens; the flicker, with its yellow-shafted wings
and dagger-like bill, drilling for grubs in the half-thawed ground.

I wonder if they might be the same individual birds you saw this time
last year, looking out from these same windows on this winter scene.

I want to tell you that they are all still here, that I am still here, that nothing
has changed—just everything inside the windows, but nothing without.

Winifred Hughes

Vectors in Kabul

The secret schools have turned to algebra,
a language for resistance. *Group theory,*
theory of rings, field theory, manifolds,

and vector spaces. Addition and multiplication
of a vector with a scaler. A girl is a vector,
but the rulers add to her silence,

then multiply by early marriage. Her eggs
are also vectors, sold to the nearest male,
his beard trailing her throat as he grunts

1, 2, 3, (pause), 1, 2, 3, (pause) 1, 2, 3,
and a theory of multiplication occurs.
In secret schools, the possibility of this vector

may be undone. Scheme-theoretically,
girls discover how *a manifold*
is a locally ringed space, whose structure sheaf,

isomorphic to the sheaf of continuous
(or differentiable, or complex-analytic)
functions on Euclidean space.

Inspectors arrive but the girls slip like ferrets
to the musty room at the back of the building,
a bucket of water between them, another

for nature's call. They memorise symbolic differences
in behaviour between finite and infinite dimensional
vector space, understand too well that if V

is the vector space of infinite sequences *(xi, x2, x3 …)*
and if VV is infinite dimensional, then there are
linear transformations $T{:}V\to V$T:V→V, one-to-one

but not onto. Meaning, their kernels are trivial
but their images not entire. Entirety is the aim.
To emerge whole, the vector space and curve

of female mind cancels words, canings,
what grinds down their algebraic dreams.
The secret schools continue. Girls seek space

on the hypotenuse as it probes
from the tight corner of the perpendiculum.
They stretch and cut space according to need,

the Fibonacci spirals[‡] within their ears,
calculating numbers and symbols
as they listen, learn.

Mary O'Donnell

---

‡ The cochlea of the ear is a Fibonacci spiral

Extinction

In stockyards, a Judas goat will lead
sheep to slaughter, while its own life
is spared; with smell
of estrus, will lure
other goats out from behind rock and scrub
so a helicopter rifle shot
can pick them out, one by one
by one— *A little world*
within itself, wrote Darwin:
with pools where blue-
footed boobies come to wade, and
tortoises old as boulders. Once,
neighbors told me of the family dog
they had to give away
when they moved.
They said she limped
back to the house they used to own,
and lay down under the laurel tree
to die. What do the leaves say
when they move like mouths
as the light changes? Little buds of jasmine
continue to give up scent
even as a different color takes over
their pale ghost bodies.
All our dead come back to us
in dreams, so we can make apology.
They hold out sheets of our tears,
so much silver warming
the grass neatly clipped where we lie down
to live out the rest of our days.

Luisa A Igloria

Emozioni

You learn them in Italian first,
from a book of expressive fish.
Curious, with shining eyes.
Nervous, all wriggly lines.
Brave, a speck of a fish in the corner
of the big black sea.
Shy, so pale, it's translucent.
Sad, like sheets of rain.
Furious, slit-eyed big-mouthed purple-red.
Proud, puffed up, pink.
Jealous, a backward-looking slithery thing.
Enamoured, rosy-cheeked and singing.
Grumpy, with bared teeth.
Happy, the whole sloppy rainbow.
Confused, turning this way and that.
Annoyed, even fish can roll their eyes.
And this little fish? I ask.
Soddisfatto. Emphasis on the
dd's and tt's. In the book,
it's big bellied,
and on the way up.

Steph Ellen Feeney

Rosetta Pebble

I watch you scour the shore, love,
eyes tough as an oyster picker's, hands
just as deft, another careful step –
and you're down again, crouching over
rarest pebbles, the mermaid's cup of an empty shell,
treasures shiny with sea-lick, glossy like
hard-boiled sweets, this pick 'n' mix beach.

I pull up your hood. We're out too early.
Over at the kiosk they're still setting up.
Seagulls shriek at the drag of plastic chairs,
the pound of lone joggers. Only the crazies are about.
A single swimmer in rubber socks and gloves
tests the water's foaming edge.

I have to point these things out.
Mid-frown, head-down, you are busy with inspection,
your pebble-victors filling my pockets.
No more now, love. I shake my head
as you press a charcoal-coloured one
into my palm, *What does this say?*

You'd be forgiven for thinking Arabic
or Hieroglyphics you might almost
read the tiny white etchings,
if you knew how,
knew enough.

All blinking eyes and wilding hair
you wait patiently for me to decipher
so sure of coming answers,
but having none, I joke about
pebble-speak and pull at your hood,
as you jerk away.

Even so, love, that was the morning –

mittened swimmer cutting far
waves, the kiosk-coffee ready,

deep ring of pebble-music in my pockets –

that was the morning
I could almost read, verily!
stones and waves and sky:

the big bad book of world.

The rising sun,
wouldn't you know,
a blood-red ball.

Tania Dain

Aground

No fresh water, just nine
sealed jars of ink salvaged
  from the wreck,
a beachy atoll deserted
but for crabs and molluscs.

By day he forages
along the scribbled strandline
  levers out a cork bung
slakes his thirst
from the stinking lip

of a carboy: rotting sepia
distilled from cuttlefish
  mixed with lampblack
thinned with spirits.
At night for warmth, piles

the tide's detritus
on top of him: a sea burial
  on land. Ear
against a gravel pillow
he listens to the bored Pacific

sucking, gasping
like a creaking water mill.
  He drinks ink, vomits ink,
shits ink, sheds ink tears.
The sea is ink, the sky is ink

pressing down
until he's sinking
  through fathoms, a fragment
lost among the ocean's roots.
Stars are drowned –

archer, herdsman, Hercules,
plough and lyre –
  even, hung among them,
Berenice's shining hair
is a rope fixed to an anchor.

When the Bajou find him
his mind is dark from sun
  and hunger, his tongue
a nub of coal
where nothing burns.

Years later in a hilltop study
in Arezzo where the sea
  cannot be seen
his quill drinks ink:
Life has written me, not I my life.

Sharon Black

(Giusto Forbici, whose story is recounted in *Seven Tenths: the Sea and its Thresholds* by James Hamilton-Paterson, travelled the Pacific between 1842 – 1857.)

I explain time travel to my son

I say, imagine simply rising from here
and walking into your future, sweeping

through the days and years
like the hand of a clock, transported

to the house where your darling children
will be born, it's afternoon you're mowing the lawn

they splash about in the plastic pool, your beloved
smiles at you from the kitchen window, your old dad

somewhere inside, confused, but not yet dead,
irritating but tolerable. Then on to the allotment

you'll later tend, experimenting with asparagus
and blueberries, your way of getting away

but which, once the kids and dad have gone,
you'll wonder why, quietly kicking yourself

as you sit looking out the window,
wondering if they'll call, the house too big now.

Even onto the care-home where you'll end,
happier than you thought you'd be.

Ready?
Here we go then.

Peter Borchers

Park Protocol

Don't leave trash on the ground.
No loitering after dark.
Pick up after your dog.
Whether posted or not, they're the rules
everyone knows.

But it's obvious to anyone
even half-serious about parks
that they have their own special set
of guidelines to be observed
in the interest of the fullest enjoyment.

Don't step too high when walking:
this will ensure you're able to hear
the sounds of your feet moving
through the rooftops of the grass
or the pebbles of the path.

Don't step on dandelions,
not even the ones without a bee on top.
But do step on pinecones, particularly
the large, dry, open ones, and step slowly
in order to hear and feel and savor the crunch.

If there are children making a commotion,
try not to let their shrieks disturb you
and remember the time in your own life
when your biggest decision was whether
to spin to the right or to the left.

Follow the flights of sparrows and of crows
until you're distracted by a bank of clouds
looking very like a whale
or by a dog, tearing around in circles,
tongue flying, for no other reason than that
of its own unplanned, imperative joy.

Scott Renzoni

No Items Match Your Search

'Hwǣr cwōm mearg? Hwǣr cwōm mago?'
'Where is the horse gone? Where is the young warrior?'
The Wanderer

I am searching for an image of the library
of Alexandria, burning. It is by John Martin.
When it was made, it swallowed the walls
of galleries, awed spectators who had never seen

skyscrapers fall or Marvel superheroes
or the annihilation of the Death Star.
Now it is a fuzzy jpg with a mediocre dpi,
its figures indistinct; even when I pinch

and drag my fingers, details merge and blur.
But the conflagration has seized the city
all the same; it is spreading upwards
through the columns stacked in rows

like candy cigarettes. The giant statue
of sinewy Alexander swinging his shield
like Captain America over the harbour
is headless now, his face a cracked egg

on the dock. Ships are foundering
and the people of the city are crowding
onto the bridges like krill. In the foreground,
a woman shrieks and leaps into the sea;

her red cloak arcs behind her like a flare.
She has no features to speak of; she is merely
a focal point for anguish, human
embodiment of loss. Is the soldier

seizing her shoulder trying to save her
or something worse? The library is closed to us,
its columns like the shelved spines of books,
blank rows of binary, their code locked.

I bookmark the page, click and close the frame.
When Twitter burns, what fragments
will they find among the ruins? What cats, what memes,
what broken threads? When Wikipedia

crumbles to dust, what dead links will remain?
In a vault somewhere in southern California
a server hums, talking to itself,
turning over its data, brooding on silence.

Catherine Spooner

Toccata for Spoons

—a sonic ballad for folk percussionist Tom O'Connor

In tro three four
Wackin' um, thwackin' um
tikki tikki takkin um
thrummin' um, flummin' um
whartelly-mortally thunkin' um

Trinky tattaloo, threp palaver do
boink abit, button yer lip
rip tarotter blue

Yellow-bellied sapsucker
doinkin' on the metal roof
yukkin' wit his band mates
fraggin' round the flag poloof

Wackin' um, etc. (refrain)

Hammer jack in hard hat
jammin' at the curb stones
dingleberry dingbat,
lemon-hearted rum proof

Pippin crusher tippin' off
caterwaulin', yak enough
plenipoten-tarian
clinkelhafta berry um

Trinky tattaloo, etc. (chorus)

Andante
Libarian philatelist
short-stopizza catalyst
rounda horn in nuttin' flat.
Plessarat, plessaroon
pleazto join me in my room.

Al dente
Ribbetty cribbage an thrup da die
shake yer cup or let it lie.
Stollee or goose tarattle em loose
spakkla shee an licketty spoon

Simmer…
Thowlen pussycat, abdul jabar
shinktiz showl onna fewnery jar.
Fiddlediz ristan riddlediz phone
boyzwit spoons are never alone.

Wackin' um, thwackin' um
tikki tikki takkin um
thrummin' um, flummin' um
whartelly-mortally thunkin' um

Trinky tattaloo, threp palaver do
boink abit, button yer lip
rip tarotter blue

Daniel Lusk

Biographies

Winner: Short Story Prize

Letty Butler

is a writer, actress, comedienne, creative coach and chronically indecisive. She's based in a tiny flat in Sheffield, writes across multiple genres and has just finished her debut novel, *Escape Artists*. Last year, she won the BPA Prize and New Writers Flash Award, and was shortlisted for Bridport, Bath and Mslexia. Her first non-fiction book, *The Jobbing Actor*, was published by Nick Hern Books in January 2023.

Second: Short Story Prize

Nicholas Petty

is a British writer living in Utrecht, the Netherlands. His short fiction has previously been listed for the Sunday Times Audible Short Story Award and the Galley Beggar Press Short Story Prize, and has appeared in *The Moth, The London Magazine*, *Short Fiction Journal,* and elsewhere. When he's not at his desk, he can be found on a sunny terrace with a plate of *bitterballen* and a tiny Dutch beer.

Third: Short Story Prize

Dylan Garity

is a writer and editor originally from Oregon, currently living in Brooklyn, New York. As a spoken word poet, he has toured around the United States, performing at a wide variety of venues and winning the College National Poetry Slam with Macalester College. He cofounded and served as vice president of Button Poetry for many years, and now works as a freelance fiction editor. *Autophile* is his first published short story.

Honourable Mention: Short Story Prize

Roger Vickery

rescued this story from a shelter. From the jump, it whined, barked, scratched, and shat out demands to be re-located to a sunny home. Drawing on his multi-vocational (ADHD?) background Roger employed marketing wiles, legal arguments, military tactics, teaching aids and sailing tacks to up-sell the ingrate. Failure. Then he remembered *The Fish*. They're a soft touch ... accepted his poetry pup in 2015 ... maybe they're open to a new stray?

Honourable Mention: Short Story Prize

Allegra A Mullan

is twenty-two years old and lives in North London. She has had work published in the *Keats-Shelley Review*, the *Penguin First Story Anthology*, the *2016 Foyles Young Poets Anthology*, and *Rotters' Magazine*. When she is not on her phone, Allegra enjoys watching film trailers and walking. She is currently studying Creative Writing at Goldsmiths and working as a chef.

Honourable Mention: Short Story Prize

Emma Neale

lives and works in Dunedin, New Zealand, as a freelance editor and occasional creative writing tutor. The published author of novels, poetry and short fiction, she is also the mother of two sons. Her husband works as a theoretical physicist; her sons like to say this family background of 'physics and poetry' has clearly led to their own divergent passions: jazz percussion and basketball.

Honourable Mention: Short Story Prize

Josephine Rowe

is the author of three story collections and a novel, *A Loving, Faithful Animal*, published in the UK by Tuskar Rock Press. She was a 2021-2022 fellow at the New York Public Library's Cullman Centre for Scholars and Writers, and a 2022 Writer in Residence at Literaturhaus Zürich. She has recently returned to Australia and is living in coastal Victoria, working on a new novel and sleep. Her latest collection of stories is *Here Until August*.

Honourable Mention: Short Story Prize

Josh Wagner

spent his early years in California before his folks dragged him off to Montana, where he learned to love a bit of solitude. He has a Masters in Creative Writing from the University of Edinburgh, and is currently living in West Cork working on a baffling PhD concerning forests, grief, embodiment and spectrality. He dabbles in music, filmmaking and theatre, but the art of fiction will always be his first and most abiding love.

Honourable Mention: Short Story Prize

Hanako Senzoku

has spent half her life in Melbourne, Australia and half as a returnee in Tokyo, Japan – her sense of what constitutes a barbecue is a present source of consternation, and writing an ever-guiding star. She is perpetually filled with wonder and confusion, and an appetite for delicious things.

Winner: Flash Fiction Prize

Susan Wigmore

– a Londoner by birth – grew up on jellied eels and cockney rhyming slang, but after spells in South Wales and Japan, has lived in Oxfordshire more years than she cares to remember. She loves writing short things, canoeing, climbing mountains (slowly) and challenging herself in all three, which can get her into trouble sometimes. She is currently working on a novella-in-flash (at pretty much the same rate as she climbs mountains).

Second: Flash Fiction Prize

Barbara P Tarrant

loves a challenge, and recently turned her attention (and curiosity) to Flash Fiction. Last year she undertook the Fish Playwriting course and has just finished writing her first play. She returned to education in her forties and received a BA and scholarship from UCD then later an MPhil in Creative Writing at Trinity. Barbara has won the Hennessy New Irish Writing award for new fiction and been shortlisted for The Francis Mac Manus.

Third: Flash Fiction Prize

Emma Goldman-Sherman

(she/they), is an outspoken Autistic, Agender, Queer, chronically ill, Feminist and Antizionist Jewish creative with plays produced on four continents. You can listen for free at TheParsnipShip.com and PlayingOnAir.org among others. Their poetry has been curated by *American Athenaeum, Non-Binary Review, Oberon, Queerlings, Writers Resist* and elsewhere. This is their first published Flash Fiction. They work as a coach and support writers and artists around the globe via https://www.bravespace.online/

Honourable Mention: Flash Fiction Prize

Mark Bowsher

is a writer and award-winning filmmaker from Gravesend in Kent, now living in Bristol. His debut novel, *The Boy Who Stole Time*, was published by Unbound in 2018. He is proudly dyspraxic and feels that it's partly his short, neurodivergent attention-span that makes him want to write escapist YA fantasy books one minute and sweary satirical whodunnit movie scripts the next. He once climbed a mountain dressed as Peter Pan.

Honourable Mention: Flash Fiction Prize

Patricia Newbery

Patricia's work has appeared in *Ambit*, the *Bath Flash Fiction Anthology*, *The Rupture* and elsewhere. She's a translator and editor and lives in Egypt.

Honourable Mention: Flash Fiction Prize

Linda Nemec Foster

lives in Grand Rapids, Michigan and was selected to serve as that city's first Poet Laureate (2003-05). Her 12 collections of poetry include, *The Blue Divide, The Lake Michigan Mermaid* (2019 Michigan Notable Book), and *Amber Necklace from Gdansk*. Her book of flash fiction, *Bone Country,* was recently published. Foster has been honored with numerous awards including first prize in the 2023 Allen Ginsberg Poetry Contest sponsored by The Poetry Center (USA).

Honourable Mention: Flash Fiction Prize

Molly Underwood

is an eco-poet and writer living in Cambridge. She was the winner of the 2019 Manchester Poetry Prize, and has been shortlisted for awards including the Alpine Fellowship Poetry Prize and the Charles Causley prize; her work appears in the *Aesthetica Creative Writing Anthology 2020*. When she's not writing, she can usually be found up a mountain or parked up in her converted campervan with a cup of tea.

Honourable Mention: Flash Fiction Prize

Martin Daly

was born in Douglas, Co. Cork to family lines of weavers and stone-cutters. He grew up surrounded by storytellers. He was a financial analyst in the construction industry and a stone mason for several years. In a nod to his ancestry, Martin's preference now is to weave words together and to cut away what is unnecessary. He has completed his first novel. Martin remains deeply rooted in Douglas, but maintains no fixed abode.

Honourable Mention: Flash Fiction Prize

Kurtis Burton

is a plague upon Colorado, USA, who's never published nor written about himself in the third person. *Kurtis enjoys hiking and skiing* is what this bio would say if he were a good Coloradan; he's frail, allergic, and, when exposed to snow or sunlight, irritable. His only cultured and respectable hobbies are reading and writing. He is thankful for his confused and concerned family, who appreciate his writing but wish he'd go outside.

Honourable Mention: Flash Fiction Prize

Ian Johnson

escaped from Strangeways prison 30 years ago, dressed as a nun, and afterwards masqueraded as a nurse and CBT therapist in various mental health establishments which were unlucky enough to have him. He found the people he worked with a joy, and inspiration for a lot of his writing. Recently retired, he is now joint Chair of Tyldesley Creative Writers whom, on a weekly basis, he burdens with his jokes.

Winner: Short Memoir Prize

Anneke Bender

is a writer, physical therapist, and adjunct professor living in Atlanta, GA. Her short stories, poems, and essays explore themes of loss, magical wandering, and the inner landscape of the body. Her work often includes encounters with creatures of ill repute who curiously offer sound advice for living. When not working, she can be found napping for pleasure, strolling the historic cemetery near her home, and riding her bike in strange lands.

Second: Short Memoir Prize **Nuala Roche**

lives in Kilkenny. She has worked in film production, multimedia, theatre and is now in the library service. Nuala writes poetry, fiction and more recently non-fiction/memoir; fitting, as she spent much time as a child in graveyards, making headstone rubbings with newsprint and crayon for her mother's genealogy research. Nuala's speculative-fiction novel, twenty-years-a-writing, provides fertile ground for rewriting, editing and playing with ideas and form.

Third: Short Memoir Prize **Sabine Casparie**

is a Dutch-born, London-based art historian who also lived in Houston, Texas, where she fell in love with campervan holidays. She currently works as a contemporary art guide and consultant for the art collection of Chelsea and Westminster Hospital, and writes a quarterly blog on art. She started writing memoir during lockdown and was previously shortlisted for the Mairtín Crawford Award, making her wonder if maybe the Dutch and the Irish are connected in spirit.

Honourable Mention: Short Memoir Prize **Thelma McGough**

is an award-winning artist and TV producer. *Blind Date*, the series she produced, won a BAFTA. In the 60s she wrote for *Music Echo*. John Lennon and she bonded over being abandoned by a dad. Macca took her to the Cavern and Jimi Hendrix's first gig. Tom Wolfe wrote of her: *Liverpool's ASTOUNDING Gift to World Beauty & Genius!* She was the muse for Roger McGough's seminal poems *Summer with Monika*. Her memoir reveals her long-supressed voice.

Honourable Mention: Short Memoir Prize **James Scoles**

James' debut poetry collection – *The Trailer* (Signature Editions, 2021), about love and loss in a mobile home – won absolutely no awards, but was called *an instant Canadian classic* on CBC Radio and considered for the Stephen Leacock Award for Humour. He has degrees from three American universities and doesn't let that hold him back. He currently teaches literature and creative writing at the University of Winnipeg, but he has lived, traveled and worked in over ninety countries.

Honourable Mention: Short Memoir Prize

Kathryn Phelan

has never had a five-year plan. She has made coffee, minded a child in Switzerland, taught English in Brazil, and waitressed at a restaurant that burned down the day she left (A COINCIDENCE). She relies too heavily on coffee and parenthesis. Her work can be found in *The New York Times, The Best American Sports Writing, The Sun Magazine, The Telegraph, The Masters Review, Wigleaf* and others. She works as a copywriter in Ireland.

Honourable Mention: Short Memoir Prize

Dani Salvadori

is a poet, photographer and video maker whose work has been shown in galleries and festivals worldwide and published in a range of poetry publications. She is studying for an MA in Poetic Practice at Royal Holloway, University of London which has given her the time to widen what she writes into memoir, manifestos and poets' theatre. She is having a great time doing it.

Honourable Mention: Short Memoir Prize

Olivia Rana

lives in Belfast, Northern Ireland with her husband and two formidable teenagers. She is currently writing a PhD in English very slowly due to a broken wrist sustained while playing crazy golf. She has her best ideas during insomniac hours and has published two novels and a number of short stories. This is her first time dabbling in short memoir. When fully mobile Olivia enjoys long walks, Pilates, and making/drinking rhubarb gin.

Honourable Mention: Short Memoir Prize

Cheryl Miller-Fitzgerald

is an editor and journalist who has written for newspapers, magazines and television news. She is particularly drawn to subjects concerning mental health and wellness. She lives down the New Jersey shore where she's raised twin sons and has seen every Marvel and DC movie – twice. When not at work or working on her novel she can be found walking the boards by the ocean or pounding the boxing bag in the gym.

cherylmfitzgerald.wordpress.com

Honourable Mention: Short Memoir Prize

Thomas Darlington Crancer

was born and raised in Lincoln, Nebraska. He has been writing since he could make all the letters. He is a high school dropout and a college graduate. He won a prize in the Midwest Writers' Conference for his short story *Victory Cafe*. His story *Required Debauchery* was published (under his pen name Thomas Darlington) in the *Stories that Need to be Told 2020* anthology. He has lived on both coasts and now lives in Portland, Oregon.

Winner: Poetry Prize

Winifred Hughes

is a reformed academic and active birder living in Princeton, NJ. The author of two chapbooks, as well as poems in scattered journals, she currently serves on the boards of two local environmental organizations and teaches courses in nature writing and ecopoetry. When she is not actually writing poems, she can be found leading bird walks and poking around in the local wetlands, or hanging out with her two grown sons.

Second: Poetry Prize

Mary O'Donnell

has published seventeen books since 1990. She was appointed Poet Laureate of Naas, Co Kildare, during 2022. Her eighth poetry collection is *Massacre of the Birds* (Salmon). An essay, *My Mother in Drumlin Country*, was listed in *Notable Essays and Literary Nonfiction of 2017 in Best American Essays* (Mariner). People say she is a kick-ass creative writing teacher. She intends to write until the energy runs out, which it hasn't – so far. Member of Aosdána.
www.maryodonnell.com

Third: Poetry Prize

Luisa A Igloria

enjoys drawing, hand-binding little books, experimenting with collage, trying out new recipes, and ripping out and re-starting knitting projects when she's not writing or teaching. She adores figs, dumplings, and tango music. Originally from Baguio City, she makes her home in Norfolk VA and teaches English and Creative Writing in Old Dominion University's MFA Creative Writing Program. Luisa is the 20th Poet Laureate of the Commonwealth of Virginia (2020-22), Emerita.
www.luisaigloria.com

Honourable Mention: Poetry Prize

Steph Ellen Feeney

was born in Louisiana and raised in Texas. She grew up in a family of fishermen, musicians and drinkers, and still dabbles in all three. She is a Board Director of Art for Human Rights. Her poems have appeared in *The Poetry Review* and *Ink Sweat & Tears*. These days, she calls Suffolk home.

Honourable Mention: Poetry Prize

Tania Dain

has spent her life filling notebooks with poems, stories, novels and plays. She studied Creative Writing at Manchester University and CitiLit, and is a member of the ZB writing group and the McGechie Duo. A secondary school teacher, her daily commute takes in – wonderfully – the fine oaks and wandering deer of Richmond Park. She is currently putting together her first collection of poetry, obligatory in a family of scribblers.

Honourable Mention: Poetry Prize

Sharon Black

is from Glasgow and lives in a remote valley of the Cévennes mountains in France. Her prizes include *The London Magazine* Poetry Prizes 2019 and 2018. She has published four full collections of poetry and a pamphlet. Her latest collections are *The Last Woman Born on the Island* (Vagabond Voices, 2022), exploring Scotland's culture and heritage, and *The Red House* (Drunk Muse, 2022), set in her adopted homeland. She is editor of Pindrop Press.
www.sharonblack.co.uk

Honourable Mention: Poetry Prize

Peter Borchers

is a retired science teacher who has lived in South Africa, Malawi and Tasmania as well as the UK. He started writing poetry in later life once all the frenzy had died down.

Honourable Mention: Poetry Prize

Scott Renzoni

is a poet and actor originally from Vermont, now based in the Berkshires of Western Massachusetts. His work has appeared or is forthcoming in *Ekphrastic Review, KGB Bar Online Literary Review, Connecticut Poetry Review*, the Library of Congress' 'Poetry 180' site, and others. Stage work has included everything from Shakespeare to farce and even a musical or two. A 4-time 'Jeopardy!' champion, Renzo also works as a bartender and bookseller.

Honourable Mention: Poetry Prize

Catherine Spooner

recently returned to creative writing after a gap of many years. In 2021-2, she took a career break to complete an MLitt in Creative Writing at the University of Glasgow and in 2022, was the recipient of the Northern Writers' Arvon Award from New Writing North. In her other life, she is an academic who writes about Gothic literature, culture and fashion. She is often found wearing black.

Honourable Mention: Poetry Prize

Daniel Lusk

is the winner of a Pushcart Prize for his genre-bending essay, *Bomb*. He is the author of eight poetry collections and other books, most recently *Every Slow Thing, Farthings* (eBook Yavanika Press, Bangalore), and *The Shower Scene from Hamlet*. Native of the prairie Midwest, and onetime preacher, sportswriter, jazz singer, cowboy, teacher and NPR commentator, Daniel lives in Vermont, USA. He is married to Irish poet Angela (Goggins) Patten.

Anam Cara Artists and Writers Retreat

Beara Peninsula, Ireland

Sue Booth-Forbes donates one week's residency at Anam Cara for the second prize winners of the Fish Short Story Prize and the Fish Poetry Prize.

Anam Cara is set amid the rolling hills of West Cork's remote Beara Peninsula. The retreat, on five acres of gardens and riverbank, is surrounded by farmland that slopes down to Coulagh Bay.

Established in 1998 by Sue Booth-Forbes, an experienced writer and editor, Anam Cara accommodates five individual residents and up to twenty for workshops. Its main purpose is to provide a sanctuary from everyday life for writers and artists. As director and host, Sue is a supportive facilitator who aims to provide what writers and artists need to 'slow down enough inside' to be productive. The north-facing bedrooms overlook Coulagh Bay, while the south-facing one faces Mishkish Mountain. One of the rooms can accommodate disabled guests.

In addition to private study-bedrooms, the house and the grounds offer many nooks and crannies for creative idylls – the bench swing in the conservatory, the sunken living room, the window seat in the gallery room, the 'island' near the waterfall, the low wall beside the stone fountain, the bench beside the duck pond.

Mealtimes provide an opportunity to share ideas and socialize. For traditional music and perhaps set dancing, the local pubs are just a walk away.

Sue Booth-Forbes: anamcararetreat@eircom.net
www.anamcararetreat.com

What Is Fish Publishing?

The Fish Short Story Prize is an open door that's inviting writers to walk through it. It has to be encouraged, celebrated, congratulated.
Roddy Doyle

Fish is doing great work. It's an inspiration for all new writers.
Frank McCourt

I hail anyone who enters the Fish Prize ... It is difficult to create from dust, as all of us writers do. I know that the best stories are those that are still untold – so keep writing, keep creating, keep the faith.
Colum McCann

Fish is dedicated to fostering and publishing new and emerging writers. Since the first Fish Short Story Prize in 1994 we have published over 800 writers from around the globe. Over the years we have added the **Flash Fiction Prize**, **Poetry Prize** and **Short Memoir Prize.** Ten submissions from each competition, as selected by the judges, are published in the Fish Anthology. These prizes are annual, as is the publication of the Fish Anthology. The prize fund is over €11,000.

Critique Service: for short stories, poems, flash and short memoir – available year-round, online or by post.

Fish Editorial Service: provides in-depth professional assistance for anthologies of stories or poems, and for memoirs and novels.

Mentoring: for fiction, non-fiction and poetry.
Mentoring offers writers a long-term, tutor-writer relationship to work on a novel, memoir, collection of stories, poems, or work of non-fiction. Our team, led by award-winning writer and poet Mary-Jane Holmes, offers professional guidance to develop and strengthen your work. Duration 3–9 months.

Writing Courses (Online)**: for** short story, flash fiction, memoir poetry and playwriting.
Courses provide useful and interesting ways to improve your craft with one-to-one tuition. The courses are structured with set exercises, and feedback on each. Whilst designed to take about three months, the courses are completed in your own time.

Details of all Fish activities are on our website

www.fishpublishing.com